DOWN & DIRTY: JAG

Dirty Angels MC, Book 2

JEANNE ST. JAMES

Copyright © 2017 by Jeanne St. James

All rights reserved.

No part of this book may be reproduced in any form or by any electronic or mechanical means, including information storage and retrieval systems, without written permission from the author, except for the use of brief quotations in a book review.

Editor: Proofreading by the Page

Cover Art: Susan Garwood of Wicked Women Designs

---

www.jeannestjames.com

Sign up for my newsletter for insider information, author news, and new releases: www.jeannestjames.com/newslettersignup

※ Created with Vellum

Warning: This book contains sexually explicit scenes and adult language and may be considered offensive to some readers. This book is for sale to adults ONLY, as defined by the laws of the country in which you made your purchase. Please store your files wisely, where they cannot be accessed by under-aged readers.

DISCLAIMER: Please do not try any new sexual practice (BDSM or otherwise) without the guidance of an experienced practitioner. The author will not be responsible for any loss, harm, injury or death resulting from use of the information contained in this book.

A BIG thank you to my beta readers:
Krisztina Holló & Author Whitley Cox

Keep an eye on her website at http://www.jeannestjames.com/or sign up for her newsletter to learn about her upcoming releases: http://www.jeannestjames.com/newslettersignup

Author Links: Jeanne's Blog * Instagram * Facebook * Goodreads Author Page * Newsletter * Jeanne's Review & Book Crew * Twitter * BookBub

ACKNOWLEDGMENTS

Thanks to author Whitley Cox for brainstorming the sketch idea for this book. Ivy needed to find Jag's sketches to see what was right in front of her face her whole life.

Jag thanks you, too.

And, as always, I thank the man who listens to my story lines (I tend to ramble) and continues to be amazed at what I come up with. I'm lucky that he answers my crazy questions about being a man (and everything that goes along with that) with complete honesty and openness. Since we both have a law enforcement background and training it's nice to bounce those ideas off him, too. Love ya, honey.

Down & Dirty 'til Dead

CHAPTER ONE

He was going to kill the bitch.
Jag pounded on the door. Again.
She was pushing him to his limit. And that was not good.
For him.
For her.
For the human race in general.
"Fuckin' open the door or I'll bust the fuckin' thing in, got me?"
He was going to knock politely only one more time, then that was it.
He *politely* kicked the door with his heavy biker boot. That was going to leave a mark.
"If you don't open this fuckin' door right—"
The door jerked open and something—or someone—tried to fly by him.
Jag reached out a hand and snagged the fleeing body. With a grip around a skinny bicep, the guy came to a screeching halt.
Jag flung him around to face him. He scowled. "Who the fuck are you?"
The already pale guy turned sheet white. With eyes wide, mouth open, he had a discarded shirt bunched in his fist and his pants hung

loosely around his hips, since he apparently hadn't taken the time to finish fastening them before the man decided to jet.

Which was a smart move. But then, Ivy tended to pick smart dudes. Though, they never hung around long. Geeky dudes and a biker babe don't mix no matter how many times she tries.

And he got it, he really did. Ivy was smart herself. Genius even. And she needed a challenge.

Other than becoming a biker's ol' lady. Or his ol' lady, more like it.

Jag looked down at the guy's bare feet. It seemed he forgot his fucking shoes in his haste.

Stupid fuck. Maybe he wasn't so smart after all.

"You touch Dirty Angels' property?"

The guy's mouth opened and closed like a guppy as he stared up at Jag, who towered over him by at least five inches.

"Asked a damn question. Did you—"

"Get gone, Jag."

His eyes slid to the woman now standing in the doorway, holding out a pair of loafers with socks tucked into them. The one wearing a fucking *robe* and probably *nothing else*.

The guy's eyes dropped to his offered shoes, then he snagged them and clasped them to his chest as if they were a lifeline.

"Get in the house. Deal with you shortly."

"The hell you will. *Get gone*, Jag."

His head twisted in her direction and he took his time inspecting her from top to toe. That fucking deep red hair of hers spilled around her shoulders, clearly messed up from a fresh fuck, which he hoped he'd interrupted. Because if anyone should be in her bed, it should be him.

Her lips were swollen and pouty. Goddamn, if she had those lips around this nerd's cock, his brain would explode. Her green eyes snapped in anger.

Whatever. She could be mad all she wanted. He was just as pissed. No, more.

"Who I fuck is none of your damn business," came out of that smart mouth.

He gritted his teeth before answering. "The fuck it isn't. Anything to do with DAMC property is my business."

Especially after she climbed into his bed all those months ago.

"Well, I'm not DAMC property. So *GET GONE!*"

Jag released the now very scared guy with a shove. He stumbled, caught his balance on the veranda railing, then ran down the metal stairs, taking two at a time. Like a scared mouse, he sprinted toward a car parked on the street.

He should've known the guy drove a fucking Prius. He should've slashed the geek-mobile's tires for dipping his dick in DAMC property.

"Fucker doesn't even ride a bike. You've got shit taste in lays, Ivy."

"Don't I know it," she muttered, making Jag's jaw tighten.

"Don't come back here," Jag yelled his warning through the dark to the guy scrambling into his car like his ass was on fire. "If you know what's good for ya," he finished under his breath. He turned back to face the pissed-off redhead dressed in black silk that hugged all her damn curves. His balls tightened as hard as his jaw. "Probably needs a dick extension to fuck you."

"I don't know if that's an insult to me or to him. Either way, you don't belong here, Jag. So, I'll say it again, get gone."

"Not leavin'."

Ivy lifted a shoulder. "Okay then. You'll be standing out here all night while I'm sleeping soundly in my bed. Thanks to you, alone. Normally, I'd say good night, but... fuck you."

The door slammed shut and Jag heard the deadbolt click. He grimaced and stared at the door.

Little did she know that her uncle, Ace, had given him the key.

He grinned, turned on his heel and jogged down the steps to where his bike was parked at the foot of the stairway in the pawn shop lot.

She may not let him in, but his mission was accomplished. He chased away Ivy's latest conquest.

And he'd keep doing it until she got some sense and realized everything she needed has been right in front of her all along.

He put his girl between his legs, hit her starter and closed his eyes for a moment, surrounded by the smooth rumble of his straight exhaust pipes.

His bike was everything to him. The only thing he wanted more between his legs was Ivy.

The only thing he loved more than his bike was... *fucking* Ivy.

And she was a fucking bitch.

Ivy leaned her head back against the door, her hands covering her face as she tried not to scream. She sucked in a deep, shaky breath in an attempt to control her temper, as well as her frustration. She wasn't having much luck.

Fucking Jag.

Finally, she heard the roar of his bike before it faded away.

Coast was clear.

She had no idea how the brother knew she had a man in her apartment. It was like he had some sixth sense. This wasn't the first time he'd chased a man away.

Probably wouldn't be the last.

The problem with being raised in a motorcycle club and being around bikers her whole life was just that... being around a bunch of misogynistic macho bikers.

Women were considered property of the club. *Property*. And being born into a bloodline of bikers made it hard to escape that.

Not that she necessarily wanted to escape. She loved her brothers and she loved her life for the most part.

She did well financially working in her uncle's pawn shop and living above it rent-free. She also had gone to school for computers and programming, so she ran the club's website, all the club's businesses' websites and fixed any of the club member's computers when needed. In all reality, she could open her own computer shop if she wanted. She knew how to diagnose, knew how to program.

The club relied on her a lot. Sometimes she even helped Ace, the club's Treasurer, run the numbers for the club's finances.

She was smart. But sometimes she just did dumb things.

Like sleeping with Jag once during a drunken mistake one night after a pig roast. She had lost her mind and dragged him upstairs to his room at the clubhouse. Ever since then, there'd been tension between them.

Luckily, Ace never found out because, even though the man was her uncle, he acted like a father to her, especially since she never knew her real father. And though he loved Jag like a son, she wouldn't put it past him to kick the younger man's ass for "defiling" Ivy.

Even though Jag was in no way her first lover.

Ace tended to encourage Ivy to date men outside the club. Though she wasn't sure why since he was an engrained member of the club himself. So, he couldn't think the brothers weren't good enough. Could he?

Maybe he was just overprotective.

Who knew.

But Ivy slipped up that night, Jag didn't fight it and now she's regretted it ever since.

Because the last thing she wanted was to be wearing a "Property of Jag" vest similar to the cuts that some of the other ol' ladies wore.

She was an independent woman, goddamn it, and intended on staying that way come hell or high water.

But she had to admit that the guy she had brought home tonight wasn't for her. He was just going to scratch an itch. The "date" they went on had been boring. He was a nice guy, sure, and cute enough. However, the spark was missing.

Both her and Jag had been drunk as all get out when they hooked up. That night there weren't sparks either. No, there had been explosions.

And that scared her to death.

———

Jag sat at the large lacquered wood table. The one that had the Dirty Angels MC logo carved in it all those years ago by one of the founding members, his granddaddy Bear.

May the brother rest in peace.

The way things were going, it didn't seem that there would ever be peace. Ever since Bear was killed by a Shadow Warrior back in the eighties, things had been a little rocky.

Which brought his thoughts to his father, Rocky, who was serving a life sentence at SCI Greene for taking out a few of those Warriors in retribution.

But even after all these years, the bad blood between the two clubs hadn't lessened. The Warriors showed up now and again to create havoc like a bad fucking penny.

And now because of recent events, the club prez, Pierce, was sitting at the head of the table talking about keeping security beefed up at all the club's businesses. Which put a bigger strain on Diesel, who was both the club's enforcer and in charge of In the Shadows Security, which provided bouncers to area bars as well as personal and commercial security to those who could afford it.

"Need to keep vigilant." Pierce glanced around the table, his eyes bouncing from one executive member to the next. "Even the ol' ladies, so spread the word to them, too. Fucker had a set on him when he tried to snag Sophie right in front of Z on a busy street. If she'd been by herself, no tellin' what woulda happened to her."

Head nods and pounding of fists went around the table.

"Can tell you what would happen if they took one of our ol' ladies, a fuckin' slaughter, that's what," Diesel grumbled.

"No doubt," Hawk agreed.

"Yeah, an' then we all end up at Greene in adjoinin' cells like Rocky and Doc," Ace, the oldest member and the coolest head in the room said to both of his sons.

Jag whacked him on the arm. "Then, brother, you and me both would get to see our pops."

Ace frowned. "Ain't funny, boy."

"Respect to Doc and Rocky," Dex shouted, causing a few hoots and hollers.

Pierce pounded the gavel on the table. "Okay, okay. Settle down so we can get through our business an' I can go bust a nut in my woman."

They all chuckled.

"Now, anybody got shit goin' down with the Dark Knights?" Pierce pinned his gaze on the large man at the other end of the table. "Diesel?"

"Nothin' new."

He looked to his left. "Hawk?"

"Only thing I got wind of is they took over Dirty Dick's Bar."

Pierce frowned. "Took over?"

Hawk leaned forward to look down the table at Pierce. "Not runnin' it. At least not yet. Mostly usin' it as a regular hangout for anyone wearin' their colors."

"That's just south of the city line." Which could be concerning since it was farther out of the city than they've been before.

"Yup."

"They pushin' shit?"

Hawk raised a brow. That was enough of an answer for Pierce. He muttered, "Shit."

Dex spoke up. "Last thing we need is them runnin' drugs or guns through Shadow Valley. Don't want 'em stirrin' up the local boys in blue."

"That's for fuckin' sure," Jag muttered. "Bad enough Axel's always hangin' 'round Sophie's bakery."

"That's 'cause he's sniffin' 'round Bella," Ace volunteered with a frown.

"I'll kill the fucker," Diesel said. The club's Sergeant at Arms was a bit overly protective of his cousin. Though, for good reason.

Ace looked at his younger son. "You ain't doin' shit, boy."

"We can just hurt 'im a bit," Hawk added.

Ace's head swung to his oldest and he pointed a finger toward him in warning. "You neither, boy. Leave him be. It'll sort sooner than later. You know better than to fuck with SVPD."

"But if they're fuckin' with DAMC—"

Pierce jumped in. "Let it go for now. Got enough other shit goin' on than Axel gettin' a boner over Bella."

Diesel's body visibly tightened and his face twisted into a scowl. Hawk crossed his beefy arms over his chest and sat back in his chair, clearly unhappy with the order.

Though no matter what their father or their president said, the brothers would always step in to protect their cousin. No question about it.

And because of that, Jag knew he had to be careful with what could happen between him and Ivy, Bella's sister. She wasn't quite on their radar like Bella was, but it wouldn't take but a misstep to put her there. And he didn't need a hassle from either of them.

Jag might not be a small man and he made sure to keep in shape, but those two could pound him into the ground before he could say "boo." Best to stay on their good side.

Pierce leaned back in his chair. "Maybe it's time for a sit-down with the Knights. See if they're willin' to clue us in on what their intentions are. We don't wanna be caught with our panties down 'round our ankles."

"That's for damn sure," Dex said.

Ace nodded. "Agreed."

"All in favor?" Pierce asked.

"Ayes," rose up around the table.

"If they're not willing to chit chat, maybe we can get someone on the inside. One of Dawg's girls or somethin'," Dex suggested. "Just a thought."

"Not sure if the Knights will easily accept an obvious stripper into their fold. But you never know," Pierce said. "Pick a bitch that ain't so obvious. But they might agree to a sit-down, we can go that route first."

Dex continued, "If we need a plant, it's gotta be one loyal to the club. No doubt. We ain't takin' them down, we're just tryin' to get a little info on their territory grab. But still need to send in snatch that ain't gonna run her damn mouth. Not sure if we can trust one of Dawg's girls for that."

"Should we even ask for a sit-down first? Might give 'em a head's up. Maybe send in a bitch, get some info, *then* ask for a sit-down once she's clear," Diesel suggested.

Pierce turned toward Diesel. "Handle it. Talk to Dawg, see if any of his girls are reliable enough. If not, we may have to approach this from a different angle."

"Got it," Diesel grunted.

"All right, enough of the fuckin' bad news. This is a fuckin' MC an' we haven't had a group ride in a while so we need to get on that." Pierce looked pointedly at Jag. "Yo Road Captain, make it happen for Saturday. Got me?"

Jag nodded in agreement. "Gotcha. Certainly could use it. 'Specially now the weather turned."

A couple "yeahs" rose from the other members of the Executive Committee.

"Good. See it done. Hawk, plan a roast for after. Get the bitches to put somethin' together. An' get Mama Bear in the kitchen to make some good grub to go along with the hog."

"Done," Hawk grumbled, clearly still stewing about Bella and Axel.

Jag might have to give his cousin a head's up. Axel may be a cop, but he was still blood.

"We done here?" Pierce asked, looking around the table. When no one spoke up, he said, "Good," and pounded the gavel on the table.

As everyone pushed back their chairs and filed out, Ace put a hand on Jag's arm and tilted his head indicating for him to hold back.

Fuck.

Ace waited until the last member left the meeting room then

turned his attention to Jag. "Brother, you're like a son to me, but we need to have a sit-down of our own."

"'Bout what?" Jag asked, but he knew.

He definitely knew.

Ivy probably ran her mouth to her uncle first thing this morning at the pawn shop.

"You showin' up in the middle of the night at the apartment."

"Wasn't the middle of the night."

Ace just gave him a look.

Jag shrugged and repeated, "Wasn't."

"No matter. You got her all jacked up this morning. Had to hear her bitchin' for twenty minutes straight. What's goin' on between you two?"

"Nothin'."

"Well, I know that's bull. No reason for you to make yourself known every time she's got some man in her place."

There were plenty of reasons, just none he wanted to spill. "That don't bother you?"

"Not my business."

Right. But if it was one of the brothers doing nightly visits to Ivy's bed, Jag just bet Ace would make it his business. "I'm just lookin' out for her like Hawk an' D do for Bella. Bein' protective."

Ace snorted and shook his head. "Right."

"Somebody's gotta protect our women."

"You know Dex is perfectly fine with watchin' out for his sisters when it comes to that."

"Dex don't care who's crawlin' in an' out of their beds."

"Then maybe you shouldn't either."

Damn.

Ace continued. "What's your end game? 'Cause you know I don't want her endin' up with a brother. Sure as shit don't want her endin' up like Bella did."

Jag blinked. "That shit'll never happen again. An' it definitely wouldn't happen with me."

"So, you got interest," Ace stated rather than asked.

Fuck. He fell right into that trap.

Nothing like looking a man he respected in the eye and telling him that he's interested in fucking his niece, who was like a daughter to him. Ace might be in his fifties but he sired Hawk and Diesel, two very big guys. And the man was no slouch himself. Plus, he didn't need bad blood between them, anyway.

"You got no problem with her apartment havin' a revolvin' door?"

That may have been the wrong thing to say. Ace's eyes narrowed and his shoulders squared off.

Fuck.

"You sayin' she's as bad as a sweet butt?"

Holy fuck. She better not be as bad as one of the sweet butts, the eager women who hung around church to service any of the brothers whenever and wherever they wanted it. Most of them did it in hopes of one day becoming an ol' lady. Which, for most, would never happen. Brothers didn't want to make a sweet butt an ol' lady. Nobody wanted something permanent with what everyone else may have had.

"Not sayin' that."

"Good. But maybe the door would stop revolvin' if you stopped chasin' every guy she dates away."

Dates. *Right*.

Ace continued, "Makes me think you're hung up on her, Jag. Makes me wonder if I should take that key back I gave you for an emergency."

"Haven't abused that key. Always knock."

"Yeah, probably have to paint the door to cover up that *knock* from last night."

"You need it painted, I'll get it done."

Ace lifted his chin. "Yeah, I'll let you know if the mark don't come off. Then your ass can fix your fuck up."

Next time, he'd just use the key when Ivy refuses to open the door. That would really get her going.

"She gotta gun?"

Ace's eyebrows rose. "Why?"

"Just askin'."

"So, you plannin' on interruptin' her next time she's got a date?"

"Yep."

Ace dropped his head and shook it. His shoulders moved with what looked like laughter. "Fuck, boy. You're lucky I like you."

Jag smiled. "Know it, Ace. Promise I won't ever hurt her."

"Better not. 'Cause I'll kick your ass myself. An' I'll kick it if you repeat this, but somebody's got to tame her wayward ways. She's restless. She ain't findin' what she's lookin' for. That's obvious by that 'revolving door' you mentioned. Maybe it's high time a brother tried to get her to settle down."

"So, I got your blessin'?" Jag asked, surprised at this sudden turn.

"Didn't say that. An' it all ain't up to me." Ace studied him for a moment with his lips pursed and his hands on his hips, making Jag shuffle his feet uncomfortably. "You know she don't do bikers. That's gonna be a hurdle right there."

Little did he know she already had done one. Once. "Just needs to do one."

Ace shook his head. "Right. If she don't want you, you gotta drop this shit, hear me? An' then let her figure out what she wants on her own."

"Hear ya. Won't be a problem."

"Just want her to be happy."

"You ain't the only one," Jag murmured.

"She'd have my nuts in a vise if she knew what we were talkin' about."

"No doubt. Don't think that nerd last night had any nuts though."

Ace snorted and slapped him on the back as they walked out of the meeting room into the common area of the clubhouse. "Surprised there wasn't a line of shit from the balcony all the way out to his car."

Jag grinned. "Yeah. Wouldn't be surprised at all if he shit his pants."

CHAPTER TWO

The roar of the motorcycles making their way into the private parking lot behind the clubhouse made Ivy's blood rush and nipples pebble.

She may tend to date anybody other than brothers, but there was nothing like a biker on a Harley to get her juices flowing. She frowned. Or one in particular.

Ivy stared into the bonfire. She wished she'd been able to ride along today. But without being one of the brothers' "bitches" or ol' ladies, her ass got left behind. Neither Diesel nor Hawk wanted their cousin hanging on their back, nor did most of the other brothers, they only wanted to haul around their own piece of ass. Otherwise, they wanted complete freedom from any female hanging on. If you weren't putting out you were dead weight.

And it wasn't like she could get her own bike and ride along with them. They would shit a brick if she tried that. If a female went along on one of the rides, it was on the back of a bike or not at all.

She could've asked Jag, but that would've made things worse between them; he already butted his nose into her business too much as it was.

Like the other night. That was the first and last date with that guy. They hadn't even gotten to second base yet when Jag so rudely interrupted. Bad enough that Ivy hadn't had any in a while. And by a while, she meant weeks, which was not the norm for her. She'd admit she loved sex and loved a lot of it. And though she may not like the misogynistic ways of bikers, she did like a man who took charge in the bedroom. And some of the guys she'd been dating lately just haven't been doing it for her.

Well, for a little while there had been Adam, but suddenly he lost interest and never called her again.

She still had suspicions whether someone from the club intimidated him. She could never get an answer out of Adam himself. He had ignored all texts, calls, carrier pigeons and smoke signals she'd sent.

So finally, she had given up.

Her brother Dex said he knew nothing about it. In fact, he had actually liked Adam as compared to the rest of the nerd herd, as he called them, she normally dated. And Adam hadn't been afraid to attend club parties like tonight, which had been a plus. Diesel and Hawk also acted like they didn't know why Adam suddenly hightailed it out of her life and bed. As the man made his way across the courtyard, her eyes landed on who she thought was guilty.

Fucking Jag. His gaze fell on her as he made his way in her direction and she gave him a frown. He gave her an answering scowl, stopped his roll, and then changed course toward the kegs and coolers along the fence instead.

Good.

She wasn't in the mood to deal with him right now, anyhow.

"You aren't ever going to get anywhere with him if you constantly pinch your face up like that when you see him," her sister Bella said as she approached, handing her another drink.

"I don't want to get anywhere with him, so that isn't a problem." She tipped the red plastic cup to her lips and sipped to test the drink. Her sister made some awesome cocktails, but she had wasted her time and talent working behind the club's bar at The Iron Horse

Roadhouse. So recently she moved on to work with Zak's ol' lady, Sophie, at her bakery in town.

No one was surprised Bella was good at that, too.

"Sometimes I think I know you better than yourself," Bella stated, settling herself into the chair next to her, staring into the bonfire.

Ivy needed to shut this line of conversation down and knew just how to do it. "How's Axel?"

Bella took a sip from her own cup and frowned. Now who was frowning?

"Point taken," Bella murmured. "You're my baby sister, Ivy. I only want what's best for you."

"Yeah, and you think a brother's it? That surprises me coming from you. Especially after all you went through."

Ivy could see Bella's jaw tighten in the glow from the fire. Fuck. She didn't mean to hurt her sister. They just needed to get off the subject of men in general. "Was Sophie out riding with Z?"

"Yeah."

"You bring anything good from the bakery?"

"Everything from the bakery is good," her sister answered.

"You know what I mean."

"Yeah. A bunch of shit. I've been experimenting with filled cupcakes, so I brought along all the 'oops' and 'whoops' that I made."

Ivy laughed. "Yeah, we'll all suffer through getting rid of the evidence of your mistakes."

Bella lifted a bare, tattooed shoulder. She had on her "Property of No One" shirt tonight. Ivy swore her sister had a closet full of them and she liked to wear them during the parties like this to remind the brothers, the prospects, and any of the hang-arounds that she belonged to no one and planned to keep it that way.

Ivy took a swallow of her drink again. It was sweet, but tangy, and went down way too easily. "What is this?"

"Long Island Iced Tea."

"Fuck. Are you trying to get me messed up tonight?"

"Someone will give you a ride home. Ace can."

"Ace said he and Janice were heading home after the ride, not sticking around."

"Call Mom if no one else is available."

The last person she was calling was their mother to come pick her up like she was some teenager. "What about you?"

"I'm drinking the same thing you are."

"How are *you* getting home?"

Bella didn't answer.

"Bella," Ivy nudged.

"I'll find a ride."

Ivy studied her sister for a moment. Her suspicion was correct when Bella avoided her eyes. "If they see him anywhere on club property, there may be a problem."

"Yeah," Bella said softly, then took another long drink from her cup.

Ivy sighed. Both of them wanted men they shouldn't or couldn't have. Bella, a brother in blue, Ivy, a brother she shouldn't touch with a ten-foot pole—a fucking hundred-foot pole—and not remain her own woman.

Ivy followed her sister's example and downed a good portion of her drink.

She turned her head toward the makeshift "stage" in the large, grassy courtyard where the band was warming up now that Nash got back from the all-day ride.

"Gonna get loud soon," Bella murmured.

"The band or the brothers?"

Bella let out a little laugh. "Both. And then the sweet butts and Dawg's girls will be out in full force grinding against whoever lets them. Expect a bunch of loud moanin' and groanin'."

"Yeah," Ivy laughed, bumping her shoulder into her sister's. "Oooh, Diesel, let me pump your piston," Ivy mocked in a falsetto voice. "Please, let me smoke your exhaust pipe, D!"

"You called?" came from behind them and Ivy jumped, her eyes wide. She turned to face her cousin.

"Just wondering if you're hijacking the bathrooms tonight since you're too lazy to take them upstairs."

"Don't want them in my bed. Hard to get 'em back out," he grumbled.

"Yeah, the bathroom's so romantic, D."

Diesel snorted. "Ain't nothin' romantic 'bout what they're offerin'."

"You don't have to accept," Ivy reminded him.

"Right," he grunted.

"At least leave the little girls' room open, please. Use the men's room," Bella suggested.

Diesel swatted a big beefy hand toward them and stalked away. D was going to do what D was going to do and no one would tell him otherwise.

Even so, all the women were tired of walking in on Diesel doing some random woman against the ladies' room wall. Ivy didn't think there were any females left who hung out at the club that didn't know what Diesel's naked ass looked like. She wasn't thrilled with knowing what her cousin's rear end looked like, either.

"Looks like someone's already going at it," Bella stated, jerking her chin toward the open pavilion.

Ivy followed her gaze to see she was right. Two people—she couldn't tell who—were already bumping uglies on one of the picnic tables in full view of everyone. Not that anyone cared. She sighed. As long as it wasn't Jag and Goldie, one of Dawg's trashy-assed strippers, she didn't care, either.

She might have to wander closer and make sure it wasn't.

No. Even if it was, she didn't give a shit. He could do whoever he wanted. Even that skank Goldie.

Ivy downed the remainder of her drink and stared into her empty cup in disappointment.

"Another?" Bella asked.

"Yeah. I'd make it myself but you're the pro."

Bella snagged the plastic cup from her fingers. "That I am. Be right back."

As soon as the seat next to her was empty, Jewel slipped into the chair, a beer bottle hanging from her fingers and a large smile on her face as she stared at the pavilion.

"Someone's really going at it over there. Sounds like a hyena in heat."

Ivy glanced over toward the pavilion again. "Know who it is?"

"No. Ain't Jag though."

Her gaze bounced back to Jewel. "Wouldn't care if it *was* your brother."

"Right." Jewel answered with a smirk. "Whoever it is, I'm jealous. I haven't gotten any in a while."

"I'm sure Diesel's looking for his next romantic bathroom rendezvous."

"Ain't gonna be me."

"You can resist his charms?"

"Yeah, if you call grunting, grumbling and chest pounding charms. And find a big-ass, badass, scary-ass, bossy-ass beast charming."

Ivy laughed. Jewel tipped the beer bottle to her lips. She reminded Ivy of Jag. It was easy to tell that they were siblings. Along with their sister, Diamond, they had stunning bluish-grey eyes that could peer into your soul and plenty of thick dark brown hair. Jag's was shorter than his sisters', of course. All the women of the DAMC sisterhood tended to wear their hair long, the longer the better. While the brothers kept theirs at all different lengths. From Hawk's very short mohawk, with the sides shaved and tattooed, to Crow's very long black, straight hair, usually kept in a ponytail.

Ivy had to admit, she wouldn't mind running her fingers through Crow's hair to see if it was as silky as it looked.

"So, I heard some shit at the shop…"

Jewel always heard shit at the shop. She was the office manager there, keeping the guys straight in both the garage, managed by Crash, and the towing company, managed by Rig. She had quite a challenge doing it, too.

Jewel looked around her to make sure no one was sneaking up.

CHAPTER 2

"Heard they're gonna get one of Dawg's girls to infiltrate the Dark Knights, try to get the skinny on their territory grab."

"Yeah?"

"Yeah. Looking for someone who's willing to do it."

"Why would one of the strippers want to do that?"

Jewel shrugged. "Money?"

"Yeah, but—"

"They not only need someone willing, but someone loyal."

Ivy snorted. "Loyal? And they're looking at one of Dawg's girls? Please. They're loyal as long as you're shoving dollar bills in their thongs."

"Agreed." Jewel pursed her lips for a second before saying, "We should do it."

Ivy's head spun toward Jewel. "What?"

"Yeah. We should go in, hang out and get some info."

"Are you fucking crazy?"

"No. What's the worst that could happen? We have to sleep with one of the Knights to get a little pillow talk? Like I said, I haven't gotten any recently, anyway."

"What's the worst that could happen?" Ivy repeated in disbelief. "You *are* fucking crazy. How about being raped? Or fucked up. Or even killed if they discover you're DAMC property."

"We're not DAMC property," Jewel muttered.

"Yeah, we shout to the rooftops that we're not but when it comes down to it, you know the truth is we are." Fuck, she hated admitting that. But that was the truth, like it or not.

"Don't you want an adventure? You're always dating those nerdy guys. Don't you want some excitement?"

"It's safer to go skydiving."

"What are you girls talking about?" Bella asked, leaning over Ivy's shoulder to hand her a fresh drink.

Ivy gladly accepted it and took a long pull at it. Because after hearing Jewel's half-cocked idea, she needed it.

"Nothing," Ivy grumbled, giving Jewel a look, letting her know to keep her mouth shut.

Jewel frowned and tugged at her beer.

"Heard Diesel's looking for you in the bathroom, Jewel," Bella teased.

"Heard Axel's out front with his legs spread and holding a boom box over his head playing a Peter Gabriel song," Jewel busted back, slapping her thigh and laughing.

"And Jag's sending threatening emails to the Geek Squad warning them from plugging into your USB port, Ivy." Bella smirked.

"You guys are freaking funny," Ivy muttered.

Bella's smile disappeared when she looked toward the stage as the band, Dirty Deeds, started their first set. "Fucking Goldie."

Ivy's head whipped toward the direction Bella was looking, her heart in her throat. It dropped back in place when the guy Goldie was sucking off in front of the band wasn't Jag. It was one of the prospects, Squirrel.

"She's doing prospects now," Bella said, shaking her head. "Can't get any lower than that."

"She's getting older, gotta try to hook her tarnished star to someone's hog while she still can. I guess a prospect is better than no one. Dawg probably won't have her stripping much longer. I heard him say she isn't a main draw anymore," Jewel said, the distaste for the woman clear in her voice.

"Squirrel isn't going to make her an ol' lady," Ivy stated, hoping that was true.

"Don't think he cares about making her an ol' lady right about now," Bella muttered.

Even from where they sat, they could see the young prospect's face was tight, his eyes were squeezed shut and his hands dug deep into Goldie's bleached blonde hair.

The members of the band ignored the show taking place at the foot of their stage as they went from one song into the next.

"Well, ladies, fuck those hos. Let's go dance and show these cavemen the moves of a real woman."

Ivy was surprised when Bella hooted at Jewel's suggestion. She was usually low-key but must be sowing a wild oat tonight. She normally stayed inside at these gatherings, working the private bar instead of being outside partying with everyone else. So, it really surprised Ivy when her sister had come outside to hang out.

Though, she was pleased to see more of the sister she remembered returning instead of Bella just being a shell of her former self.

She wondered if it had anything to do with Axel.

Didn't matter if it did. If Axel made Bella happy, fuck anyone who was against it.

"Yeah, let's go dance!" Ivy yelled, downing a good portion of her Long Island Iced Tea before snagging Jewel's hand and pulling her out of the chair.

F ucking Ivy.

Jag sucked his teeth in annoyance as he leaned against the wood post of the pavilion, his eyes peeled to the woman dancing around the crushed grass with a bunch of the other women. They were all officially drunk off their asses. Singing. Swinging their hips. Shaking their tits. And Nash's band, Dirty Deeds, was playing whatever song would make them do it more wildly.

He knew it wouldn't be long before some of the sweet butts and hang-arounds, not to mention some of Dawg's women, were dancing around topless. The weather was warm enough for it. Even if it wasn't, he doubted that would stop them. It usually didn't.

If Ivy took off her damn tank top, he would blow a fucking blood vessel.

Zak sidled up to him, sucking on a bottle of beer. "Better than hanging out at Heaven's Angels."

"Right." He turned to his cousin. "Where's Sophie?"

"Crashin' in my room upstairs. She was up early bakin' an' then that long ride took a lot outta her."

"Been a while since we rode that long an' hard."

"Yeah. Needed that."

"Hear ya, brother. Sophie did good, though, for bein' new."

A proud smile pulled at Z's lips. "Yeah, she did." He angled his body toward Jag. "When you puttin' Ivy on the back of your bike?"

"Why? So she can scratch my fuckin' eyes out when I'm tryin' to ride?"

Zak snorted. "Ain't that bad."

"Bad enough."

"She just needs a bit of tamin'."

"Funny, Ace said the same thing."

Zak's brows rose in surprise. "Yeah?"

"Yeah."

"He tap you for that?"

Jag nodded. "Think so."

"Damn, cuz. You're the first brother to get the go ahead for any of the women he *thinks* he's responsible for."

"If he's like that with them, good thing he never had any daughters of his own."

Z blew out a breath. "Ain't that the fuckin' truth."

"Damn," Jag muttered, watching Kelsea and Ivy grinding on each other and throwing their heads back in laughter. "Goddamn, gonna give every male on the property a fuckin' hard-on that won't quit."

"Look at Diesel havin' a shit fit across the yard."

Jag glanced in the larger man's direction. Even from where Jag stood, he could tell the club's enforcer was not happy with what the women were doing out in the grass. Not that he had a lot of room to talk, he probably just got boned in the bathroom. And Jag didn't think he was disturbed by the women letting it all hang out. Maybe he was just being his usual overprotective self with Bella. Though he seemed to be glaring in Jewel's direction.

That was new.

When Jag looked back to see if his sister noticed, she was oblivious, now dancing with Bella, having a good time. When Jag's head swiveled back to Diesel, the man was gone.

Huh.

But his attention was quickly drawn back to the women and his body went tight. Ivy was now dancing by herself, her arms waving over her head, her curvy hips swinging, her head swaying, her eyes closed as she followed the music. He felt that all the way down into his dick.

Goddamn.

He swallowed hard. Then out of the corner of his eye, he saw it. One of the regular hang-arounds named Pete making his way closer to the women. Jag pushed himself off the post, his fingers gripping his beer bottle tightly as he watched the guy stalk directly toward Ivy, his eyes glued to her ass.

"Oh, fuck, no," he muttered. He took a swig of his beer and wiped the back of his hand across his mouth before swinging the bottle towards Zak. "Hold my beer."

"Nothin' good ever comes from that sayin'."

"No shit," Jag grumbled and moved. Before he made it to the group of women, Pete was standing behind Ivy, his hands on her hips, swaying along with her, grinding his *fucking dick* into her ass.

He bumped his shoulder hard into Pete, not quite knocking him off his feet, but definitely dislodging him from Ivy's ass.

"What—" The man looked over his shoulder at Jag and his eyes widened.

"Get gone, Pete," Jag growled. "Before you permanently disappear."

Pete lifted his hands in surrender. "Didn't mean to trespass."

"You know better than to touch club property." He tipped his chin toward some of Dawg's girls dancing in a group on the other side of the bonfire. "Have at it," Jag muttered, then the man scuttled in that direction.

Ivy ignored him, continuing to move to Dirty Deed's cover of AC/DC's *Shook Me All Night Long*. Jag took Pete's place behind Ivy, but instead of holding onto her hips, he brushed her long, red hair out of the way and pressed his lips to her ear. "You'll just take it from anyone, won't you?"

She stilled and looked over her shoulder, her flashing green eyes narrowed. "Anyone but you."

Just then, the band started their own slow rendition of *Knockin' on Heaven's Door.* Perfect. He grabbed her bicep, swung her around and directly into his arms.

"What the fuck?" she griped, trying to pull back.

Jag tightened his embrace, his hands sliding from her arms to her hips. He jerked her tight against him. "If you're lookin' for some dick, I got what you're lookin' for."

"*Jesus.* You know how to make a girl melt."

"Don't know about melt, but I can make 'em sweat an' come."

"Funny how I don't remember any of that."

"Need me to remind you?" He pressed his now hard-as-a-rock erection into her belly. Her eyes went from hot and angry to hot and... something else.

Damn. She *did* want him. She might fight it like a wildcat but it was unmistakable.

"If I give you this, will you leave me alone?" she asked.

"Leave you alone?"

"Yeah. You get what you're chasing and then you'll move on."

Jag's brows lowered. "That what you want?"

"Will getting me flat on my back get you off mine?"

No. But he wasn't admitting that out loud. "Sure."

She pursed her lips as she studied his face, which he purposely kept blank. "Liar," she said barely above the loud music. She shook her head. "Go away, Jag."

"You really want that?"

"Wouldn't say it if I didn't mean it."

Jag leaned in until his lips were directly above hers. "Now who's lyin'?"

"Not me," she whispered.

"Right," he whispered back. He wanted to kiss her right there in front of the band, the women, the brotherhood. He didn't care who was watching when he did it. But if she smacked the shit out of him, he'd mind who saw that. And he had a feeling that might happen.

"Let me go, Jag."

That was never going to happen. He was never letting her go. Not as long as he was breathing.

But, again, he kept that to himself and reluctantly released her.

He studied the woman he wanted almost his whole life, but kept herself out of his reach. At least until that one fateful night, when he thought things were changing, swinging in his favor. Turned out he couldn't have been more wrong. After that, she put even more distance between them. "Don't let me see you leavin' here with anyone tonight."

"You don't have a say in the matter."

Jag dipped his chin and gave her a hard look. "That wasn't a challenge."

"I need a drink."

"Yeah, that's exactly what you need," he muttered, shook his head and headed back to his waiting beer.

Jag dragged himself up the stairs toward his room at the clubhouse. The bonfire had died down to just coals, the kegs were kicked, the band was packing up their shit, and the common area downstairs was littered with bodies, either drunk or simply crashed.

After the all-day ride and then the pig roast, his ass was beat and his bed was calling to him.

Too bad he was hitting it alone. Goldie had offered him some company, but after seeing her blow a prospect, he wasn't near drunk enough to consider what she offered. A couple of the sweet butts had made it known they were available, but Jag wasn't in the mood for them, either. Diesel had the right idea... fuck them where they stood and don't let them near your bed, because they were hard to get out afterward.

Anyway, his mind was only on one woman and he had spent most of the night keeping an eye on her. At least, until she hit the head and never returned. A quick check of the parking lot showed her car still out there. Though, she may have slipped out with someone else.

Maybe she caught a ride home since the last time he saw her she wasn't fit to drive as it was. Nor were any of the other females that continued to dance and raise hell the rest of the night. And hell wasn't the only thing Ivy was raising. Jag had sported a hard-on most of the night as he watched her dance to just about every song Dirty Deeds played. Hard rock, heavy metal, classic rock. She didn't give a shit. She was letting herself move with the music.

It took everything he had not to grab a handful of that red hair of hers and drag her upstairs to his bed.

As he made his way down the corridor of rooms, he heard grunts, groans and squeals. His lips curled up at the corners and he shook his head as he reached his room. At least a few of the brothers were getting "down and dirty" like their club motto: "Down & Dirty 'til Dead."

Though that motto had a deeper meaning than just getting laid, it worked in that respect, too.

He dug deep into his jeans' pocket and found his key. He let himself into his dark room and hit the light.

Then froze.

There was no mistaking the wild red hair that tumbled over his pillows.

Fucking *goddamn* Ivy.

He slammed his door closed and slid the bolt lock home before turning to the bed, hands on his hips.

"What the fuck you doin' here, Ivy?"

When he didn't get an answer, he stalked to the bed and ripped the sheet off her.

Fuck, she was laying in his bed in just her panties and a bra.

Fuck.

Fuck.

Fuck.

"You lost?" he snapped.

Her green eyes blinked open in slow motion as she tried to focus on him. "No." Her answer came out thick and slow and it was not from sleep.

She was smashed.

CHAPTER 2

Once again, she was in his bed drunk as fuck. But this time he wasn't. Because if he was, he'd be sliding right in next to her to make her pay the rent for taking up space on his mattress.

Like last time.

But tonight he was way too sober for this shit. Her extreme temperature changes set his teeth on edge. Hot one minute, cold bitch the next.

Fuck that.

"All the fuckin' rooms up here, you had to break into mine."

"Needed a place to crash," she mumbled, then stretched her arms out over her head, yawning.

Jag watched as the generous mounds of flesh almost spilled out of her bra. He got to see those amazing tits once. And, for fuck's sake, he wanted to see them again, but not like this.

He wasn't doing this shit again.

Nope.

"Too inca... inca... pacitated to drive," she volunteered. Not that he needed to ask. It was a bit obvious.

"Incapacitated," he echoed.

She sucked in a deep breath then pushed herself into a seated position, her long fiery hair falling around her shoulders.

He cursed his dick when it started to rise.

"Yeah... Means drunk."

He frowned. "Know what the fuck it means. How'd you get in here?"

She shrugged sloppily. "Picked the lock."

She fucking *picked* the lock.

He wondered who taught her that and how often she's done it. He shook his head.

She patted the mattress. "You comin' to bed?"

He bit his bottom lip and dropped his head, staring at his boots as he warred with himself. "Fuck, Ivy. Not again," he muttered, more to himself than her.

Hell yes, he wanted to join her. But this was not how he wanted her.

He was not making that mistake again.

Last time, even though neither of them were completely sober, he had this mistaken idea that being with him meant something to her.

But it didn't.

It had meant nothing and she continued to chase every computer nerd, accounting geek, and pencil pusher from Pittsburgh to the West Virginia line.

His jaw tightened. "If you gotta be drunk to be with me, don't want you."

She tossed her head back, her hair flying and she glared at him.

Glared at *him*. What the fuck?

"No... you'd rather fuck that... that... Goldie... on the couch... in front of everyone."

"Ain't fuckin' Goldie."

She flung an arm in his direction. "Yeah... you already did."

"You got room to talk. You were draggin' some little boy around that night. I'm sure you rocked his world after you left here in a huff."

"Certainly did."

"Not enough for him to stick around, though."

She winced, then her face got hard. "Got a feelin' it wasn't me he... tired of... *Jagger*."

He gritted his teeth at the use of his full middle name, but she continued before he could stop her.

"Got a feelin' someone in this club chased him away... Maybe even threatened him..." She swung a hand in his direction again, her eyes narrowed. "Know anythin' 'bout that?"

Ah, fuck. "Nope."

"Liar."

"Whatever, Ivy. Seriously, I'm beat an' don't feel like dealin' with your shit right now. You wanna crash here, go ahead. If you're gonna puke, hit the head. Don't want to come back to chunks in my bed. Got me?"

CHAPTER 2

Without waiting for her to answer, he spun on his heel and headed toward the door.

"Where you goin'?"

He could have sworn that was an actual whine. Without looking back, he threw over his shoulder, "Somewhere else."

"But—"

He jerked the bolt lock open, pushed the lock button on the knob so no one else would wander in while she was passed out—because he was sure she'd pass out real soon—and stepped out into the hallway, slamming the door shut behind him.

It would serve her right if he went and crashed at her apartment.

CHAPTER THREE

Ivy eyeballed the Harley parked at the foot of her stairs. She glanced around first and then up the steps. No one was in the pawn shop lot but her and no one waited for her at her apartment door.

No one meaning Jag. She recognized his bike since it was custom and there could be no mistaking it since it was one of the nicest bikes in the club. But then Jag was the Road Captain, so he took pride in his baby more than most.

And that was the man's specialty... customizing bikes. He was well known in the industry for doing some damn good work. Customers came from all over for him to trick out their bikes.

Not that she cared.

Right? Right.

Maybe he was meeting Ace in the pawn shop for whatever reason. Most likely bitching about her actions last night. Like her uncle would care.

However, neither Ace's bike nor his truck were anywhere to be seen.

She climbed the steps slowly, her hangover still raging.

She admitted it, she had done a stupid thing.

Okay, a few stupid things.

The first being that she sucked down too many of Bella's easy-to-drink Long Island Iced Teas and getting shit-faced. The second was breaking into Jag's room while being shit-faced. The third was waking up alone in Jag's bed, no longer shit-faced but feeling the effects of being shit-faced instead.

Right now, she needed a date with the coffee pot in her kitchen and a jug of water.

Even though she hadn't slept with anyone last night—and apparently, not for lack of trying with Jag—she still felt like she was taking a walk of shame up to her own place.

She pressed the heel of her palm into her throbbing eyeball as she dug out her keys. Just the jingle of them made her wince.

Damn it.

After unlocking the door, she shoved it open, but closed it gently, trying to make the least amount of noise possible.

She dropped her keys and wallet on the kitchen counter and dragged the coffee maker out, set it up, and turned it on to brew.

Snagging a bottle of water out of the fridge, she cracked the lid and guzzled half of it down, then headed toward her bedroom as the soothing smell of coffee started to fill her small apartment.

A cup of coffee, a couple bottles of water, some aspirin and she'd soon be feeling some relief. And maybe more like herself.

She was never drinking again in her lifetime.

Though, before the coffee, she needed a shower desperately. She still smelled like the bonfire, booze, and sweat from all the dancing she did with the girls.

She rounded her couch to head down the hallway and then almost fell flat on her face as she tripped over something on the floor.

Flinging out a hand, she caught herself on the couch and stared at not only *something* but *two* somethings. Boots. Not just any boots. Fucking biker boots.

In her apartment. In her living room. On her floor.

Fucking Jag.

CHAPTER 3

She kicked them out of her way and beelined to her spare bedroom. The door was cracked open, but the room was empty. She moved to the next door, which was *her* bedroom, and the door was closed.

Oh. No.

No.

No. No. *No.*

She turned the knob quietly and shoved it open.

That fucker was asleep in her bed.

Her bed.

She looked down at the plastic water bottle in her hand, then at his head which looked way too comfy on two stacked pillows. And before she could control it—not that she wanted to—her hand whipped forward automatically.

Surprisingly, even with a lack of practice and a horrible hangover, she hit her target.

Jag yelled and rolled up to a seated position, holding his head. Now they both needed aspirin.

"What the fuck!"

She decided to state the obvious. "You're in my bed."

He glanced at the bottle lying next to him, then up at her. "What the fuck, Ivy?"

"You're in my bed," she repeated.

"Yep." He grabbed the water, unscrewed the lid, then downed the remainder as if being in her bed was nothing out of the ordinary.

"*Yep?* How did you get in?"

He grinned. "Picked the lock."

She opened her mouth then snapped it shut. She deserved that. "Why here?"

"Why *my* bed?" he threw back at her.

She opened her mouth then snapped it shut. Again.

Damn it.

She certainly wasn't going to tell him the truth about why she ended up in his bed. That would make him crow with victory. And all it really was was a moment of weakness.

Or so she kept telling herself.

"You need to get gone, Jag."

His eyes flicked to the clock radio on her nightstand. "It's only eight."

She planted her hands on her hips. "Yeah? And?"

"It's Sunday."

"Yeah? And?"

"Always sleep in on Sundays." With that he plumped both pillows, slid back into a reclining position, settled his head on *her* pillows and closed his eyes.

No. He. Didn't.

Maybe he needed a taste of his own medicine.

She stalked to the bed, took a fistful of the top sheet and whipped it down.

Fuck.

The man was only wearing his tattoos. Even though there were plenty of them, there weren't enough to cover all his male goodness.

And by male goodness, she meant male *goodness*.

If she was a cat, she'd be licking her whiskers.

She stepped back from the bed as he opened only one of his eyes. "Don't need sheets to sleep, just so you know." Then he closed that one eye, a smile curving his lips.

"You're not sleeping in my bed, Jag."

"Already did," he answered matter-of-factly, not opening his eyes.

"Well, you can stop now."

"When I wake up, I'll stop sleepin'."

Ivy groaned and pressed both heels of her palms into her eyes, grinding them hard. When she stopped, she saw spots. But they weren't big enough to block out his freaking awesome naked body in her bed.

And she hadn't seen that many tattoos since...

Since the last time she had been with Jag.

Damn. She forgot how well he wore them. "You gotta go. I have to shower."

"Yeah, I can smell you from here."

Her spine snapped straight. "What?"

"You stink, Ivy," he mumbled into the pillow, his eyes *still* closed.

Her mouth dropped open.

"You want me to do you before I leave today, you need to shower."

You want me to do you before I leave...

You want me to do you...

"Don't hear the water runnin'," he muttered.

She snapped her mouth shut.

"Don't forget the soap. Wash good. 'Specially if you want me to go down on you."

What...

The...

Fuck...

He did not just...

Nope.

"You think I want you to go down on me?"

Both steel-blue eyes popped open, he rolled to his side and propped a hand under his head to look at her. "Yeah, why wouldn't you?"

Goddamn, he looked good in that pose. She could... He could... *No.* "Because you're leaving, that's why."

"Ain't leavin'. So, go take a shower, get naked, then get in bed. Don't got all day. Need to catch up on some sleep."

He "don't got all day."

"Your bed is now empty back at church, you can go there to sleep."

"Not if it smells like you right now. Gonna hafta wash the sheets first."

Damn.

"Look, you were in my bed last night for a reason. But I'm not doin' you when you're drunk like that. Not again. This time when we bump uglies, you're gonna be wide awake an' you're gonna remember everything."

"You think I was in your bed because I wanted to sleep with you?"

One side of his mouth pulled up. All cocky-like. "Not sleep."

She blew out a breath. "Okay, then... Fuck you?"

"Yep. Why else?"

"Maybe because it was an empty room and I needed to crash."

"Bullshit, Ivy."

Yes, it *was* bullshit. Damn it.

"Baby, get in the shower. Time's a tickin'."

Jeez. Like he had an important appointment or something. The only thing he had to do was put his head back on *her* pillows and go back to sleep in *her* bed.

Fucking Jag.

With a frown and a curse under her breath, she kicked off her shoes and headed to the bathroom. She'd deal with him after she freshened up and felt a little more put together.

"Brush your teeth, too."

Ivy flipped him the bird over her head, then slammed the bathroom door.

Ivy dug her heels into Jag's tattooed back as her hips shot off the bed. And not for the first time, either. The man was certainly a master with his tongue. She also couldn't ignore his fingers, which were deep inside her, curved perfectly to make sure he hit the right spot.

No complaints there, he was *definitely* hitting all the right spots. The tip of his tongue flicked at her clit, his fingers worked in and out and his thumb pressed hard against her anus, teasing but not taking.

Fuuuuuck.

Had he been this good the first time around? Not that it mattered, because if he hadn't been, he was sure making up for it now.

She curled herself forward and dug her hands into his hair, grabbing a handful in each, holding him tightly against her as she cried out nonsense.

"That's it, baby," he murmured against her pussy. "Feel you comin'."

She felt herself coming, too. And it was a good one. Her body clenched tight around his fingers as she bucked against his face, an orgasm ripping through her. A moment later, she collapsed back onto the mattress with a long sigh, her chest rising and falling at a rapid pace.

She stared at the ceiling and thought, *I'm so screwed.*

No one previously in her bed had done what he just did so well.

Though, again, she kept that to herself.

On his hands and knees, he moved up until his face was directly above hers. He dropped his shiny lips to her mouth and dragged his tongue against hers so she tasted herself.

She moaned and cupped his cheek, but he pulled away to dip his head down, capturing one of her nipples. His tongue stroked the tip as he sucked it deep.

She closed her eyes when he rolled her other nipple between his thumb and forefinger.

Damn, why didn't he suck in bed? It would make it easier for her to avoid him. She didn't want a biker. Mostly because she didn't want to be some man's property. Or be treated like a second-class citizen.

She wasn't going to be caught dead wearing a "Property of Jag" cut. No fucking way.

She shook herself mentally. As far as she knew, he wasn't trying to claim her. So, hopefully after they got done "bumpin' uglies," he'd just leave and they'd both go on about their lives.

She snorted. Yeah, right.

Jag's head lifted, his grey-blue eyes narrowed. "Somethin' funny?"

"Nope. Are you going to fuck me or what?"

His eyes darkened and his lips curled in that delicious way they did. "Yep."

"Then get going."

He arched a brow. "You in a rush?"

"You said you need to catch up on your beauty rest."

"Yeah, an' this will help me do that. But no need to rush."

"Want my bed to myself."

"Told you I ain't leavin'."

"Oh, that's right. You *told* me." She rolled her eyes. "Sorry, I forgot."

He stared at her for a moment, his smile long gone. "I'm assumin' with all the dick you got comin' an' goin' in this joint, you got wraps."

All the breath left her suddenly and she felt the sting of tears. And she was *not* a crier. She blinked them away as she whispered, "Seriously, Jag?"

He went practically nose to nose with her, his face dead serious. "Yeah, seriously. That shit's gonna stop. Got me?"

Ivy's body went solid underneath him, the threat of tears instantly gone. "Why's that?"

"'Cause from now on, it's just me in here. An' I'm not talkin' about your apartment."

"Really."

"Really," he echoed with a sharp nod of his head.

Guess she was wrong about him trying to claim her. It wasn't going to happen, but with both of them being naked in bed, now was not the time to make it clear to him. "Are you going to finish what you started?"

"Yep."

"The condoms are in the top drawer."

He turned his head, looked at the nightstand, then leaned over to rip open the drawer, pulling out a large box. Which happened to be already opened.

And only half full.

He peered into it.

"Goddamn," he muttered. "This box is half empty *an'* it's warehouse sized. What the fuck, Ivy?"

"My sex life isn't your business, Jag."

"Is now."

She rolled her eyes again. "You trying to make me feel like a... a... *sweet butt?*"

His lips thinned as he pulled a condom out of the box. "If the shoe fits."

Her jaw tightened and she slammed both palms into his chest. He grunted from the impact but hardly moved. She struggled beneath him, but his hips pinned her tightly to the bed.

"Knock it off, baby, before you knee me in the dick."

"Don't tell me to knock it off. Get off me."

"No."

She slapped her palm on the mattress. "Jag."

"No."

"Jag..."

"No, baby. I'm gonna fuck you good, then we're gonna sleep."

"Well, maybe now I don't want to fuck you. And I definitely had no plans to sleep with you afterward."

"Okay."

Her brows shot up. "Okay?" Couldn't be that easy.

"I hear you but don't agree with you."

Ivy groaned and slammed her head back on the pillow. "Jag."

"Yeah, baby?"

Damn. Every time he called her baby, it tightened her nipples even more and made her break out in goosebumps. "Please don't call me that."

"Okay, baby."

Ivy blew out a breath. "Now you're just being an asshole."

"Yep." And then he had the nerve to smile. *Smile*. "Can I fuck you now?"

"And if I say no?"

"You sayin' no?"

"Goddamn it," she muttered.

"Thought so." He ripped open the wrapper and rolled the condom over his cock. He went nose to nose with her again. "You want the bottom or you wanna ride me like the wild woman you are?"

Ivy blinked up at him, but considered her options. "Start at the bottom then finish on top."

"*Fuck,*" he breathed. "That's my girl."

Nope. "Just today."

"What?"

She needed to lay down some ground rules. "Just your girl this moment, right now. That's it."

He studied her for a second, then smiled his cocky smile. "Okay, baby, whatever you say."

Right.

Then the thick crown of his cock bumped her slick folds and Ivy figured she'd worry about all that other stuff at another time. Like after she tossed him out on his ass later.

When he pushed inside her, everything melted away between the two of them. He moved slow and gentle, his hips finding a rhythm that made her want him even more. He pressed his forehead to hers and their gazes locked.

When he whispered, "Baby," her toes curled and lightning shot down her spine.

Damn. She wasn't expecting it like this. Not from him.

Tender. Gentle. Loving.

Her heart seized.

He had to be screwing with her. Faking her out. Playing a game. Something.

He leaned on his elbows and took her cheeks in his large hands, pressing his lips to hers, brushing against them softly.

What the hell was going on?

They were supposed to be fucking. That's it. *Fucking.* This wasn't fucking.

Ivy found it difficult to swallow as she stared at the man above her. Where was this biker pulling out finesse like this to actually make love to her?

Never in her life had she been made love to. It had only ever been sex, a mutual physical satisfaction. Even with Adam, who stuck around longer than most guys, she wouldn't allow emotions to get tangled up between them.

But this tattooed, badass biker knew just how to move his hips. He wasn't just slamming her hard. No. He was drawing out her responses gently. He was forcing her to keep eye contact, to keep a connection.

He wasn't playing fair.

Not at all.

"Nobody else in here, baby. Nobody but me. Got me?" he said softly.

She opened her mouth, however, nothing but a gasp escaped as he thrust and held it, grinding deep, making her squirm.

"Got me, Ivy?"

No. No. He was not going to claim her. He was not going to own her. She was not going to end up an ol' lady. Jag's or anyone else's.

No, she was not.

"Jag..."

"Mine, baby."

Panic started to claw at her. She couldn't allow this connection to happen. "Jag... Fuck me."

"I am."

No, he wasn't. He wasn't. He was fucking with her head. He needed to stop with the sweet stuff and just get down to business... getting them both off.

That's the only reason she had slipped into bed with him after her shower.

"Jag, don't do this," she whispered, her voice cracking.

"Do what, baby?" he murmured against her neck, his hips moving slow, coaxing a response from her. The heat of his breath beat against her skin.

"What you're doing."

"What am I doin'?"

Oh, shit, he was destroying her. That's what he was doing. Peeling away the hard layers that she had put in place to keep him and any other biker out of her heart. They weren't like this. They weren't.

They weren't loving and caring.

He was just trying to soften her up enough that he could claim her, then he'd change back into his real self. The misogynistic asshole who treated women like property like the rest of them.

Because even though she loved them and considered them family, they were all just that.

"Harder, Jag."

"'Kay, baby."

But he didn't go any harder.

"Rougher, Jag. Faster. Give it to me good."

"Givin' it to you."

No, he wasn't.

"Fuck me like you mean it."

He finally lifted his head and shifted to look down into her eyes. "Mean everythin' I'm givin' you, baby."

That's what she was afraid of.

"Please, Jag, don't make this special," she begged, then bit her lip when he stilled, his body tense above her.

"Just a dick in your bed, that what you want? Just like any other dick in your bed? Gettin' you off? That what you want, Ivy?" He slammed his cock deep once, and they both grunted with the impact. "That what you want? Hard, fast, an' furious? Just a fuck?"

She winced at his words. "Yes. That's what I want. That's the only thing I want from you."

His nostrils flared and his eyes narrowed. "Goddamn, you're a fuckin' bitch, Ivy."

She closed her eyes and sucked in a breath. "Just fuck me, get me off, and then get the fuck out." It came out softer than she meant it to, but it still had the same effect as if she had spit it in his face.

He went so solid, he didn't even breathe. But she couldn't open her eyes, she couldn't look at him.

She just couldn't.

Then he was off her but before she could open her eyes, he

CHAPTER 3

flipped her onto her belly and yanked her hips up until she was on her knees. "Can't stand to look at me? Fine. Play it your way." He slammed into her hard and she gasped. "Wanna get off? Fine. So do I." He rammed her deep again. Then again. There was nothing soft about his movements now. "Just want me to be a dick? I can be a dick. More ways than one." Now it was just raw fucking, just physical contact. Nothing more. "Got you, Ivy."

She should be relieved. But she wasn't.

The breath rushed out of her every time he thrust hard. He grunted, slapped her ass, moving faster, rougher, making sure what he did couldn't be mistaken for anything but a fuck.

"That what you want? Just to use my dick? Well, you got it, babe. You get my dick an' nothin' else." He shoved her face down, keeping his large hand at the back of her head, pinning her into the pillow, not letting her move. Not that she struggled. She had no need to. She took every slam of his hips against her. Though she wasn't going to get off that way, not from behind. Not like this. But she wasn't going to tell him that.

She wasn't going to ask for anything more from him than what he was giving her.

This was what she wanted, asked for. Wasn't it?

She reached between her legs pressing two fingers against her clit, circling, wanting to get off before he did. Because it was obvious with the anger making his body tight, he wasn't going to wait for her to come.

At this point, he was in no way concerned with her being taken care of.

He grabbed her wrist, squeezing hard, and yanked it away from herself. "That what you want, Ivy? To just get off?"

He took over, roughly pushing his thumb against her, circling, pressing and she cried out.

"Wanna come, Ivy?"

"Yes," she hissed as she took the brunt of his thrusts and the rough handling of her sensitive clit.

This was what she expected from him from the beginning. Not that sweet, caring stuff.

"I feel you tightenin' around my dick, squeezin' me. You close?"

She was afraid to tell him that she was. She feared he'd pull out and leave her hanging to prove a point. "No. Fuck me harder."

"Liar," he grunted, slamming her faster, their skin slapping together. "You just wanna be pussy, Ivy? Just a hole to bust a nut in?"

No, damn it, that's not what she wanted. She closed her eyes and bit her bottom lip. "Jag..."

"Shut up, Ivy. You said enough."

CHAPTER FOUR

Jag sat on the end of the bed and dragged a hand through his hair. He was doing everything he could not to look over his shoulder at Ivy.

He wanted to strangle her, that's what he wanted to do. Knock some fucking sense into her.

The stubborn woman was always searching for the wrong thing. Always chasing the wrong type of guy. She seemed determined to buck her fate.

What she didn't realize was that there was no way she could end up permanently with someone like the men she brought home. The geeks, the nerds, the pussies.

They could never satisfy her in the end. Her personality would roll over them. It was one reason they never stuck around long. Jag intimidating them was another. Though, it wasn't just him that pushed them away. She couldn't drag a non-biker to club pig roasts and parties and expect them to fit in. Or even feel comfortable.

Ivy was Dirty Angels MC through and through. It was in her blood as much as it was in Jag's. The same as it was her uncle's or her cousins', or even Dex and Bella's.

Though, he hated to admit it, he'd waited a long time for his shot with her. Way too long. And he was not a man who had a lot of patience. Especially when it came to that spitfire.

He'd watched her through the years desperately trying to avoid ending up with one of the brothers. Did he understand why?

Yeah. Sorta.

Was he going to accept it? Fuck no.

When the day finally came that she admitted she belonged to the club in every way possible, she couldn't belong to just any one of them. No fucking way.

She was his.

She'd always been his. All the way back to when they were kids and she had a crush on Zak, who'd never make a move on her. Whether she realized it or not, no other brother, or even prospect, would ever approach her, even if she wanted them to.

It was called respect. And it was the glue that bonded the brotherhood.

And, as for respect, Ivy wasn't showing him any right now. Nothing new, though, he was used to it.

But that wasn't what bothered him. What stuck in his craw was that he finally had his chance with her when they weren't drunk and she turned something that could've been good into something ugly. It was nothing more than a transaction for her.

He stared down at his hands which were curled into fists on his thighs and blew out a breath.

He needed to get dressed, walk out, and slam the door behind him without so much as a *see-ya-the-fuck-later*. Cleanse her poison from his system.

He needed to get over her and move the fuck on.

But fuck him, he couldn't.

He closed his eyes and sighed. "Ah fuck, Ivy."

"Don't make this into something it's not, Jag."

His jaw tightened and he could barely get out, "Tell me what it is then."

"Nothing."

Nothing. This was nothing to her. He was nothing.

He jumped to his feet and rounded the bed to where she sat back against the headboard. He stared down at her.

Something flickered behind her eyes as she met his.

She was so full of shit.

This wasn't nothing.

This was everything. And it scared her.

"If it's nothing, why'd you break into my room?"

She shrugged a bare shoulder. "We already had this discussion."

"If it's nothing, why'd you climb into bed with me after your shower?"

"It's my bed."

"You don't want me that bad, you gotta spare room."

"I just wanted to get off."

He gritted his teeth. "Yeah, you got that."

"Yes, I did." She raised her hand toward the door. "Now you can leave." She dropped her hand into her lap. "And anyway, I probably stink again, so I don't want to offend your sensitive olfactory system."

He frowned. His what?

"Your nose," she clarified.

"Smell like me now. Left me on you. I can live with that."

"Maybe it's a smell I can't live with and need to wash it off me."

Sometimes she just acted like a cold fucking bitch.

But inside... inside he knew she wasn't. Inside she burned as hot as the color of her hair. She just didn't burn for him.

And once again, it hit him that he needed to get dressed and get gone. From her apartment. From her life.

But before he left, he needed to show her the error of her ways. Or at least try to make another attempt.

Show her what she'd be missing if he walked out the door and never came back. Yeah, they'd see each other at church. Yeah, it'd be hard to ignore each other completely. And it would be bad for him when she dragged her next nerdy conquest to a club party.

So, if he couldn't have her again after today, he wanted to make it good enough that neither of them would forget.

Not like the fuck that they just did. It could've been any woman under him earlier. And Ivy wasn't just any woman.

"You just going to stand there with your junk hanging out? Or you going to get dressed and get gone?"

"Not goin' anywhere. We're gonna do this right an' then I'll leave."

"What do you mean, do it right? We just did it."

He climbed onto the bed and went face to face with her. "We're going to do this right, babe."

"I don't see—"

He cut off her words when he took her mouth hard. Taking advantage of her surprised gasp, he shoved his tongue between her lips to tangle with hers. A noise rose from the back of her throat.

He didn't care if it was a complaint or encouragement. This time they were doing it his way.

She grabbed his shoulders, digging her nails into his flesh. He flinched but didn't let up. Instead, he straddled her legs while burying his hands into her hair, holding her still.

Then she bit his bottom lip, he jerked back, tasting blood.

Her body was tense, her eyes narrowed and before she could bitch him out, he claimed her mouth again. But not before saying, "Mine," against her lips.

He explored the inside of her mouth, hoping she didn't bite his tongue off. Because that would suck.

But she didn't. The longer he kissed her, the softer she became, her nails raking down his back, this time not in anger, and it made him hard for her. When her hands slid up his back, she didn't stop until she had fistfuls of his hair.

He waited for the painful tug. But it didn't come. And when she moaned into his mouth, he knew he had her.

He had her.

Her fingers curled against his scalp and with a tilt of her head, she took the kiss deeper.

This. This was what he wanted from her.

CHAPTER 4

He pulled back enough to grumble, "Gonna do this the way we should've earlier. On your back, then you on top."

Her eyes were unfocused, her lips swollen and shiny, and damn, he wanted them wrapped around his dick.

When he shifted to put her on her back, she slipped quickly from under him. Before he could grab her, she shoved a hand against his chest and pushed him down, then settled between his legs.

Yes. She'd read his mind.

When her hot, wet mouth encircled him, he threw his head back and barked, "Fuck," at the ceiling. Then his eyes rolled back in his head as her tongue did some wicked fucking dance over his length and down to his balls.

Holy mother fuck.

His breath caught and he lifted his head enough to see her thick, red hair spread across his lap. He grabbed a handful of it and rubbed the silkiness over his stomach. Satin. Warm satin. Just like her pussy.

As her teeth scraped along the head of his cock, his hips jerked and he slammed a hand down on the mattress. "Fuck!"

But it was when he parted her mass of fiery hair so he could see her face, when she tilted her eyes up to his and held them as her cheeks hollowed out, he just about lost his shit.

That sight was going to be burned into his brain for the rest of his life. If he walked out of there today and never saw her again, this was what he'd remember. Her red hair, her green eyes, her lips stretched around him.

Goddamn heaven, it was.

And then she squeezed his balls...

He fought with himself on whether he wanted to just come down her throat or fuck her again. He wanted both, but he knew he may not get that choice.

He had to take what he could get, what she was willing to give him at that very moment. Because even though now she was eager, hot and bothered, in a few minutes, she might turn cold as ice.

And he didn't want the Ivy he had right that minute to disappear. He had to keep her as long as he could.

But it wasn't him that made the decision on how to finish. It was her as she moved away and went to the open box of condoms, snagging one and tossing it onto his chest.

Her voice was thick when she urged him to hurry.

He usually didn't take orders from any woman. But this was one he'd allow. He might be a hard-headed biker, but he wasn't stupid.

He tore the wrapper open, rolled the condom on and before he could raise his gaze, she was there... Pushing away his hands, mounting him, then *sliiiiiiiding* slowly down his cock.

Holy mother fuck.

And when she finally had him fully inside her, she stilled, closed her eyes, and he could feel her pulsating around him, the warm, wet silk of her pussy squeezing him tight.

He flexed his dick deep inside her and her eyes popped open, a smile crossing her lips as she met his gaze.

Then, suddenly it hit him that she'd done this with other men. Been on top like this, looked exactly like this with someone other than him. More like with many someones. And he had to squeeze his eyes shut to let the fury run through him. Otherwise they would be back to where they were earlier. Just two bodies fucking and getting off.

He was determined it wouldn't be like that this time. He needed to remember that. He needed to concentrate on this moment. This time, this place.

"Jag," she whispered, and he opened his eyes to see hers with a question in them. "Isn't this what you wanted?"

"Yeah," he said just as softly, trying to keep the anger from his face.

Her brows furrowed. "Then why does it look like someone kicked your puppy?"

He sucked a hard breath through his nostrils. "Ain't nothin'."

When she started to move, he couldn't help but let the anger go. He reminded himself that he'd been no angel, either. In fact, he'd done some stupid shit when it came to other women... like letting

Goldie ride him on the couch in front of everyone, including Ivy and the man-boy she was dragging around that night.

Ivy's tits bouncing as she rose and fell on his dick took him out of his thoughts. They weren't huge, or heavy, but they were big enough to fit his hands perfectly and they were the perkiest tits he ever saw. He cupped them in his palms and ran his thumbs over the tightly beaded tips.

Since it caused her mouth to part, and her eyes to darken, he did it again. Then he rolled them between his fingers and pulled. Her fingers clamped around his wrists tightly and she encouraged him to pinch her nipples harder, to twist them roughly and he did.

Fuck.

No other man's hands belonged on her tits. On her body. No other cock but his belonged inside her.

He bucked his hips up and knocked her off balance, then twisted until she was now under him. He slid deep inside her and stilled, meeting her green eyes.

Then he thrust slowly, all the way in, all the way out until he barely nudged her with the tip.

"Jag," she breathed.

"Like that?"

"Yeah."

Yeah she did. So did he.

All the way inside her, then all the way back out, teasing her opening with the crown again.

"Fuck," she groaned.

He did it once more. This time staying outside of her warmth for a beat. She squirmed against him, pushed her hips up.

"Jag," she moaned.

All the way in. All the way out. Even though she tried to follow his movement, not let him escape, he did. He pulled out and away. Far enough she couldn't impale herself, which she was trying desperately to do.

This time when he seated himself into her heat, he stayed deep within her. He pressed his face into her neck, his breath ragged. His movements might be driving her crazy, but they were pushing his limits, too.

She squirmed beneath him, whimpering, clawing at his ass, trying to get him to continue.

When he finally moved, he found a rhythm that was slow, complete. It wasn't hard or fast or rough. It was what he did earlier when he wanted to show her how good it could be between them. That they were made for each other, how well they fit together.

This time she let him have his way, shifting her hips with his, wrapping her arms around his neck, whispering in his ear, "That's it, Jag. Oh, *God*, that feels so good."

Surrounded by her wet heat, his brain turned to mush and his thoughts spun as he listened to her sweet voice egging him on.

Her heels dug into the backs of his thighs as she arched beneath him. Then his balls tightened as she breathed his name against his skin.

Fuck.

Fuck.

Fuck.

This was his Ivy. "Ah, *fuck*, baby."

"Make me come, Mick."

His hips hiccupped at the use of his real name. One he hadn't heard since they were little. In fact, a name most people didn't even know existed.

One his parents thought would be "cool" to name him since it was after the rock star.

His heart squeezed painfully. "You tryin' to forget who I am?"

She drew her fingers down his spine and grabbed a handful of his ass. "No."

"Tryin' to make me into somethin' I'm not?"

"No, Jag. Fuck me. *Please*."

He dragged his tongue down her neck and sucked a tight nipple into his mouth. He flicked at the tip, then lifted his head. "What's my name?"

She hesitated, but finally breathed, "Jag."

He rolled the now wet nipple between his thumb and forefinger and moved to tease the other one with his mouth. He ground his hips against her making her toss her head back and wail, clenching tightly around him.

Fuck.

Fuck.

Fuck.

"Say my name."

"Jag."

"Again."

"Jag."

"*Fuck*, baby. Say it again."

She released another low wail, wiggling her hips beneath him, encouraging him to move faster. "Jag."

Fuck that. He was taking his sweet fucking time.

No matter what she said, what she did, she wasn't going to change that. He had never taken it this slow with anyone before. And he had to admit, it wasn't easy. Especially with Ivy, who drove him nuts in more ways than one.

"Jag, *please*."

He shoved his face into her neck and smiled as he continued with his slow, steady rhythm. He inhaled her scent and locked it into his memory. He slid a hand between them, finding where they were joined and tweaked her clit, then circled it with his thumb.

She tightened down on him and he had to fight the urge to move faster, to make it to the end as soon as he could. It took everything he had not to take them over the edge as quickly and fiercely as possible.

"Damn you," she groaned, arching her neck back.

He sucked the skin at the base of her throat, then murmured, "Want me to stop?"

Ivy went still beneath him. "Don't you fucking dare."

He grinned against her ivory skin as her legs tightened around his hips. But the grin quickly turned into a hiss when she clenched her muscles around his dick tight. Then she did it again.

And again.

Ah fuck, she was playing dirty.

His balls pulled tight when she did it again.

Even though he had stopped thrusting, her actions were about to make him blow his load.

Was she that worked up or did she just want this to be over?

He hoped it wasn't the latter. Because, fuck him, he was in deep. And not his dick, either. It was more than that. It always had been.

Fucking Ivy.

He worked his thumb faster, circling her clit. She clenched down so tightly on him he muttered a curse then gave up all control, pounding her hard and fast and finally giving her what she wanted.

"Yessss," she hissed, digging her nails into the flesh of his ass. "That's it, Jag. Right there. Oh, right... there." Her hips tilted it up and she cried out, "I'm coming," as her orgasm radiated around him.

And fuck him, those words were his undoing. He thrust once more and let loose deep inside her. "Me, too, baby." And for once in his life he wished he wasn't wearing a condom. He wanted to make her his completely.

Moments later, he peeled himself off her, sliding to her side, attempting to catch his breath, watching her chest rise and fall rapidly as she tried to control hers.

She stared up at the ceiling as she confessed, "I don't sleep with bikers."

Was she trying to convince herself or him?

Jag drew a sharp breath through his nose. "Know that, babe."

"Not one."

Well, one. But he got where she was going with it.

"Then you happened."

His chest got tight. He assumed she was talking about that first time with their drunken hookup. "Sorry for you, baby, that it happened. But it did. No takin' it back." He twisted his head toward her. "Was it so bad?"

"No, that's the problem," she muttered, avoiding his eyes.

He fought back a grin. "Don't sound like a problem to me."

"It wouldn't," she answered softly.

"When's the last time you had it that good?"

She pursed her lips before saying, "It's all what you make of it."

His eyebrows pinned together. "Whadaya mean?"

She covered her eyes with her hand. "Nothing. Never mind."

He closed his eyes for a moment trying to keep his shit together. It was a losing battle. Finally, he grumbled, "Fuckin' goddamnit, Ivy, let me in."

"I can't," she said so softly, he almost didn't hear it.

It wasn't that she couldn't, she wouldn't. Which ticked him off even more. "If I was someone named Mick, would you?"

Would she accept a guy named Mick Jamison instead of Jag Jamison? It wasn't the name itself, it was the possibilities of the man behind the name. If he wasn't DAMC, would he go by Mick instead of Jag?

Who fucking knew. But no matter what, he *was* DAMC. Always was, always will be. That would never change whether she accepted it or not.

She lifted her hand from her face and her eyes slid to him. "Maybe. If you were Mick. But you're not." She rolled onto her side and went face to face with him. "But you're not Mick. You're Jag because you're a brother. And as a brother, you're a part of this club. As a brother, you treat women like property. As a brother, you keep shit from us, you dictate to us. You treat your fucking bikes better. In this club, it's better to have an engine than a vagina."

He frowned at the trace of pain in her voice, the hurt in her words. "Bullshit."

Throughout the years, there were plenty of brothers who loved their ol' ladies. Once a woman was established as an ol' lady they were treated with respect. Yeah, they were supposed to be kept out of club business, though Jag was sure some shit slipped out during pillow talk, but for the most part, they were kept in the dark from things that didn't concern them.

Some ol' ladies revered their status. Wore their ol' man's cut with pride. A lot of the women, whether sweet butts or others, who hung around church, did so to try to get in good with one, find a permanent spot on the back of a bike. Some brothers even married their ol' ladies, like Zak was going to do with Sophie.

Not that he blamed his cousin there. Sophie was worth keeping. Loyal, smart, sexy, successful, everything Jag was looking for in an ol' lady, too.

If he was going to be tied down with a ball and chain, it had to be the right one.

And he was lying naked next to the one who had everything he was looking for. He could see himself waking up next to her every morning and falling asleep after they fucked every night.

But if she was looking for him to be Mick, an average Joe, someone he was not, instead of Jag, she'd never accept him.

He was not changing for anyone. Even her.

They grew up together, so she'd never known him to be anyone other than Jag. He was DAMC through and through.

And whether she wanted to admit it or not, so was she.

"Think Z treats his bike better than Sophie?" When she didn't answer he continued, "Think Ace treats Janice like property?"

"Bella—" she started, but he cut her off.

"That shit ain't right no matter who you are, Ivy. Can't use that as a comparison."

"It happens," she said softly to the ceiling.

"Yeah, it happens." He sucked in a breath to bring up something she did last night while she was wasted. Something she may not remember but was going to have to deal with. "Speaking of Z, you started hangin' all over him. Sophie hears about that shit, she ain't gonna be happy."

"Fuck," she groaned and put a hand over her eyes, rocking her head back and forth.

"Yeah, 'fuck.' Was bad, Ivy. You're lucky she's a nice girl. Anyone else, you'd get a knife in your ribs. The sisterhood only goes so far when you're fuckin' with a bitch's old man."

"I need to apologize to her."

"Wouldn't say a word unless she comes to you. Hear me?"

CHAPTER 4

She nodded, still staring at the ceiling. "Why didn't you stop me?"

Jag closed his eyes and took a calming breath. "Z did. Was nice about it. I stop you, it ain't gonna be nice. No matter what, you gotta get your shit together. You're outta control."

"I'm not out of control."

"I'm not the only one who thinks so."

She turned her head toward him, her eyes flashing. "Who thinks I'm out of control?"

"People concerned, that's all, Ivy. Need to settle down."

Her eyebrows shot up her forehead. "*Settle down?* With who? You?"

"Know you've had a crush on Z forever." Shouldn't be so painful for him to say it, but it was.

Her body jerked next to him. "Jesus. When we were kids."

Jag snorted. "Right. Thinkin' that's why you're so restless when it comes to dick. Won't be happy until you get Zak, even though he's already got an ol' lady he's crazy over."

"No." She shook her head. "No, Jag. That's not it at all."

"I'm wonderin'. An' if that's true, then I never had a shot."

Goddamn, he just said too much.

She stilled. "You want me to be your ol' lady, Jag?"

Oh, that was a fucking trap. He wasn't going to answer that. Because his answer was sure to come back to bite him.

Fucking Ivy.

She was setting him up for a slam dunk. And he wasn't going to play that game.

No way.

His lips thinned and he looked away.

When he refused to answer she finally said, "I don't need a man. I'm smart and I'm quite capable of doing things for myself."

"Know you are, but don't mean you should."

"Not looking to get tied down, Jag. With you. With any of the brothers."

He pushed himself up to a seat and looked down at her. "Yeah.

You're makin' that clear." Then he climbed out of bed to find his jeans and boxer briefs. After jamming his legs into them, he zipped his fly and fastened his silver DAMC belt buckle. He didn't glance up until he was done.

Ivy had sat up in bed, the sheet tucked around her chest. But she was watching him.

Yeah, she was. So he took his time looking for his T-shirt and moved even slower when he pulled it over his head, making sure she didn't miss a thing. He snagged his cut, which was thrown over a chair and shrugged into it.

He glanced over his shoulder at her. She looked good enough to kiss.

Fuck, she looked good enough to eat.

But he had enough of her shit for today. But that didn't mean he didn't want to keep chipping away at her hard, stubborn exterior.

"Next time you got an itch for dick an' you ain't drunk, call me. Don't be sleepin' with strange, Ivy. It's dangerous." With that he stood and walked over to her nightstand, picked up the open condom box and counted.

Eight.

"Better be eight in that box when you call me to come take care of your *business*. Got me?"

Her eyes narrowed as she watched him toss the box onto the bed next to her. Then he strode out of her bedroom, snagged his boots on his way out of her apartment, and slammed the door without even a goodbye.

CHAPTER FIVE

Ivy sat perched on the desk at Shadow Valley Body Works, where Jewel ran the office.

Even though Jag worked there, she was hoping she didn't run into him today. Not with how they left it last Sunday.

But she brought her girl some lunch, and she wasn't going to be able to avoid Jag forever. Plus, even though she might be nuts, she was actually thinking about taking him up on his offer. Or more like demand.

She wasn't looking to be tied down, so as long as he didn't make a play for her to be his ol' lady, what was wrong with them knockin' boots every once in a while? No one had to know but them, right?

Right.

And the guy was good in bed, too. That was a plus.

A big one.

If she had to admit it, probably the best she'd had in a while. Adam was good but Adam was no Jag.

Though, Adam wasn't really into biting and nails. She bet Jag would eat that shit up. As well as probably give as good as he got.

Heat rushed through her at the thought.

Just then, Crash did what he did best and crashed through the door between the shop and the office. He stopped short when he saw Ivy.

Then he looked down at the burgers and fries they both had in front of them. His golden-brown eyes popped back up to her with a frown. "Brought Bangin' Burgers for Jewel, but none for the rest of us?"

Ivy felt heat rush into her cheeks. In truth, she hadn't even thought about it. "It was a last-minute thing. I didn't have time to get an order together."

"That's just wrong, Ivy. You know we love that shit. Can I have your fries, Jewelee?"

Jewel quickly covered her fries with her hands and hunched over her desk, protecting her food. "No! You know I love this shit, too. Get gone, Crash."

"What the fuck," he muttered, his eyes narrowed. "That's just cold."

"No, what's gonna be cold is my fries if you don't leave me alone."

With a grunt, he turned on his heel, heading back out to the shop.

"I wonder what he needed?" Ivy asked, watching his retreating back. She made a face when she saw the man was wearing his dirty-blond hair in a man-bun again. Ugh. Man buns. Sure, he had to keep his long, luscious hair out of his face when he worked... but still. Ivy shuddered.

Jewel shrugged. "Don't know. Don't care. They bug me all day for no reason." She shoved a fry in her mouth. "Mmm. No way I'm sharing any of these fries. They give me a damn orgasm."

Ivy laughed, dragging one of hers through a puddle of ketchup and popping it into her mouth. She agreed, they were some of the best burgers and fries in the area. Angus beef. Hand cut fries. Just a whole lot of yum. "Guess I should've at least stopped at the bakery and brought a dozen cupcakes from Sophie's." And while there, felt out whether Sophie knew about her hanging all over her man at the party.

CHAPTER 5

Jewel's eyes lit up. "Oh, damn, yes. Though, between this and a cupcake, it would wreak havoc on my hips."

"You've got great hips. The kind a man likes to grab on to in bed."

"Oh fuck. Didn't just hear that about my sister," came the grumble from the doorway.

Ivy's head twisted that direction, a napkin pressed to her mouth. Oh fuck was right.

Whether the man was in jeans, a tee, and his leather cut, or he was wearing blue work coveralls, he looked damn good. And the color of his coveralls brought out the blue in his eyes. Those eyes which were traveling down her body and making her toes curl.

Double oh fuck.

She tossed the napkin on the desk and crossed her arms over her chest to cover her now hard nipples. Not that he missed them. Which was quite obvious when his lips curled into a sexy smile.

"Crash is out there bitchin' up a storm 'bout you bringin' food from Bangin' Burgers an' not askin' us."

"She's not obligated to bring you guys shit," Jewel told her brother. Then she leaned toward Ivy, whispering loudly, "Need to put a lock on that damn door to shut them out of my office."

Ivy bit back her smile, which was quickly lost when Jag approached and pressed against her to snag her burger. Her eyes followed it as he lifted it to his mouth and took a big bite out of it.

What. The. Fuck.

"Well, that's fucking rude, Jag," Jewel said, shoving her own burger in her mouth then rolling her eyes in ecstasy.

"No, was rude that she forgot the rest of us," Jag said around a second bite of her burger. Then he laid it back onto the open burger wrapper and grabbed her fresh-squeezed lemonade and slurped a third of it through the straw into his gut.

"Excuse you," Ivy said, whacking him on the arm. "I don't want your backwash."

Jag cocked an eyebrow at her. "You worried 'bout my spit now?"

Jewel set down her burger. "What does that mean?"

Ivy frowned at Jag. "Nothing."

Jag gave her a cocky smile before snagging two fries and dipping them into her ketchup.

Then he wrapped his long, warm fingers around the back of her neck and pulled her closer, leaning down to murmur into her ear, "Haven't gotten that call yet, baby."

Shock waves rushed through her and her nipples peaked even harder under her shirt. He gave her a squeeze before releasing her and straightening. He grabbed two more fries and turned to leave.

"Eight," Jag shot over his shoulder before the door slammed behind him.

Jewel's eyes flicked to Ivy. "Eight what?"

Ivy looked at her now ravaged fries and shrugged. "No idea."

"Right." Jewel tapped a crispy fry to her lips, thinking way too hard for Ivy's liking. "My brother wants down your pants. It's so obvious."

"That's your *brother* you're talking about."

"So? At least I didn't see him busting a nut in Goldie on the couch at church that night. Ugh. Now, *then* I would've been scarred for life."

Ivy winced. "Wasn't pleasant. That was for damn sure."

"Why? Because it was someone fucking Goldie or because it was *Jag* fucking Goldie?"

Ivy picked up her half-eaten burger and inspected it where Jag's teeth had been. Did she want that mouth on her again? Should she call him and have him come take care of her *business*? Or should she continue to look for someone less complicated? Someone she wasn't constantly butting heads with?

But then that would be boring. Another con when it came to being with the men she dated.

"Still waiting on that answer," Jewel prodded.

Ivy quickly shoved the burger in her mouth so she couldn't answer and pointed to her full mouth. By the time she was done chewing and swallowing, Jewel's attention was now focused out of the front office window into the large paved lot of the business.

"Wonder why the beast is here?"

Ivy's head spun toward the window. "The beast?" Diesel was climbing off his bike and looking in their direction. Her gaze went back to Jewel. "You call Diesel the beast?"

"Yeah, 'cause he is one."

Ivy laughed but agreed. Diesel did seem to be a beast in his own way.

"Never heard you call him that before."

Jewel murmured, "It's a new nickname."

"Aaaah."

"Ain't like that," Jewel quickly said.

Ivy shrugged. "Okay."

She frowned. "Nice way to deflect off the subject of you and Jag."

"There is no me and Jag."

Jewel opened her mouth to respond but snapped it shut when the exterior door was pulled open and Diesel pushed his way into the room. With him in it, the room shrunk in half.

Diesel's eyes landed on Jewel first, held for a second, then his gaze swung to Ivy. He did a chin lift. "Cuz."

"D, how's it hanging?" Ivy asked her cousin with a smile.

She got a typical grunt as an answer. That meant "good" in Neanderthal.

"That good, huh?" Ivy teased.

She got another grunt, then his eyes dropped to their almost gone food. "Bangin' Burgers." His massive hand reached out and the rest of her food was history. Down his gullet in a flash. The few fries, the mouthful of burger and the little bit of lemonade disappeared instantly.

Ivy shook her head and sighed, then held out a napkin to him. He grunted again and his eyes swung back to Jewel, then dropped to her food.

"You touch mine, I'll kick you in the balls," she warned before quickly stuffing the rest of her burger in her mouth.

"What are you doing here, D?" Ivy asked, curious why the club's enforcer was stopping in at the shop in the middle of the day.

"Club business," he grumbled.

Uh huh. So basically he was saying club business was none of her and Jewel's business. So typical.

Jewel held out a fry to him. "Give you a fry if you tell us what's going on with using one of the strippers to infiltrate the Knights."

Diesel snagged the fry and had it swallowed before she could even react. She looked at her empty fingers in surprise. "Damn," she whispered. "You need a woman to make you meals if you're that hungry."

"So, make me a meal."

"I'm not your house mouse! Get someone else to cook for you." Jewel pointed to the remaining five fries in front of her. "You get the rest if you give us info."

He eyeballed the fries and then grumbled, "It's a no-go."

"I need more than that for five whole fries, D."

"No one trustworthy. Girls scared of gettin' in the middle of war between Knights an' us."

Jewel's steel-blue eyes, just like her brother's, slid to Ivy and she gave her a look, which meant her mind was turning and she was getting ideas.

Which may be good, may be bad. It could go either way with Jewel.

"So you need someone trustworthy and not scared," Jewel stated.

Diesel's eyes narrowed as they landed on Jewel. "Will fuckin' cuff you to a bed if you even think 'bout it."

Ivy's brows rose. *Interesting.*

Jewel swatted a hand in his direction, dismissing him. Which you did not do to Diesel. "You're not cuffing me anywhere. And it wouldn't be up to you, anyhow."

He took a menacing step closer to Jewel. "Get it out of your head."

"It would be up to Pierce," Jewel continued, ignoring the dark look crossing Diesel's face.

"Pierce agrees to that, it'll be the last thing he does as prez," Diesel grumbled. "Last thing," he repeated, standing directly over

CHAPTER 5

Jewel now, staring down at her, while she stared up at him, her eyes hot.

Very interesting.

"An' you won't be able to sit down for a week," D's growl rumbled through the room.

Damn. Her cousin was laying down the law on Jewel. Yes, he was the club's Sergeant at Arms, yes, he managed In the Shadows Security, but Ivy never saw him be this protective about any woman before, even Bella.

Very, very interesting.

"You have no say," Jewel whispered, not breaking eye contact with him.

Boy, did she have a set of balls on her. Ivy loved Diesel, as both her cousin and her club "brother," but didn't think even she would challenge him. Jewel called him a beast, and he was exactly that. A no-bullshit type of guy, he was one of the few members who wore his hair brutally short. Soldier-like. Ivy didn't think she ever saw scruff on that man's face, even when he was younger. He liked to keep his shit tight. But he certainly was wound tight like a spring, didn't take much to blow his top, and Jewel was clearly pushing his limit.

"Woman," was all he grunted as if a warning.

"Beast," she answered him softly and his large body jerked as if she struck him.

Suddenly, Ivy felt the need to escape the office. The air became thick and electric and she found it hard to breathe as she watched the two of them in a stare down.

But before she could move, Diesel turned, wearing a dark scowl, and went through the shop door, slamming it so hard the wall shook.

Jewel, appearing a bit shaky, gave her wide eyes.

"What the fuck, Jewel?"

The younger woman's mouth opened but nothing came out. She sat back in her office chair and stared at the five fries that still remained on her desk. She grabbed the wrapper they sat on, crumpled it up, and threw it in the garbage.

"You okay?"

Jewel's gaze met hers. "Yeah."

"Are you going to talk to Pierce?"

She hesitated, her eyes sliding sideways to the door that Diesel stomped out of, like a pissed off bull. "No. I don't think that's a good idea."

"Not if you want to be able to sit down for a week," Ivy murmured, then laughed, trying to break the remaining tension in the room.

Jewel's eyes widened even more, then she burst out laughing. "I know, right? These guys… You'd think we'd be used to their grunting, chest-pounding ways. Me man. You woman."

Ivy snorted. "Tell me about it." She deepened her voice to mock them. "Club business, babe. Not for vaginas with ears."

Jewel shook her head, still laughing. "Fucker made me waste five Bangin' fries, damn it."

"Sacrilege."

Jewel sighed. "So, I wonder what Pierce is going to do about the Knights now that they can't find any of Dawg's girls to do it?"

Ivy shrugged. "Ask for a sit-down, I assume. That's what I heard Ace telling Dex."

"Oh, damn! If they find out you're eavesdropping, they'll put chastity belts on your ears."

Ivy grinned. "Can't help but overhear them. They talk like they're hard of hearing. They could be standing next to each other at the shop and they're booming back and forth."

"You should do it, Ivy."

Ivy gave her a look. "Uh huh."

"Yeah, you don't have any man breathing down your neck. Talk to Pierce, tell him you're interested. I'd do it in a second."

"So, besides being dangerous and a really bad idea, you're not going to do it yourself because D just told you no? Really? Don't you think he'd say the same thing to me if he knew I was interested?"

"But he doesn't know."

"And you heard what he said about it being the last thing Pierce would do as president."

"Yeah, but that was about me. Not you."

"Damn, girl, you're splitting hairs."

"Maybe. Can't hurt to ask." She hesitated, an excited look in her eyes. "Don't you want an adventure?"

"Your idea of *adventure* is fucked up."

"You're super smart, too. You could figure out ways to get info out of them."

"Probably a simple blow job would do it. No need to be smart for that."

Jewel laughed. "Though I'm sure you're good at it, I doubt that's enough to make them spill club business."

Probably not. Not that she was doing it. Even if she was crazy enough, she certainly wouldn't go into their ranks planning on giving head to a bunch of bikers from another club.

She looked at the clock on the wall. "Shit. I have to get back to the shop."

"Like you'd get fired for being late."

"No, but I'll have to listen to Dex whine about being left alone to run it. I think Ace had to take Nana to the doctor or something."

"She good?"

"Yeah, just a checkup, I think. Still the same crotchety old woman as ever."

"Well, there's a relief."

Ivy arched a brow at Jewel. "Says you."

Jewel laughed. "Anytime you want to stop by with Bangin' Burgers, don't hesitate."

"I hear ya, sister. See you soon." With a wave, Ivy pushed out into the bright afternoon light and headed toward her car.

A parts truck must have arrived when they weren't paying attention and squeezed between D's Harley and her Dodge Charger. As she rounded the box truck, she came to a sliding halt.

Jag leaned against her driver's door, arms crossed over his chest, dark sunglasses hiding his eyes.

"You're not getting grease on my car with your filthy self, are you?" she asked as she unfroze herself and moved forward.

"An' if I did, whatcha gonna do 'bout it?"

"Kick your ass."

He stared down at his boots for a moment and when he looked back up, he wore a half smile. "Lookin' forward to you tryin'."

Unless he moved, she'd never be able to get into her car to leave. She stopped right in front of him and planted her hands on her hips. She hated that she couldn't see his eyes behind his dark shades.

Before she could react, his hand snaked out, snagged her waist and pulled her to him until she was pressed between the V of his outstretched legs.

Ivy panicked. Not because she was close to Jag, because his heat seared her, because her pussy just went into a spasm, and her nipples started to ache. Nope. Wasn't that.

Her gaze swung around the parking lot. Luckily no one was outside and the box truck blocked them from being seen by anyone in the office.

Like Jewel.

"What are you doing?" she hissed in his face, trying to pull back.

"Havin' a conversation," he answered, holding on to her tighter.

"We don't need to be touching to have words."

"True enough."

She attempted to jerk away from him again with no luck. "So, let go. Someone is going to see us."

"Don't give a shit."

"I do. If you need to say something, say it, then let me go. I need to get back to the pawn shop."

"What time you workin' 'til?"

Her brows knitted together. "Why?"

He blew out a frustrated breath. "Can't feel why?" He moved his hips slightly. His cock was hard and long as it pressed into her belly.

Oh, yeah, she could feel it. "I don't remember calling you to come over."

"Can hear my phone right now," he murmured as he grabbed his cell from the front pocket of his coveralls and pressed it to his ear.

"Yeah, baby? That right? You want me to come over an' give you some? You got it. Be there at eight. Wear somethin' sexy."

He pulled the phone from his ear and slipped it back into his pocket, giving her a cocky smile.

She couldn't decide whether to be amused or annoyed at his pushiness.

When he dropped his head toward hers, her breath caught. Was he going to kiss her right here in the body shop lot?

Holy shit, he was.

His lips crushed against hers while one hand tightened on her waist and the other squeezed her ass. *Hard*. She gasped into his mouth and he took that opportunity to slide his tongue in and find hers.

Her gasp turned into a groan. Then both hands were on her ass, pulling her even tighter against his erection.

Finally, he pulled away enough to groan, "Fuck, baby. Could do a quickie in the back of your car."

For a split second she considered it, then reality hit her like a splash of cold water.

Last thing she needed was to get caught fucking Jag in the back of her car in the parking lot of an open business where everyone knew them. And she could just picture the parts truck driver getting into his cab and seeing them going at it like cats in heat in the back seat of her Charger, which wasn't very big in the first place.

No.

No.

Hell to the no.

Though, the thought did make her wet and her breasts ache, damn it.

"And, baby, just so you know," he brushed his tongue over her bottom lip, "not bringin' me an order of Bangin' Burgers is a punishable offense."

She cursed her pounding heart as she whispered, "Punishable, how?"

He pressed his lips to her ear, murmuring his promise of,

"Tonight."

She frowned as a shiver ran through her. "Right." Like she would let him into her apartment.

Shit, she probably was going to let him into her apartment.

The thought of having more awesome sex with this man made her weak in the brain. And she could feel that bad decision coming on.

She just wished the promise of awesome sex wasn't with Jag.

Or any male chauvinist biker.

Damn it.

"Maybe I have a date."

"Yeah. At eight. Your apartment. With me." He pushed away from her car and guided her back a couple steps. But before he let her go, he leaned close and said, "Don't make me come find you."

With that, he let her go and stepped around her, heading back toward the shop door. She quickly got into her car, the rumble of the Hemi engine soothing her nerves when she started it.

She sat in the driver's seat watching him walk away. After rolling down her window, she shoved it into drive and pulled up next to him.

"Jag!" she called out her window. He stopped mid-stride and glanced over his shoulder. "Let me remind you of something. Just 'cause we're having—correction, we *had* sex doesn't mean you own me."

His lips twitched, and he continued on his path back into the shop, his head shaking.

Son of a bitch. That didn't look promising.

Jag pounded on the door. Again.

She was pushing him to his limit. *Again*.

Yeah, he was late. But she should be used to the brothers never being on time. They got up when they wanted, got to work—for the most part—when they wanted, and certainly didn't go to bed until they damn well wanted to, either.

But, hell—he hit the power button on his cell phone to activate the screen—it was only ten. It was early yet.

And it wasn't like she had to get up to open the pawn shop in the morning. Ace was an early riser. He opened the shop early, closed it late. Anything to avoid going home to take care of his cranky old mother.

That's what his ol' lady, Janice, was for, anyway. To do shit like that. And both of his sisters lived on the farm, too, helping take care of Lonnie, Doc's wife. She used to be a bearable woman until Doc got life without parole for murder. Since then, she's been unbearable.

He sighed. He was going to knock politely only one more time then that was it.

He *politely* kicked the door with his heavy biker boot. *Again.* Leaving another mark *again* next to the one he left last time.

The woman had to be so damn difficult.

He closed his eyes and sucked a long breath through his nose. This time he wasn't going to yell any threats. Nope.

This time he was using his fucking key. Though, he hated the fact that she'd now know he had one.

And no doubt, would probably change the locks.

Fuck.

He dug deep into his jeans' pocket and pulled out his bike keys, singling out the one he needed.

Then he inserted it into the deadbolt and turned. His progression came to a quick halt by the chain she had secured the door with.

With a curse, he stepped back, lifted his boot and then kicked with all his weight. The door slammed open, the jamb splintering where the chain had been hooked.

He pushed his way inside.

The apartment was dark. But if Ivy was sleeping, there was no way that crash just didn't wake her ass up.

He stalked down the hallway to her closed bedroom door. He turned the knob. Locked. What the fuck? Who locked their bedroom door in their own place?

He lifted his boot again and this time the door gave away much easier, but not much quieter.

The bedroom was dark, too. He slapped at the wall until he found the switch and lit the room up.

Ivy was sitting up in bed, her flaming hair falling around her, and he felt that deep down in his dick. She blinked at him in surprise.

"You gotta be shittin' me," he growled.

"Ace isn't going to be happy about that."

"Yeah, well, I ain't happy 'bout you lockin' me out."

"Who said I locked you out? Maybe after waiting up for an hour, I gave up and went to bed and secured my apartment like any sane single woman would."

"Right. Who the fuck goes to bed this early?"

"Me. When I'm alone."

The "alone" part turned him solid. "Unless I'm here, you should always be alone in your bed." He shrugged out of his cut and tossed it on the nearby chair.

Her eyes had followed it but they quickly landed back on him. "Is this something new?"

The bed sank as he sat on the edge to unfasten his boots and yank them off. "Nope, but it's something you need to start followin'."

"Do I get a say in this?"

He pushed to his feet, tugged his worn Harley tee over his head and dropped it on the floor. "Nope. Told you from now on you need dick, you get mine."

"Maybe I don't want yours."

"Tell me that again in about an hour."

Ivy snorted. "Won't take you an hour."

"Whatever, woman."

"Is the front door hanging wide open?"

"Yep."

She arched a brow. "Do you think you should go secure it?"

That was probably a good idea. Never know when the Shadow Warriors were in the area. He didn't need to make it easier for them to do something like fire-bombing Ivy's apartment. Or coming in when the two of them were getting busy, knocking him the fuck out and kidnapping Ivy.

Then he'd end up in SCI Greene for murder. Because no one was touching his woman.

No one.

He stalked out of the bedroom, closed the front door as best as he could, then shoved a recliner against the door.

Good enough. At least now he'd hear someone trying to break in.

He unbuckled his belt, unbuttoned his jeans and was sliding the zipper down as he reentered her bedroom.

Fuck.

Seeing Ivy still sitting up in bed, taking him busting into her apartment in stride, he realized how much she did it for him. She would be his ultimate ol' lady. She was already part of the biker life, so she knew the rules, she worked hard and was smart as hell.

And fuck if she didn't give him a constant hard-on. Not to mention, her pussy was as sweet as fuck.

She was perfect.

He just had to convince her that he was perfect for her.

Though, she might need a bit more convincing in that respect.

Tonight would be another step toward that goal.

He shoved his jeans down and left them where he stepped out of them. Hooking his thumbs into his boxer briefs, he shoved them down, too.

The whole time she just watched him, not saying a damn word. But he could see the heat in her eyes as she checked him out.

She was in no way immune to his *charms*.

He wrapped his fingers around the root of his *charm* and stroked himself once, twice, then thumbed the precum at the end.

"Get rid of the sheet," he ordered. He was dying to see what she was wearing. He had told her to wear something sexy, and he hoped she had listened, but, honestly, would be surprised if she had.

However, when she flipped the sheet off her, he squeezed his dick harder.

Fuck.

She was wearing a tight pink camisole top that not only didn't contain her cleavage, but it didn't do anything to hide how hard her nipples were, either. She also wore some little shorts that almost looked like boxers. Boxers that looked way better on her than any man.

"You normally wear that to bed?"

She ran her fingers absently over the thin strap at her shoulder. "Yeah."

"So you didn't do what I asked." Not that he was going to complain about what she *was* wearing, but he was disappointed she didn't wear it just for him.

"You didn't ask. You demanded."

"Sounds 'bout right."

"You don't like what I'm wearing?" she asked.

Oh, he liked it. His dick liked it, too.

But when she pouted, a jolt shot through him. Ivy never fucking pouted. She didn't play sex kitten games like that. What the fuck was her play?

His eyes narrowed. "What's your game, woman?"

Her eyes widened, her face a mask of feigned innocence. "What do you mean?"

"Don't fuck with me," he warned in a grumble.

"I'm not fucking with you. I'm waiting for you to get in bed and fuck *me*."

Jag hesitated. This was way too easy. "You drunk?"

Ivy laughed sharply and shook her head. "Stone cold sober."

"What's with the turnabout?"

"I'm thinking you're right. When I need dick, you give it to me. But that's it. Nothing more than that."

He frowned.

She continued, "Here's the deal… I call. You come. We fuck. You leave. Keep it simple." She wasn't done yet. "But there's more… Stay out of my personal life, I'll stay out of yours."

He wasn't liking the sound of that.

"I'm not your property. I'm not your ol' lady. Think of me as an

CHAPTER 5

independent agent."

He wasn't liking the sound of that, either.

"You don't claim me at church."

He hated the sound of that.

"Take it or leave it."

Fucking goddamn.

P issed or not, Jag was thinking about what she just offered him. *That* she could clearly see written on his dark, angry face.

But, she also could see him agreeing to her terms then not far down the road trying to claim her in front of the brothers. Even going as far as asking the club officers to vote on her being his ol' lady.

And, normally, they wouldn't even give a damn if she wanted that or not. She belonged to the club, like it or not, and they could decide her fate.

But if he tried that, she'd have to rely on Hawk and Diesel to vote it down, as well as her brother Dex. Though, Dex could be a wild card. Knowing him, he'd probably think it was a good idea that she be tied down to Jag.

She couldn't imagine Ace agreeing with it, either. But just to be safe, if it came down to it, she'd just need to do some politicking with her blood.

Hell hath no fury like a woman scorned.

And if Jag proposed it and they agreed, she'd make their lives a living hell.

Never fuck with a redhead.

She looked at the naked man standing in the middle of her bedroom stroking his cock.

Someone may need that lesson sooner than later.

But first, she did have a man naked in the middle of her bedroom. And he just happened to be stroking his very nice cock.

One he was extremely skilled with.

And, if she had to admit it, he was just as accomplished, if not better, with his tongue. Which made her wet, as did his full sleeves of colorful tattoos, including the flames that ran up both forearms. And if he turned around, he sported all the same patches that were the club colors in black and grey on the skin of his back, too.

And, if she had to admit it, that was fucking hot as hell.

Damn it.

But it was those club rockers and patch that made him who he was.

Which was a misogynistic Neanderthal.

"Are you going to stand there all night, or are you going to get over here and take care of business?" she prodded.

When he finally moved, his eyes remained hot and focused on her, but he moved *around* the bed instead of onto it. He opened her drawer and dug out the box of condoms.

And right there in front of her, he counted them. He certainly did. Out loud, too.

Ivy rolled her eyes. "Now I know that you're smart enough to count."

When he got to seven, his gaze met hers and his eyes narrowed. "Missin' one."

"Maybe I spoke too soon. You can use your fingers if you need to."

"Babe, I know you're bein' a smart ass, but there's only seven."

"That can't be right. Anyhow, just grab one and let's go." She snapped her fingers. "I don't have all night."

With a scowl, he tilted the open box so she could see inside. "Seven," he repeated in a deep growl, sounding a bit miffed. He stepped closer to the bed. "Had this discussion. No one in here but me. Musta misunderstood me, not heard the words I was sayin'."

"I heard you. I never said I was going to listen."

His spine snapped straight. "You think I want in where someone else just was?"

"You fucked Goldie. There were a whole lot of *someone elses* in there. I didn't think you were that picky."

His nostrils flared, and she knew she was playing with fire. And he was stoked red hot.

"If you don't like to hear the truth, you know where the door is. You know, the one you kicked in."

"Ain't gonna get off that easy."

"I'm sitting here waiting for you to get me off, and you're not making it easy. So you are correct."

"Gotta smart mouth."

"Nothing you didn't already know, Jag."

He sighed loudly and ran a hand through his hair. "Fuckin' with me gets you goin', don't it?"

"Yeah, it's like foreplay. So. Let's. Go." She patted the bed.

He hesitated, staring at her. Probably fighting with himself whether he should just leave and find someone easier to deal with. Most likely wondering if she was worth the hassle. But in the end, he shook his head, threw the box on the nightstand and climbed onto the bed, his cock hard and hanging between his muscular thighs.

Clearly, he ate up the shit she gave him.

He didn't want easy. He could get that any night of the week with one of the sweet butts at church.

Or he could get that with one of Dawg's girls. He only needed to make a call.

No, he didn't want easy.

His kicking her door in—hell, both of them—proved that.

And she certainly was good at making it hard for him. In more ways than one.

She didn't want sweet sex from him. She wanted it hard. She wanted it rough. She wanted it angry and hot.

She could get the boring shit anywhere else.

That's not what she wanted from Jag.

And if she had to torque him up a little to get what she wanted... So be it.

Ivy watched him continue to stroke his cock. Every movement of his hand made her clench deep inside. She wanted that hand, those fingers, on her.

"Are you going to keep that to yourself or are you going to give it to me?"

"Fuckin' gonna give it to you, baby. You're still dressed."

"I didn't know I had to undress mys—" Before she could finish, he grabbed her ankles, yanking her onto her back and down the bed. He ripped her shorts down her legs and off her feet, throwing them somewhere over his shoulder.

Then he shoved her cami up over her breasts, burying his face between them, snagging both nipples between his thumbs and forefingers, rolling them hard, making her cry out in both pain and pleasure.

Yes. This.

This was what she wanted from him. Not that sweet shit he tried to give her last time.

His teeth scraped her skin before sinking into the side of her breast. Her body bowed in response, and she threw her head back, crying out once again.

"This what you want? This?"

"Yes. Yes. *Yes*," she yelled, her eyes rolling back.

"Fuckin' Ivy," he muttered before pulling one of her nipples deep into his mouth, scoring the tip with his teeth. She grabbed onto his thickly muscled shoulders, digging her nails in, then raked them up his neck.

He shuddered against her and groaned around her nipple. Nipping along her skin, he came nose to nose with her.

"Want it rough, that what you want?"

Something flashed in his eyes when she hissed, "Yes."

He finished tugging her cami over her head and flung it across the room. "Your tits are so goddamn sweet," he murmured before sucking the other nipple into his mouth, he gripped her other breast and squeezed hard.

Yes, that was how she liked it.

His cock pressed against her thigh and she couldn't wait to have him inside her. But first...

"Are you hungry, yet?"

He lifted his head, met her gaze with a smile. "Starvin', baby."

Pushing back to his knees, he shoved her legs up, throwing them over his shoulder, and buried his face between her thighs.

"Fuck yes," she shouted to the ceiling. She squirmed when he chuckled against her swollen, soaked lips. He sucked her clit hard, and she dug her heels into his back, sinking her fingers into his hair, holding him close, encouraging him to get even closer.

Her whole body jerked with each flick of his tongue against her overly sensitive nub. Then skilled fingers were inside her, curling, finding the spot that made her hips dance even more. He teased her with his mouth, his tongue, tortured her with his fingers... until she couldn't take any more.

"I'm coming," she wailed as the blood rushed through her, her body vibrated against him, around him. He bit hard into the flesh of her inner thigh. "Oh fuck!"

"My baby likes it rough."

She ignored the "my" part of "my baby" when he sank his teeth into her other thigh. "Fuck, Jag, yes!"

"Goddamn," he whispered, pulling himself up and over her, going face to face. "Grab a condom," he demanded, his eyes dark, heated.

Ivy slipped her hand under her pillow and held one up with a smile. "Number eight."

"Fuckin' Ivy," he muttered, shaking his head, but she didn't miss his grin before he slammed his lips down on hers. His tongue plundered her mouth and his hands dug deep into her hair, pulling her head back, arching her neck. He broke away and tugged on her hair even harder.

He sounded out of breath when he asked, "Like your hair pulled?"

Fuck. "Yes."

"Like your ass spanked?" He scraped his teeth along her throat.

Ah fuck. "Yes."

He lifted his head. "Those nerd boys of yours give you what you need?" When she didn't answer him, he tugged her hair again. "Answer me, Ivy. They give you what you need?"

She was damned if she answered him, damned if she didn't. She knew the thought of her being with other men bothered him. It shouldn't since she had lost her virginity a long, long time ago. But she knew it did. And at twenty-eight, she'd been through quite a few men, but she was sure his conquests outnumbered hers by at least triple. If not more.

The old double standard reared its ugly head.

And though some of the men she'd been with could get as "down and dirty" as a biker, most of them didn't. Or couldn't. It just wasn't in them.

"Takin' your silence as a no," he said, pushing himself back on his knees once again. He snagged the condom she had hidden earlier, ripped it open, and rolled it on. When he was done, he met her gaze. "I can give you what you need, baby." He smacked his palm against his bare chest. "*Me*. I'll give it to you any way you want it. Long as I'm the only one in here."

There he went again, demanding exclusivity. The fear of being tied down to one man, hell, tied down to a biker to boot, went through her.

She was young. She had more life to live yet before she settled down.

If she ever settled down.

At this point, she saw no reason to do just that. Be with only one man for the rest of her life.

She enjoyed her freedom. Or as free as she could be being part of an MC.

But what was staring at her right now was the opposite of freedom.

"Not promising you jack," she whispered, knowing it would piss him off, but it had to be said.

A muscle twitched in his hard jaw and his eyes narrowed. Then he grabbed her and flipped her over roughly, yanking her hips up and back, then with not even a slight hesitation slammed into her with a grunt.

"Fuckin' woman's gotta fight me at every turn." With each slam, he grunted. With each impact, the air rushed from her lungs. She buried her head in her pillow, her lips parted as she struggled for breath.

The crack of his hand against her ass surprised her more than hurt her. And when she laughed, he froze mid-motion. She twisted her neck to look behind her. He was staring at her with what sort of looked like a confused expression on his face. But his nostrils flared and his eyes burned like coals. Then, with a grimace, he dug the fingers of one hand into the flesh of her hip and smacked her hard again with the other.

Her body shifted forward with the impact, but she shoved herself back, impaling herself on him. "That's it, Jag, fucking give it to me."

"Goddamn," he grunted and did it again, just as hard. Her skin began to burn where he spanked her.

"The other side, too," she encouraged him, breathing hard now, tilting her hips, taking him as deep as she could.

He switched sides and smacked her again.

"Fuck, yes," she screamed into the pillow, gripping the sheet tightly in her fists.

"For fuck's sake, Ivy," he barked.

"Shut up and do it!" she yelled at him.

He did it again, not as hard this time. Then his body collapsed over her, covering her, and he sank his teeth into her shoulder. She quivered uncontrollably beneath him, her groan muffled. She squeezed him hard with her inner muscles and he grunted against her skin.

"Again," she encouraged.

When he bit the back of her neck, she cried out. She released her grip on the sheet and found her own clit, pressing, circling, rubbing until her body vibrated on the edge. And then she found what she was looking for... release. Her pussy clenched hard around him and he groaned, straightening back up, now holding onto both hips, but holding still as she came down from her high.

Once he slipped from her, she moved quickly to her back, spreading her thighs, inviting him to come back to her, but he shook his head, his hair falling across his forehead, into his face. She swept it away and seconds later, she was on top of him, straddling his belly, his cock pressed against her.

Rising to her knees, she shifted back and while he held his cock in place, she slowly lowered herself and sighed when she hit the end of him. Of her.

She planted her palms on his heavily tattooed chest and used that leverage to ride him hard and fast, never breaking eye contact with him once. Not even when she came for the second time and didn't break her rhythm.

His face was twisted in a grimace, and she knew he struggled to keep her gaze because he wanted to close his eyes and blow his load. But he didn't. She could see the battle to keep his shit together, to prove to her that he could be everything she needed.

But this was just sex. Nothing more.

Nothing more.

He dragged his fingers through her hair and then palmed both of her breasts, thumbing the nipples until they were hard peaks. And to Ivy, they felt as though they had swelled larger, filled his hands fuller.

Out of breath and her pulse pounding in her neck, she ground down hard against him, driving him as deep as possible.

"Lemme watch you come again." His voice was low, grumbly, and caused a shiver to run through her.

She grabbed one of his hands kneading her breasts and brought it down to where they were connected. She guided him as they both stimulated her clit, their fingers meshed, pressing her hard, making her grind even harder until she exploded around him.

"That's it, baby. Squeeze me like a vise with that tight, little pussy. *Fuck.*" He grunted as his hips rose off the bed. "Fuck," he barked to the ceiling. "Fuck, fuck, *fuck!*"

His head lifted off the bed as he watched their hands moving as one, then he bucked her off, flipped her onto her back and sank fully inside her once more.

He dropped almost all his weight to her, shoving his face into her neck, scraping his teeth over her skin.

This man knew how to move his hips. She drew her legs around his thighs and followed his rhythm. Which wasn't as hard and as rough as she wanted it.

No, it was slow and careful again.

Like last time.

No. Not again.

No.

She raked her nails down his back and he bowed against her. Then she continued to his ass, digging them in hard, tearing at his flesh.

He lifted his head, grabbed her face and kissed her deep, taking possession of her mouth. She squirmed underneath him, fighting this play of his. Whatever he was doing to get her to fall for him.

It wasn't going to work.

It. Was. Not.

When she sank her teeth into his bottom lip, he didn't pull away. Instead, he grunted into her mouth, sliding his fingers into her hair and pulling painfully until she released his lower lip.

"Fuckin' bitch," he grumbled, but gave her a cocky grin, a dot of crimson appearing on his mouth. "Keep fightin' it, baby, but I'm determined to win this war."

"You're not winning shit."

His eyes flashed. "Love a challenge."

A thrill ran through her. "Me, too."

He grabbed both of her wrists and pinned them over her head, holding them tightly to the bed with one hand.

He dipped his head down low enough to grab the flesh of her left breast into his mouth and he bit her so hard, she knew it was going to leave a mark.

He marked her as his.

Fuck.

His tongue soothed the bite before he went nose to nose with her once more. "You on the pill?"

What the fuck? Why was he asking that now? Was he worried about the condom failing?

"If it breaks, no worries," she said. It wasn't a direct answer, but the only one he was going to get.

Then he pulled out of her, ripped the condom off and with a grunt, came deep inside her.

Ivy went completely still, even her breath. Her pulse thumped in her neck as hard as his cock pulsated in her pussy with his release.

"What the fuck did you just do?" she whispered in shock.

"Did what we're gonna do from now on. Nothing between us. You takin' everything I give you. Gotta problem with that?"

"Yes!"

"Too fuckin' bad."

She slammed both palms into his chest. "Get off me."

"I'll get off you when I'm good an' ready."

"Jag," she whispered, her voice shaky and her lips trembling. "You can't do this. You can't claim me like this."

"The fuck I can't."

"It isn't going to work."

He grunted his answer. And she knew exactly what that grunt meant, which made her furious.

She slammed his chest again. "Get the fuck off me." He ground his hips into her again, reminding her of how he spilled inside of her. "Now I have to wash you out of me."

"Ain't getting rid of me so easily."

"Whatever, asshole," she grumbled. "I can't believe you." Her fingers curled into a tight fist.

He chuckled. "You gonna punch me, baby?"

She blew out a breath and slowly relaxed her hand. "I should."

He snorted. "Ain't gonna hurt me, gonna hurt you since I have a thick skull."

She squeezed her eyes shut and murmured, "You've got that right."

He brushed a knuckle over her cheek and said softly, "Baby, look at me."

Ivy blinked her eyes open. Then regretted it when he had the gentlest of looks in his eyes. Her heart squeezed painfully.

Shit. Shit. Shit.

"We need to make it clear—"

He cut her off sharply. "No need to repeat yourself. Heard you the first time. You call, I come, we both come, then I leave. Got it."

It sounded so simple.

Both of them knew it wasn't.

"You get what you want then I get what I want." He reached between them and cupped her mound firmly. "Nobody else in here, Ivy. I'm serious." He pressed his lips to hers and she tasted the blood she had drawn. He pulled away just enough to say, "Don't ever lock me out again, either."

With a grunt, he rolled off of her, off the bed and onto his feet. He gathered his clothes from the floor and his cut from the chair and walked out of her room. She heard the water running and the toilet flushing from the hall bathroom.

When the door squeaked open, she yelled. "If I don't call, are you still going to show up?"

"Yep."

Fuck.

"Gonna get one of the prospects to stand outside your door until I can get them to fix it tomorrow," he yelled from the living room.

He was going to do what? "You're going to make one of them stand out there all night?"

He peeked his head around the broken bedroom door. "Yeah. Don't let 'em in. An' for fuck's sake, let 'em do what they need to do. They wanna patch in, they need to do what I say."

Then his head disappeared, and she heard his boots thumping down the hallway, the scrape of something heavy being moved, then the clatter of what she could only assume was left of her front door.

"I'm not going to be yours, Jag," she yelled, hoping he was already out the door.

"Too late."

"Fuck!" she screamed.

She swore she heard a chuckle. She slammed her fists into the mattress and screamed.

She was afraid he may be right.

CHAPTER SIX

Pierce leaned back against the glass display case that housed handguns. A lot of them.

After Jag left last night, Weasel had shown up to "stand guard" at her broken front door. Despite what Jag said, she invited him inside to hang on the couch. She wasn't going to have him standing outside all night long.

Ridiculous.

Now three of the prospects were in her apartment replacing both her front door and bedroom door.

Instead of stopping down and having to explain to Ace about why her doors were kicked in, she had texted her brother Dex to tell him she needed to run an important errand and would be in later.

Ivy knew this *errand* might bite her in the ass, but her frustration with Jag was apparently driving her to do stupid things.

Though she was far from stupid.

Pierce had his arms crossed over his broad chest and his ankles crossed as he perused her. "When you gonna come work for me? Could use the help."

She would never work for Pierce. He was a biker who wanted to remain in the old ways. Women were nothing but a doormat and a hole to bust a nut into. "Recruit more prospects. They're cheap labor."

"Doin' that, but this is a gun shop, gotta trust everyone workin' here an' can't have a record."

"Annie's helping you out still, right?" Speaking of Annie, Ivy wondered where she was. She didn't want her aunt overhearing what she came to talk to Pierce about.

"Yeah, only part-time, though. Has to help take care of that bag o' bones that's your grandmother."

She sighed. "You're such a gem, Pierce."

He shrugged. "Truth, though, right?"

Ivy shook her head. But she had to stay on good terms with the club president, so she bit her tongue.

He jerked his chin in the direction of the glass display case. "Need a gun?"

"No."

"Sure? Can teach you to use it."

Right. That's what she needed... To have him teaching her how to shoot in his indoor range with no one else around. To him, she was club property and with him being president, he'd think he could have her whenever, wherever, he wanted. She wasn't claimed by any of the brothers, so in his mind she was fair game. Didn't matter if he already had an ol' lady. Wasn't unheard of for Pierce to take what he wanted.

Also didn't matter to him that he was old enough to be her father. Pussy was pussy to a man like him.

Which reminded her to state her business and get the fuck out of Dodge before she regretted this whole thing. But she needed to handle it delicately. She really wasn't supposed to know club business. None of the women were. Though, they did find out some of it... But if the brother who spilled the beans was caught? Not good for him.

However, this time it was Diesel that kind of gave up some of the info to her and Jewel, the rest she overheard from Dex and Ace. Plus,

CHAPTER 6

Jewel was a pro at sneaking around the garage, listening for anything interesting.

Luckily, Diesel could sing like a canary and no one would do anything to the man, except maybe pull his rank of Sergeant at Arms. Though if Pierce did that, he'd be stupid. Diesel was the best and scariest enforcer the club ever had. No one on the Executive Committee or even any of the brothers would back the president on a decision like that.

"If you ain't here for a gun an' you got somethin' to say, say it, woman."

She almost rolled her eyes at him, but she was proud of herself when she didn't. "I accidentally overheard a conversation about getting one of Dawg's girls to infiltrate the Knights for intel. Did you find someone?"

He cocked a brow at her. "Expect me to answer that?"

Fucker. "Yes, and I'll tell you why... I have a proposition..." She pursed her lips as she gathered her thoughts. "You probably can't trust one of the strippers to do the job right or know what info you need... so..."

"Fuckin' woman, get to the fuckin' point." The impatience ran deep in his gruff voice. "All you bitches talk in circles."

Ivy sucked in a breath and counted to five. Five wasn't long enough but it would have to do. "I just think you should send someone in who's not only smart and loyal to the club, but is part of the club, too. Someone who has some skin in the game."

"You sayin' Dawg's girls ain't smart?"

It was her turn to cock a brow.

A wide smile crossed his face. "Hear what you're sayin'. You proposin' somethin'?"

"Yes."

"Who you suggest?"

"Me."

Pierce quickly pushed away from the display case and Ivy instinctively stepped back, her heart racing.

"You?" he barked loud enough that she flinched. "You fuckin' crazy?"

Probably. "No."

"You don't think they know who you are? With that fuckin' red hair of yours? They don't know you're DAMC property?"

"I've never met any of them." At least she didn't think so.

"Good thing, that."

"So why would they know who I am?"

"Hard to miss, Ivy. Any of 'em ever come into the pawn shop when you're workin'?"

"Not that I'm aware of."

"Couldn't miss 'em if they did. All of 'em are black an' would be wearin' their colors."

She already knew the Dark Knights were an all-black MC. That was no secret and hard to miss. And since she had a college education, she was sure she could read the words "Dark" and "Knights" on their cuts. Not that she was going to say that to Pierce. Now was not the time to be a smart ass.

"Then no, never saw any of them, never ran into any of them anywhere."

"Lucky, then. Probably like a girl like you. All that white skin an' red hair with that temper to boot."

Temper? She didn't have a damn temper.

Okay, maybe just a little one.

Before she could respond, he continued with a thoughtful expression, "Though, probably *would* like a girl like you. Probably swarm you like flies on shit. Try their chance at some sweet white pussy surrounded by a red bush."

Ivy struggled not to roll her eyes, or even heave at his words. Sometimes Pierce was just a plain old obnoxious asshole. More than sometimes. How he ever got the gavel, she'll never know. That's what happened when you let men run things.

"Well, there you go. I'm perfect for it."

"Why do you want to do this?"

Why? Because she's crazy, that's why. Did she want to help the club out? Sure. But that was just the excuse, not the real reason.

She didn't want to admit to herself the real reason. And if she couldn't face the truth herself, she certainly wasn't admitting it to Pierce.

"Show my loyalty to the club," she said simply.

He frowned. "When was that in question?"

She shrugged. "I'm not saying it was. But you guys need someone, right? Who better than me?"

He uncrossed his arms and ran a hand through his short salt and pepper hair, and down to his tattooed neck, which he squeezed as he stared at his boots for a moment. When he looked up, his gaze pinned on her hard. "Need to bring it to a vote."

Shit. No. That wouldn't work. She should have just done it and not told anyone, but she needed someone to know she was going in. Someone other than Jewel.

"No vote. You bring it to the committee and it'll be shot down. And then what? Even if the Knights agree to a sit-down, you'll be going in blind. Wouldn't it be better to have some intel on what's up first? Go in prepared?"

He shook his head. "Fuckin' Ivy. Too damn smart for a female. Could run this club if you had a dick."

"But I don't. So let me do this."

"Ace know you're here?"

"No. No one knows."

"Might wanna keep it that way." He stared at her long enough she wanted to squirm. Finally, he sighed. "You go. Get what you can. Get out. Report directly to me."

She nodded, trying not to smile.

"Careful what you gotta do to get intel, Ivy. Don't need any of your blood breathin' down my neck if you get knocked up by one of those Knights."

She no longer had to fight back a smile, now she frowned. "It's not going to get that far."

"Hope not. Ain't like they ain't gonna try for a piece of you though. You bring fresh pussy into Dirty Dick's, you know they gonna be sniffin' hard. Maybe even fightin' over you. Be prepared. Sure you don't want a gun?"

"No, I'm good."

Little did he know that she already had one. Ace got it for her a long time ago and taught her how to shoot it. She hardly ever carried it, though, and kept it locked away in one of the pawn shop's safes. It was a little .38 snub nose and she doubted she could do much with it in the midst of a brotherhood of bikers who was sure to be packing lots of fire power. But she'd bring along a small container of pepper spray, just to be safe. And to give her a little peace of mind.

Suddenly Pierce stepped closer and before she could back up, he reached out and flipped a finger through the wavy ends of her hair.

"Damn, your hair is hot and feisty like you. Bet you're searing hot in bed, too, ain't ya? Jag get a piece of you yet?"

Should she say yes to get him off her back? If Jag claimed her as his, Pierce wouldn't express interest. At least out loud. But she also didn't want anyone in the club to know that Jag and her had hooked up.

Plus, Pierce would probably change his mind about her heading into Knights territory if he thought she belonged to Jag. He wouldn't want to create any static with his Road Captain.

"No."

"Sure you know you're on his to-do list. Maybe you can give me a little taste first."

When he reached for her, she shimmied away from his grasp and rushed to the front door. "Gotta go. Ace is waiting for me to get to the pawn shop. I'm late."

"Right," he grunted, looking a little put out.

Before the door almost shut completely behind her, she heard, "And, woman, we did not have this talk, got me?"

CHAPTER 6

Jag gritted his teeth so hard he thought they might shatter. He parked his sled close to but not exactly in line with all the other bikes that sat in front of Dirty Dick's. Even the glow of the neon beer signs didn't do shit to light up the stone parking lot. But he could see a Dark Knights prospect standing guard in the shadows at that line of Harleys. The young guy was doing his time and whatever he was told to do to in order to patch in.

Been there, done that, he thought. He'd gone through all that bullshit himself over a decade ago and survived. This guy would, too.

The prospect probably texted someone when Jag rode in. Most likely their President or Sergeant at Arms. Someone who, no doubt, would greet him as soon as he stepped through the door.

After he kicked his stand down, he turned and noticed Ivy's Charger parked in a very dark corner of the lot. That made his jaw tighten even more. She could be ambushed there, raped, and no one would see it or maybe not even care if they did.

The woman was fucked in the head for coming here alone. Hell, for coming here at all. Of all the hair-brained ideas she could come up with to piss him off... this was at the top of his list.

Putting herself in known danger.

And what was worse, not getting permission to do it. Or letting any of the brothers know. Diesel would bust a blood vessel for sure when and if he found out.

However, right now, he needed to get her out of there. And in one piece. If anyone was going to tear her apart for this stunt, it was going to be him. Not a Dark Knight.

And, for fuck's sake, if she slept with any of them...

He bit back a curse, his fingers clenching into fists.

Though he would never hit a woman, the thought of her fucking a Dark Knight to get information made him want to explode. He would make Diesel look like a newborn kitten.

He stood next to his bike and sucked the night air through his nose. He needed to get his shit together before walking into this nest of Knights to confront her. And maybe even them. All by himself.

He'd decided to come alone because he figured he could get in, get Ivy, and get out. If he brought a bunch of brothers with him, the Knights might see it as a threat and war could break out.

They weren't enemies at this point, and he wanted to keep it that way. He didn't want to have their club added to DAMC's list of rivals right below the Shadow Warriors. Things were tense enough when it came to that nomad MC.

As he approached the badly lit entrance, the young prospect had his arms crossed and legs spread, attempting a look of strength. Jag could easily take the guy down, but that would be a bad start to his mission. As well as counter-productive.

Jag did a chin lift toward the guy.

"You got business here?" the young recruit asked.

"Yeah, somethin' inside belongs to me." Whether that *somethin'* realized it or not.

"You or your club?"

He knew it was risky wearing his colors to the bar, but he needed to establish a claim on Ivy. "Both."

"The redhead?"

Jag's spine stiffened and his chest tightened. "Yeah," he grunted.

"Been here last three nights."

A muscle in his jaw popped. "Figured as much."

"Gonna get greeted on the inside."

"Figured that, too."

The prospect then did his own chin lift as if giving him permission to proceed. Jag returned it. A silent way of saying thanks for the heads up.

He yanked the old, cracked wooden door open and was immediately assaulted by loud music, the stale smell of beer and heavy cigarette smoke, as well as the muted sounds of conversations.

But there was no mistaking it when eyes turned toward him and a majority of the conversation halted.

He steeled himself and stepped deeper into the grungy bar. He ignored the attention and let his gaze bounce around the dimly lit room.

Her back was to him, her unmistakable red hair falling around her bare shoulders. She was wearing a snug black tank top, tight black leather pants and thigh-high black suede boots with probably a three-inch heel. She must have gone shopping with one of Dawg's girls at Hookers-R-Us.

He was going to strangle her.

It took everything in his power not to rush over there, grab that hair of hers and drag her out of that bar on her ass.

Then teach her a lesson she would never forget.

Instead, he found himself face to face with one big black dude blocking his way. Their gazes met—though, Jag had to raise his a bit—and the guy did a chin lift.

Jag returned it reluctantly.

"Magnum."

Jag didn't miss the Sergeant at Arms patch on his leather cut. "Jag."

The club enforcer's head turned to where Ivy was talking to three Knights in the back corner. "Can't help but notice why you're here. She belong to you?"

She belongs over my knee, that's where she belongs. "The club."

The man cocked a thick, dark brow. "Then she lost her way."

"That ain't the half of it."

His beefy hands landed on his hips. "What she doin' here?"

Jag might be able to take the prospect but there was no way he could take this guy. He needed to keep things cool. "Bein' a pain in my ass."

The larger man cracked a smile. "Ain't they all?"

"Fuck yeah."

"My brothers have takin' a likin' to her."

Jag sighed and his eyes slid back to Ivy, who still didn't know he was there yet. "I'm sure."

"She doin' it just to piss you off? Or is there another reason she's been hangin' here makin' nice?"

Hopefully they had no idea she was there trying to grab intel on their territory grab.

"Doin' it to piss me off. Truth is, she's not just the club's. She's mine. She just likes to be difficult."

"Difficult bitches are usually the best fucks."

"That she is."

"Be a shame for none of my brothers to try her out then."

Fuck. The guy was testing him. Once again, he reminded himself to restrain his temper. "Prospect out front said she's been here last coupla nights."

The enforcer grunted, "Yeah."

With a calmness he didn't feel, he asked, "None of your boys got a taste?" Strangling wasn't going to be good enough if this man said they had.

Instead of answering, Magnum asked, "You said she's yours, why she out lookin' for strange?"

"Like I said, likes to piss me off. Likes an angry fuck."

"Hear you there. Sure can't piss a white brother off more than his woman chasing a black brother. Once she gets a taste, she may never wanna come home."

This was no time to be comparing dick sizes.

When Jag didn't answer him, the Knights' enforcer did a chin lift to one of the guys Ivy was talking to, one who faced their direction.

The guy did an answering chin lift and leaned toward Ivy, saying something close to her ear.

The tension in Jag's body ratcheted up a hundred notches at that. But then the guy pointed in his direction and he couldn't miss Ivy's spine straighten like a steel rod. She slowly turned around.

Even from where he stood and in the bad lighting, he could see she wore heavy makeup. Her eyes were dark, her lips as red as her hair.

She looked like a damn whore.

"Jesus," he muttered.

Her eyes had widened when she first spotted him, but they narrowed as she stalked toward him in those hooker boots.

It hit Jag then that she wore no fucking bra, and he knew every man was watching the bounce of her tits as she approached him.

"Looks like you're gonna get an angry fuck tonight, too, brother." Magnum laughed and whacked him hard enough on the back that the air fled his lungs.

"No shit," he muttered.

"Think I'm gonna go piss off my old lady so I get some of what you're gonna be gettin'."

Jag gave him a nod of thanks as the larger man stepped away when Ivy got to him.

"What are you fucking doing here?" she whispered angrily.

Jag cocked a brow in disbelief. She had some nerve. "You fuckin' kiddin' me? You gonna back talk me right now?"

Ivy pressed her lips together as he grabbed her arm and yanked her toward the entrance and out the front door to a bunch of catcalls and whistles.

He did a cursory nod to the young prospect, who now wore a large, knowing smile, and pulled Ivy through the parking lot as fast as he could walk. She leaned back but couldn't stop his forward motion.

"Slow down! I can't keep up like that in these boots."

"Think I give a shit? Those damn hooker boots are goin' in the damn garbage."

"The hell they are. I paid a fortune for them."

He glared at her over his shoulder, but didn't stop walking until they got to her car. He spun her around and pushed her against the driver's door, his knee between her thighs and his hands holding her arms tightly. Just in case she tried to start swinging.

"Have you lost your damn mind?" he yelled in her face, his breath coming hard and fast.

She winced. "No."

He dropped his head, tried to steady his breathing and counted to ten. Of course, it didn't help. "You didn't think you'd be recognized? *Fuck.* You could've blown this whole thing. Even started war between us an' the Knights."

"Thought I could slide in there."

"Slide in..." The pressure in his head became unbearable. "Slide in where? Into one of their beds? How else you think you goin' to get info? You think they just gonna get a loose tongue around some white bitch hangin' around their bar? Fuck no. If anything, you'd have to be doin' one of 'em to get anythin' out of 'em."

"I'd do what I have to do."

His head jerked back at her response. She did not just say that. "Stop being a whore, Ivy," he said through gritted teeth.

"I'm not a whore."

"Then stop acting like one."

"You know, I'm sick of the double standard. No one blinks an eye when you fuck Goldie in front of everyone at church."

Holy mother fuck. "That shit again?"

"And I know you've had plenty of women in your room at the clubhouse. It's okay for you, but not for me."

"Right," he grumbled.

Ivy shook her head, looking like a pissed off hellcat. "Right."

"When were you watchin' me, Ivy? How do you know who's up in my room?"

Her expression quickly became a blank mask. "I don't watch you."

"Must be. Keepin' tabs."

"I'm not."

"Haven't been with anybody but you since the night you broke into my room. Didn't notice that, though, did you?"

Jag heard her suck in a breath. He leaned closer. "You keep tabs on me. I keep tabs on you. Must mean somethin', baby."

She shook her head. "How do you keep tabs on me? Do you follow me?"

"How do you think I know when you got dick up in your place?"

"You follow me?" she repeated much slower this time.

"Not always. Sometimes. Should've been following you the last few nights, but thought we had a deal. Should've known better. Could've stopped you before you even set foot in that place."

He tilted his head and wished he could see her face more clearly. Though the heavy makeup on her face would probably piss him off all over again. She needed to wash that shit off.

Reminded him of one of Dawg's girls. And that's not what he wanted in his bed. That's not who he wanted as his ol' lady.

"You don't belong here," he said softly. "Dirty Angels' property don't belong in a Dark Knights' bar. You know that, Ivy. That's why one of Dawg's girls was gonna go in. You played with fire by doin' this."

"Nothing happened." She shrugged. "Made some new friends."

Jag snorted. "Made some new friends? You gotta death wish? What do you think Diesel or Hawk would do if they found out you were here? Messing with Dark Knights?"

"I wasn't messing with anyone."

"It was stupid. Grow up, Ivy, before you make a mistake you'll not only regret but won't ever recover from. Got me?"

"I'm not DAMC property."

He shook his head at that same old song and dance. "The fuck you aren't. Always been. Always will be. Don't need to tell you that you were born into it. Hell, you got Doc's blood runnin' through your veins. You don't get any more DAMC than that. But even if that wasn't enough, the second you dragged me upstairs that night and climbed into my bed, you cemented it."

"A drunken mistake."

He released her arms and stepped back. "Right."

"You want to talk about regrets? There you go. Biggest one ever."

"You're a fuckin' fool, Ivy. And a fuckin' bitch. Go home." He spun on his heel to leave.

"That's right, I'm a bitch. And apparently a whore. So move on, Jag."

His shoulders straighten and stiffened before he said over his shoulder, "Nothin' to move on from. You just killed whatever was there."

Ivy winced.

"Go home, Ivy. I'll follow to make sure you get home safe, then that's it. Done with your ass."

"About time," she muttered, yanking open her driver's door and sliding in.

Jag watched her for a moment, then shook his head, stalking back to his bike. He didn't doubt she'd take off without waiting for him.

And he was right.

Fuckin' Ivy.

CHAPTER SEVEN

He was done with her.
He was done with *her*!
Like she cared.
No, she didn't.
Fuck him. She was sick and tired of goddamn nosy bikers. All up in her business all the time.

Sometimes she just wanted to be free of this club. Free of this life. Run away. Find a new life somewhere else. She had her Bachelor's degree, she was good at computers and programming. She could get a job anywhere. Do anything she wanted.

She paced her kitchen, her stomach twisted in knots.

There was no way that Jag followed her tonight to Dirty Dick's. If he had, she never would have even made it through the front door. He would've stopped her long before then. Jewel must have spilled the beans.

It certainly wasn't Pierce, or Jag would've said so.

She didn't blame Jewel. The brothers could be demanding and relentless if they wanted info. And quite possibly she started worrying about Ivy's safety.

Whatever. She just wished she'd had more time to dig deeper

into the Knights. She had caught a few tidbits but nothing concrete. But the little she did hear, she'd have to report to Pierce, to give him the heads up.

She rushed to the door when she heard straight pipes rumbling into the pawn shop lot. He'd followed her home like he said he would. Not that she waited for him. Most likely she was part way home before he even got his Harley started. And she certainly didn't go the speed limit. Hell no. She had pushed that Hemi engine so she'd get home with the speed of lightning.

She yanked open the door and stepped out onto the second-floor landing, hands on her hips, watching him park his bike next to her Charger and quiet the engine. He ripped the bandana off the lower half of his face and yanked off his goggles to squint up at her.

It was clear he wasn't a happy camper. Well, fuck him, neither was she.

"I'm home safe. You can go now," she yelled down the metal staircase.

He didn't dismount, didn't even move. Simply stared at her. A shiver shimmied down her spine.

He was done with her? No way.

Finally, he spoke, "Givin' you five minutes to wash that shit off your face, hide those fucking boots where I can't find 'em, an' change out of those pants that emphasize your camel toe. You got five. Hurry up."

"I don't know who you think—"

"*Five*. Go."

He didn't yell it, no. He growled it softly which made her realize how pissed and serious he truly was.

"If I gotta get off this bike before those five minutes are up, Ivy..." He dropped his head and shook it.

She swallowed hard. She could continue to stand there and argue with him, or she could go inside and lock him out, which would mean she would need another front door.

Or she could go do what he demanded. Though, that wasn't her first instinct. No, every bone in her body wanted to continue to fight him, but she realized it may be smarter to just get done what she was going to do, anyway. Remove the heavy makeup and get undressed for bed as she originally planned.

At least that's how she rationalized it.

She threw up her hands in a show of disgust and stomped inside, slamming the door behind her. She didn't bother to lock it since she figured the prospects who changed out the door gave him a key. She didn't bother to chain it either because that had proven to be a joke when it came to a biker's boot.

She ripped off her new thigh-high boots, threw them in the closet by the door and then headed to the bathroom.

Ten minutes later, she opened the bathroom door to find her apartment quiet. She peeked down the hallway and was surprised to find he wasn't there taking up space in her living room. Nor was he drinking a beer in her kitchen.

Huh.

She pulled the tie on her black silk robe tighter and tiptoed down the hall to her bedroom. The door was open, the bed empty.

She sighed as every muscle in her body relaxed. Maybe he *was* done with her. Maybe she finally got what she wanted. Because that was exactly what she wanted, right?

Right.

Fuck. Her. Life.

In frustration, she scrubbed her hands over her now squeaky-clean face and moved into her bedroom. It was two AM, and she needed some sleep so she could deal with this whole thing of getting caught at Dirty Dick's more clearly in the morning.

She yelped when a hand came out from behind the door and grabbed her by the throat. After shoving her into the wall, Jag came nose to nose with her.

His voice rumbled out low and growly like his straight pipes. "I know you like it rough, baby, but one of 'em coulda raped you. Left you beaten an' bloody. Torn apart. Possibly even dead."

Her fingers pried at his grip on her neck. "You said you were done with me."

"I am."

"You slamming me against the wall of my bedroom proves otherwise."

His nostrils flared, and he blew out a harsh breath. He dropped his hand like it was on fire and stepped back. "Coulda been seriously hurt or dead, an' no one woulda known," he said it so softly Ivy's heart squeezed.

"Jewel knew where I was."

He barked out a harsh laugh. "Yeah, that's how I found out. No one knew but her. Somethin' went sideways, she couldn't have done shit. An' by the time the rest of us found out, woulda been too late. *Fuck!*" She winced at the rawness of his screamed curse.

Well, Jewel wasn't the only one who knew. Pierce did. But still she had no indication that he was aware of that.

He pinned his gaze on her. "What'd you find out?"

She wasn't expecting that question. She was only supposed to report to Pierce. "Nothing."

He tilted his head as he stared at her. "Nothin'. So, you went in amongst the enemy for *nothin'*."

"They're not the enemy."

"Not yet. Will change if they keep grabbin' territory closer to Shadow Valley."

And, unfortunately, Ivy had a feeling from what little she did hear that was their plan. But she needed to talk to Pierce first.

Suddenly, he was there in her face again, his heat searing her as did his words. "You touch any of 'em?"

Her voice shook as she whispered, "No." He was untying her robe and sliding his hands over the bare skin of her waist. She pressed herself tighter against the wall, trying to prevent his hands from skimming over her ass, trying to fight the need she felt for him.

It was a losing battle.

Her breath hitched as he gripped her ass and jerked her against him. His cock was hard and hot against her flesh, even through his jeans.

"You drive me crazy, Ivy. Know that?"

"I don't know why. There's plenty of other females who are willing."

He slid his hands up her ribcage, cupped her breasts and gently brushed both nipples with his thumbs. "Don't want any other females."

Her heart squeezed again then thumped all the way into her throat. Her body was a traitor. Her nipples hardened to painful points, her pussy clenched and began to throb.

Why, why, *why* did this man have such power over her?

Why couldn't she find a nice nerdy guy with a regular job, who was responsible and wanted the white picket fence?

Fuck!

Because she didn't want that either.

I'm so screwed.

He rolled one nipple between his thumb and forefinger, slipping his other hand between her legs, dipping it between her now traitorous slick folds. He leaned his forehead against hers, his breath coming fast and ragged as he groaned, "Fuckin' Ivy."

She parted her thighs slightly, giving him better access to slip a finger, then two, into her. She panted as he slowly worked them in and out, and when his thumb brushed against her swollen clit, she cried out.

"Goddamnit, why you gotta be like this?" he murmured, almost sounding as if in pain.

"Like what?"

"So tempting. Need to walk away from you, baby, an' I can't. But you're such a bitch. Make me want you but make me hate you at the same time."

Even though the feeling was mutual, she'd never got this wet for anyone before. Never wanted anyone else so much.

He was like candy. Tempting, addicting, but oh so bad for her. If she fell for him, it would be like falling into a deep, dark hole. She'd have a hard time climbing back out to save herself.

"Why you gotta be such a bitch to me, Ivy?"

God, he sounded wounded, and it cut her to the quick.

But it was hard to think when he was tweaking her nipple and fucking her with his fingers. "I— I have to be," she whispered.

"Why?"

"I don't want to be any man's property."

"Not any man's," he clarified with a grunt.

She sucked in a breath as his fingers curled and he proved he was skilled in a different type of body work other than bikes and cars. "Not yours, either. *Ah, fuck.*"

"Like that?" he murmured against her lips.

"Yeah."

"Hard to be a bitch when my fingers are deep inside you."

She ignored that.

"Even harder when my dick is inside you."

"When's—" the words caught in her throat. She tried again. "When's that happening?"

"Want me inside you, baby?"

"Yes," she hissed.

"How bad?"

Her hands came up and fisted his leather cut in an attempt to jerk him closer. His knee separated her thighs a little more and as she gave him more access, he pulled his hand away and lifted it to her lips. "Open."

She did as he demanded and he slipped his fingers into her mouth.

"Tastes good, right?"

She didn't answer, just locked her gaze on his as she sucked his fingers deep into her mouth and circled them with her tongue, the tip teasing along his slick digits.

He pulled his hand away and dropped to his knees, gripping her thighs to separate them even more, then he separated her folds and his mouth found her center. He sucked her clit hard, and when she wasn't expecting it, slipped his still wet fingers between the cleft of her ass until he found her tight rim.

He didn't ask, he just took. One finger, then two. His mouth worked her front, his fingers her back, and her knees simply buckled.

CHAPTER 7

She grabbed at his shoulders to hold herself up, and used the wall to prop herself as he quickly made her forget everything that he was, everything that he believed, everything that he was about.

For a split moment, he was Mick the man, not Jag the biker, the Road Captain, the misogynist.

She knew it wouldn't last, but she'd take whatever moments she could get.

But the problem was, every time they were together, every time she let herself forget, she slipped a little more. Skidded down that slippery slope, toward that black hole, to that point of no return.

She needed to hang on to the edge, even if it was only by her fingernails.

However, the precipice she was currently teetering on collapsed around her, and slamming her head back against the wall, she came hard, squeezing him tight, pulsating against his mouth, crying out his name. Not Mick's name, no. But Jag's. Digging her fingers into his hair, she pressed him closer until the last wave faded away.

She opened her eyes and glanced down at him. His eyes met hers and he smiled. "That's the real you, Ivy. What you just gave me is you, baby. That's what I fight for."

She closed her eyes as she took in his words and tried to slow her breathing, her pounding heart. After a moment, she blinked them open. "And who's the real you, Jag?"

"Never shown you anyone but who I truly am. You're either gonna accept that or you're not."

She was either going to accept him or she wasn't.

"Are you going to fuck me?"

He pushed to his feet, leaned in and kissed her, sucking her bottom lip into his mouth and snagging it in between his teeth. When he let her go, he asked in a gruff voice, "That what you want?"

"I wouldn't ask if I didn't."

A slow grin crossed his face. "We had a deal about me takin' care of your business. So, if that's what you want, glad to oblige."

"Well, if it's going to be a chore—"

He scooped her into her arms, startling her, took two long strides to the bed and tossed her onto the mattress. Before she could catch her breath, he had his cut off, his shirt pulled over his head and tossed aside.

Damn, the man not only had mad skills in bed, he was certainly easy on the eyes, even with all the ink. Though, she didn't mind the ink at all. She grew up around heavily tattooed men and women, so she appreciated good body art. Crow probably did almost all of Jag's tattoos and he was one of the best ink slingers in the western half of Pennsylvania.

Crow had even done the couple tats that she had. The poison ivy vine that wrapped around her ankle and down her foot. And the small DAMC logo she had on her shoulder. She had gotten that second one when she was stupid drunk one night. And, of course, Crow wasn't going to talk her out of getting something that branded her DAMC property, drunk or not.

Crow was another brother who was easy on the eyes, but he wasn't the one standing in her bedroom stripped down naked at the moment.

No, he wasn't.

She reached over to her nightstand drawer, but he was there in a flash, grabbing her wrist and shaking his head. "No. Told you last time. Just me an' you. Nothin' in between." He wrapped her fingers around his erection, sliding her hand up and down his length. "Nothin' but this, baby."

She shook her head. "Not smart."

"Ain't a problem if it's just us."

Her heart flip-flopped in her chest. *Just us.*

Those two simple words should bother her because once again he was demanding exclusivity. But, damn it, right now, right as he stood naked before her offering himself to her and only her, she could actually imagine being with only him.

And that scared the living shit out of her and she didn't want to think about it. Not now.

Instead, she just wanted to take what he offered her in her bedroom at that moment. Nothing more.

Without releasing his cock, she shifted to the edge of the bed and guided him into her mouth. His fingers dug deep into her hair as he let out a low groan, "Fuckin' Ivy."

She gripped the root tighter and stroked her tongue along the underside of his length, savoring the salty, musky smell and taste of Jag.

"Fuck, baby. Your mouth... *fuck*."

She sucked so hard her cheeks hollowed out, then bottomed out when she took almost his whole length. Relaxing the back of her throat, she released the root, taking everything that was him.

"For fuck's sake," he growled.

She tipped her eyes up, but his were squeezed shut, his head tilted back, his jaw tense, the tendons in his neck bulging.

He just might be enjoying what she was doing to him.

Then in quick succession, she cupped his balls and hummed around his length, his eyes popped open and he shouted a curse at the ceiling. With a loud grunt, he shot his salty load down her throat.

After a few quick deep breaths, he slipped from her mouth, gave her a languid smile and brushed his thumb over her bottom lip. "Damn, woman. Anytime you wanna hum a tune, don't even gotta ask. Now get rid of that robe."

"What do you want me to hum?" She shrugged the robe off her shoulders and before she could toss it aside, he grabbed it out of her hands and slid the black silky tie from the loops.

"Longest song you can think of." *Then* he tossed the rest of the robe aside.

She eyed the tie in his hands. "Do you plan on doing something with that?"

He wound it around his fist then let it unwind on its own. "So many things I can do with it. Gag you, blindfold you, tie you up."

A thrill ran through her, constricting her nipples into tight buds. She arched a brow in his direction. "And?"

A grin spread slowly over his face. "Fuckin' Ivy," he murmured and climbed onto the bed to come face to face with her, his now semi-soft cock hanging between his thighs.

It made her want to cup him and suck him all over again.

"Gonna fight me if I truss you up?"

"Is that what you want? For me to fight?" she whispered. When she was done asking, she couldn't stop the puffs of hot breath that escaped from her lips in rapid fire.

His grin died, his steel-blue eyes turning dark and stormy. She watched as his throat undulated as if almost in slow motion. A sound came from the back of his throat that sounded like a combination of a groan and "Ivy." Whatever it was made heat explode from her core all the way to her fingertips and toes.

When his head dropped, and he sucked an aching nipple hard into his mouth, she arched against him. "Fuck. *Yessss*," she hissed softly.

He shoved a knee between her legs to part her thighs, reaching one hand down to slide a finger through her wetness. She had a feeling he'd find her pretty damn slick. The other teased her nipple with his thumb, the hard nub so sensitive, every brush of his thumb felt directly connected to her pussy, which only made her more eager.

She was close to climaxing as his fingers played along her slick labia, pinched her clit, then dipped inside for a split second.

"So fuckin' wet," he mumbled against her breast. Then he was gone. Nothing but the room's cool air touched her.

She didn't even realize she'd had her eyes closed until that moment. She only had a second to look at the ceiling before her face ended up in the pillow as he flipped her over, snagged both arms and crossed her wrists at the small of her back.

"Wanna spank that ass, baby. Wanna spank it so fuckin' hard."

She turned her face to the side so she could breathe, but he kept pressure on her back so she couldn't turn enough to see him. She jerked at her arms, but he tightened his grip. Then the smooth silk of her robe tie was being wound around and around, binding her hands together.

Goosebumps broke out all over her body. "Jag..."

"Yeah, baby?" he asked softly. "Scared?"

Scared? No. Excited? Holy hell, yes!

She couldn't be docile though, even tied up. Especially tied up. So, she tried to kick him in the back with her heels, then wiggled hard underneath him as he straddled her thighs.

"Jag," she repeated, this time his name came out on a ragged breath.

"I'd gag you, too, but like hearin' you say my name. Gonna like it even better when you're screamin' it when you come."

He knotted the tie and let go. Immediately, she tested the binding and couldn't believe it didn't slip even a little. His tongue, wet and warm, worked its way up her spine from above her bound hands all the way to the back of her neck, where he pushed her hair to the side and he sucked her skin at the top.

A moan escaped her as he sank his teeth gently into the back of her neck. He then kissed her where he bit her and pressed his mouth to her ear.

"Woulda liked one of those Knights doin' this to you?"

"No."

The tip of his tongue traced the outer shell of her ear. "Sure?"

"Yes... I'm sure."

He sucked her earlobe, then released it, his warm breath making her shiver. "Don't know... The way you were dressed, baby... Kinda throwin' yourself in their face. Hard to resist temptation like that."

"Nothing happened." She had taken a risk, yes. She knew that going in. Pierce knew that. But it wasn't anything she couldn't handle.

Though Jag would probably disagree.

He dropped his weight so his cock, which was now hard again, slid in between her ass cheeks.

"Was stupid, baby. Admit it."

She was having a hard time thinking when he thrusted against her like that. She wanted him deep inside her.

"Are we going to have a conversation or are we going to fuck?"

He sat up and his body shook against her as he chuckled. "Gonna fuck. But don't think this conversation is over. It isn't."

"Well, let's get to it. I don't have all night, Mick."

His body stilled above her and she heard a loud, long sigh. If she had to push his buttons to spur him into action, she'd do it.

Suddenly, he was pulling at the knot at her wrists, loosening and unwrapping the binding. She twisted her head to look at him.

No doubt about it, he was unhappy with a capital U.

"What are you doing?"

He shook his head, but wouldn't meet her gaze. Instead he stared at the black tie in his hands. "Can't do this shit with you, Ivy. I can't. If an' when you want me..." His eyes then shot to hers and pinned her. He slapped his chest with the flat of his palm. "When you want *me, Jag*, you let me know. Until then, you can go fuck yourself." He climbed off her thighs, off the bed and snagged his jeans from the floor. Slipped one leg in and then the other, tugging them up over his thighs and his hard-on, struggling to fasten them.

She flipped over and sat up, pushing her wild hair out of her face. "What are you doing?"

"Gettin' the fuck outta here. You were right, plenty of other willin' women at church. Didn't want easy, though. Wanted you. *You*, Ivy."

She climbed to her knees and flung out an arm. "You can't just leave—"

"Fuck I can't. Got a perfectly good palm."

"Mick—"

He pulled his Sturgis tee over his head with jerky movements. "See? There you go again, Ivy, callin' me somethin' you know pisses me off. Tryin' to get under my skin. But you know what? You're already there. Been there for way too long. Need to get rid of you like a goddamn rash."

She pushed herself off the bed, grabbed his arm before he could snatch his cut off the chair. "Stop. Jag! Stop."

When he looked down at her, she closed her eyes, stepped behind him and wrapped her arms around his waist, pressing her naked body to his.

"Fuck," she whispered. "*Fuck.*"

CHAPTER 7

He circled her wrists with his fingers and tightened them until they were slightly painful. "Let go, Ivy."

She pressed her cheek to his back and murmured, "No."

His muscles were tight, his body stiff, but she didn't care. She had something to say and when she opened her mouth, the words just rolled out. "Going to Dirty Dick's was stupid. You're right. It was risky. We knew that."

Jag's body jolted against her at the "we," and she realized she may have just slipped up. She could only hope he thought "we" meant her and Jewel. She continued on before he could ask. "I want you, Jag. I do. It..." She lost her words because she didn't want to admit this out loud, not to him, not to anyone. "It scares me."

His body tensed at her words and then just as quickly everything about him softened. He released her wrists and turned in her arms, his fingers combing through her long hair, pulling it away from her face. With a thumb under her chin, he tilted her face up. His expression spoke volumes, and that scared her even more.

"Nothin' to be scared of."

"Easy to say when you're a man and treated as such. It's one thing to be a part of the club, to be born into it. As it stands now, I can do what I want when I want for the most part. It's another when you become someone's ol' lady, become someone's property. And you know that shit happens. Don't lie and say it doesn't."

"You're too proud for that shit, baby, I get it. It happens; it's the way of the club. Has been, always will be. Can't do shit about it." He paused, his lips flattened as if he thought hard about saying what he said next. "Don't wanna either. I claim you as mine then you're *mine*. In all ways."

She sucked in oxygen and tried to pull back but he locked her tighter against him by wrapping his arms around *her* this time.

"How about we just keep our initial deal? When I need dick, you supply the dick."

He went solid once again as he stared at her, his face not revealing anything. Then his nostrils flared and his brows furrowed. "Can't be havin' you runnin' around doin' stupid shit like tonight.

Can't watch it, Ivy. Can't watch you dancin' while you're drunk gettin' everyone's dick hard. An' I'm supposed to sit there an' not do shit? Ain't gonna happen. Sorry."

He released her and took a step back. His eyes raked her from top to toe. He bit his bottom lip, shook his head, grumbling, "Shit. Want you like no other, but fuck, baby... Gotta be in or out. Not goin' to deal with this half-assed shit. In?" He leaned close enough that she could feel his warm breath brush against her cheek and he narrowed his eyes. "Or out?"

Out.

Out.

Out.

Goddamn it.

She couldn't give in. Not now. Not ever.

"I can't," she said under her breath. But she knew he heard her because his face changed to a mix of disappointment and frustration. He started to step closer but stopped, put his hands on his hips and dropped his head to stare at the floor. He nodded, avoided her eyes, then grabbed his boots and cut.

As he walked out of the room, her stomach twisted and her chest felt as though a heavy biker boot had stomped on it.

Then a crashing sound came from outside that made the hair rise on the back of her neck. She snatched her robe and slipped it over her shoulders, cinching it with the belt, before rushing out of the bedroom to see Jag rip open her door and run out.

The metallic scraping and screeching continued to be heard through the open doorway but sounded like it was getting farther away.

Then she heard Jag shouting from the top of her steps, "FUCKING MOTHERFUCKERS!"

CHAPTER EIGHT

Jag stood in the way too early morning light, hands on hips, staring at what was left of his baby.

The sight was almost cruel enough to shed a damn tear. But he wasn't upset. No. The air may be humid, but he was steaming.

Dex, Diesel, Hawk, Rig, Crash and Jag's sister Jewel, all appearing as if they were in mourning, also circled the hunk of metal that used to be his customized Harley.

Rig had brought the rollback during the night and they had loaded the pieces up and hauled them back to the garage. Now they were in a pile. A fucking pile. The chain that the Warriors had hooked to his sled to drag it through the pawn shop parking lot and down the road, effectively scattering pieces of metal for about a tenth of a mile, was still wrapped around what was left of the handlebars.

His baby. Forty thousand dollars and two years of work. His custom baby was destroyed. Royally fucked. And it wasn't some simple fix. It was totaled.

What good was a Road Captain without a ride?

"See nothin'?" Diesel asked in grunt speak.

Jag blew out a breath trying not to drop to his knees and pound the pavement with his fists until they were bloody. "No."

"Too busy with your ears between her thighs?" Jewel asked, her lips curved slightly at the corners.

Out of the corner of his eye, Jag saw Dex's head pop up and twist toward him. His brows knitted together. "You fuckin' my sister?"

The heavy gazes of Hawk and Diesel landed on him. He didn't need to have his body parts strewn alongside his bike's either.

He dragged a hand through his hair. "Yeah." He eyeballed Dex. "Gotta problem with that?"

Whacking Jag on the back, Dex barked out a laugh. "Fuck no. 'Bout time."

He turned to Hawk and Diesel. "You two gotta problem with it?"

Even though both brothers were Ivy's cousins, they tended to be more protective of her than her own brother.

Diesel cocked a heavy brow. But before he could grunt his answer, Jag said, "Don't matter anyhow, shit's over before it began."

"What do you mean?" Jewel asked, her mouth hanging open, her eyes round.

Jag ignored his sister and glanced around the circle of his brothers. "Wasn't just Warriors I dealt with last night. Dragged Ivy out of Knight's territory. Was hangin' at Dirty Dick's."

The air changed around him. Both Diesel and Hawk's spines straightened and suddenly they appeared taller, broader and definitely scarier than usual.

"What the fuck?" Hawk asked. He turned to Dex. "You know about this?"

Ivy's brother shook his head. "Fuck no. I did, would've stopped her."

Hawk gave a sharp nod and his eyes fell on Jewel, who abruptly became pale. And when Diesel's gaze fixed on her, she took a step back. "I— I gotta go back to the office."

"Don't you fuckin' move," Diesel growled, his brows pinned low, his face twisted in a scowl.

Jewel spine straightened as she slammed her hands on her hips and faced him. "Can't tell me what to do, D."

His nostrils flared and his jaw tightened. "Fuck I can't."

"Beast," she said under her breath and he took a threatening step forward but stopped.

Jag had no idea what the hell that meant, but Diesel certainly didn't like it and usually no one challenged him. Not even the man's father, Ace. At least not since Diesel outgrew him when he turned sixteen.

"Spill it," Diesel shouted.

Jewel's body jolted. "Nothing to spill," she whispered, her voice a bit shaky. She looked at Jag and raised her eyebrows, a silent plea for his help.

Jag frowned at his sister. He hadn't stuck around last night after overhearing Jewel mention that Ivy was at Dirty Dick's to one of the prospects. But he had questions of his own.

He'd let the club's enforcer get the answers from her. He wasn't really happy with his own blood right now. Especially since she knew Ivy was going to Dirty Dick's on her own.

"Woman. Talk or else. Got me?"

Jewel pursed her lips, tilted her head as she considered the large angry man in front of her, then said, "She went to Pierce and he okayed it. That's all I know."

"Fuckin' bitches gotta meddle," Crash said, shaking his head. He looked at Jag. "They fuck with her?"

"Not that I can tell. She says no. Dragged her ass outta there as soon as I found out. Talkin' all sweet to three of 'em dressed an' made up like a goddamn hooker."

Jewel's mouth dropped open. "No, she wasn't," she whispered like she didn't believe him.

"The fuck she wasn't. No bra, tight tank top, leather pants an' thigh-high hooker boots. Makeup so thick, need paint thinner to remove it."

Diesel's expression became more intense and crazier as he

confronted Jewel that even Jag began to worry. "You women dress like that when you go out?"

Her eyes flicked up to D then slid to the side. "No."

A sound escaped Diesel that even made Hawk raise his brows in his direction. "Fuckin' better not," Diesel practically roared. "Now get gone, woman. Get back to the office. We gotta talk."

Jag was pretty sure Diesel meant "we" as in the men, but he wouldn't doubt D's "we" had a double meaning.

Jewel scrunched her face up at Diesel, but after a quick eye flick to Jag, she turned and headed back toward the office. Slowly.

"Hurry up," Diesel yelled at her.

Without turning around, Jewel flipped him the bird over her shoulder, but she started to walk faster. A couple of the guys snorted, and Rig bent over in laughter, slapping his thigh.

"She's another one that needs tamed, just like Ivy," Crash mumbled. When Diesel's gaze dropped on him, he threw his hands up. "Not for me to take on, though. *Noooo* doubt. Like my pussy a lot easier and agreeable. Gotta be a helluva good fuck to want to put up with that hassle."

A-fucking-men, Jag thought, that "hassle" from last night still fresh in his mind.

"Fuckin' women," their VP, Hawk, grumbled. "So we gotta deal with two issues. First one bein' Pierce allowin' Ivy to head into the Knight's territory. Supposed to be one of Dawg's girls goin'." He looked toward his brother.

"Couldn't get one to cooperate," Diesel said, his eyes still pointed the direction Jewel went, though she was no longer in sight.

"Think Pierce approached Ivy or think it was the other way around?" Rig asked, scratching his barely-there beard.

"Knowin' my sister, she probably went to Pierce," Dex answered.

Diesel grunted.

"Even if any of us were okay with it, he needed to bring it to the table. He didn't," Hawk said. "Bad move for a prez."

"Gonna need dealt with," Diesel said, his attention finally back on the group of men.

"Pierce is fucked," Jag muttered.

Hawk raised a placating hand. "Yeah, well, let's not do anythin' stupid. This is gonna have to be a bigger discussion than just the few of us. Can't accuse Pierce on Jewel's word alone. Ivy coulda told her a story about Pierce okayin' it when she just went an' did it on her own. Let's get to the bottom of it first. Then deal with it at a later date once we got all the facts."

"Agreed," Crash said and some other assenting grunts rose up around the circle. "Second problem..."

"Yeah, that," Hawk continued.

Jag chimed in. "Doubt it was the Knights' retaliation for me draggin' Ivy's ass out of Dirty Dick's, stealin' away some possible fresh pussy. Or even for DAMC violating their territory, be it a bitch or not."

"Got Warriors written all over it," Diesel said, kicking the heavy chain that laid next to the destroyed bike parts. Another round of grunts rose in agreement from the brothers.

"You don't fuck with my woman or my bike," Jag muttered, though he felt like screaming it at the top of his lungs.

"Anyone call 5-0?" Hawk asked, his eyes on Jag.

"Not me," Jag answered. "An' none showed their pig faces before Rig picked up me an' what was left of my sled."

"Goddamn shame," Rig grumbled, kneeling down and patting what was left of the custom gas tank that had one side crushed in and most of the custom paint scraped off. Road rash.

"Good," Diesel spoke up. "Keep this on the D.L. We'll handle it."

Hawk turned to Jag. "Guess you'll be in four wheels for a while until you get a new sled. Grab a loaner cage from Crash."

Jag nodded, although he wasn't happy about being stuck driving a car. Especially one of Crash's junkers.

However, unless he bought a temporary bike, it would take him another two years to build something like he already had. His pride and joy. His baby. All that work, all that money, gone in minutes by those nomad assholes who had a chip on their damn shoulder.

But better his bike than them grabbing Ivy. Bad enough she had been hanging with the Knights. He would have lost his mind if the Warriors had snagged her. No telling what would have happened. To her, anyway, because there was no doubt what would have happened to the Warriors. They'd all be dead. And he would be holed up at SCI Greene with Doc and Jag's father, Rocky.

"Guess you're gonna have to make another custom."

Jag lifted his eyes to Crash, and he grunted in agreement. His mouth flat-lined at the thought of all the work that was involved. It was one thing to build a custom bike for a customer. Building customs was his passion, but it was something he got paid to do and paid well. He was always in demand and never had a lack of work. People came from all over to get a custom from him. Even the biker cops did, too. He'd take their money, it spent like anyone else's. Quite a few of the Blue Avengers MC members had a custom from him. Even Axel, his cop cousin and Zak's brother, had one. The man had spent a small fortune to get what he wanted. And Jag had *loved* taking Axel's hard-earned money.

However, when it came to building his own bike, he had to do it on his own time. Nights, weekends, and every spare moment. Plus, he had to dump his own money into it. He'd been squirreling away some scratch so he could move out of his room at church and buy a house. Not a big place, but something that was his and not the club's. Now it didn't look like that would happen anytime soon. A new sled came before a house. As club road captain, not having a bike was like missing an arm or a leg.

Fuck.

Hawk clapped him on the back. "Wanna say a eulogy before we recycle her?"

Jag snorted and with a last look at his baby in ruined pieces, he shook his head and walked away before he broke down in front of his brothers.

He lost both Ivy and his bike in one night. He needed a drink and didn't care that it wasn't even nine yet.

CHAPTER 8

"Sit," Pierce barked, tipping his chin toward the chair to his right. He sat at the head of the polished wood DAMC table.

Ivy shook her head. She wasn't getting comfy with Pierce in the club's meeting room, especially with the door closed. "I'm not going to be here long."

He tilted his head and ran his heated gaze up her legs, over her breasts where he hesitated, then finally met her eyes. That was after staring at her mouth for a few seconds. Ivy had fought not to lick her lips.

"Anythin' happen?"

"Jag found out and dragged me out of there last night."

He lifted one brow, picked up the gavel in front of him and spun it absently in his fingers. "Yeah?" He tilted his head and asked, "He pissed?"

"Let's just say he wasn't thrilled finding me there."

The corner of his mouth twitched. "Told you you're on his to-do list."

Ivy ignored that.

"D'ya find out anythin'?"

"A little bit of chatter. I wasn't there long enough to get anything good."

He shook his head. "Fuckin' Jag, gotta let his dick screw shit up."

Ivy was sure that Pierce's dick had screwed things up before, too, so he had no room to talk. "Yeah, well, I kind of told a couple of the Knights I lived in Baldwin. They seemed to know the area well, so makes me wonder if they've been scoping out the town."

Pierce released a low whistle. "Baldwin? Shit."

"Problem is, I'm not sure if they're going to be suspicious since Jag came in claiming me as DAMC. If the Knights compare notes, they might figure out I was lying to them. It might put the club in a bad spot."

"Nothin' we can't handle."

"Right... Sorry I couldn't get anything more."

He studied her. "Like I said, probably wouldn't get more unless you took some Dark Knights' dick. Least we know to watch Baldwin. They grab that town, we know they're headin' in this direction. Doesn't mean they won't push our boundaries, though. Or they might stop there. Hell, they can have Baldwin."

Ivy kept her face neutral but she couldn't believe Pierce was telling her this stuff. Usually they didn't share shit with the women. But he was talking to her like she was one of the brothers. Because of that she wasn't going to interrupt him.

Suddenly a look came over his face and he narrowed his eyes. "That doesn't leave this room, got me? Don't be flappin' your lips to the other bitches 'bout what you heard at Dick's or in here. Club business ain't your business. None of ya."

And there it was. He was running his mouth in front of a vagina with ears and realized his mistake.

Asshole.

Ivy closed her eyes in a struggle not to roll them. When she had it under control, she opened them and asked, "Are we done here?'

"Unless you want me to fuck you over this table, we're done. Close the door behind you."

The man was probably going to whack off when she left. Her stomach turned and so did she as she rushed to leave the room. Quickly closing the door behind her, she was relieved to see Grizz sitting at the club's private bar in his normal spot.

She ducked behind the bar, grabbed his almost empty pint glass and poured him a fresh draft, sliding it in front of him.

"Where's Mama Bear?"

He lifted his bearded chin toward the kitchen and grumbled, "In the kitchen where she belongs."

Ivy didn't stop her eyes from rolling this time. She made sure Grizz saw it.

He swatted a hand towards her in dismissal, but his heavily wrinkled eyes narrowed in her direction. "Watcha doin' in there? You an' Prez fuckin'?"

All the blood rushed from Ivy's face. "No!" She shot a glance toward the closed door to make sure Pierce had remained inside and didn't hear that.

"Watcha doin' with him alone then? You know that's no good."

She dropped her eyes to an empty shot glass that sat on the bar. "Just talking."

"'Bout what?"

She picked the shot glass up and sniffed it. Jack. Someone had been hittin' it already this morning. "Nothing."

Grizz slammed his palm on the bar top, causing Ivy to jump out of her skin. "Ain't *nothin'*, girly. Spill it. Or I'll tell everyone you doin' him on the sly. Wait 'til his ol' lady hears that. She'll pull out your hair an' scratch your face." Then his eyes became distant like he was imagining the two women getting into a cat fight. His lips twitched.

Crazy old man. Though, she loved the big old bear no matter what a grump he could be.

She jammed her hands on her hips and frowned at him. "You wouldn't."

He swiped at the beer foam clinging to his overgrown grey mustache. "Fuck I wouldn't. Tell me. If he's hidin' club business, I gotta know. Don't trust that slimy fucker. Especially after..." His gravelly voice faded off.

"Especially after what?" she prodded.

He shook his head and pulled at his long, raggedy salt-and-pepper beard. She could hardly see his lips buried in all that untrimmed wiry hair but she could tell he was now frowning.

"Just listen to me, girl. Don't be alone with him. That's all I'm sayin'."

A chill ran through her. She looked over her shoulder back to the closed meeting room door. "He's prez though," she whispered.

"Yeah." He tilted his pint glass to his lips and downed half his beer, then slammed it back onto the polished wood bar top. "Now... spill it or I will."

"You're ruthless, Grizz."

"Yep." He nodded. "How the fuck you think I survived long enough to get this grey?"

She leaned over the bar toward him and murmured, "Can't tell anyone."

"Right," he grunted.

Right. He would run his mouth as soon as he could. Because of that she needed to make something up that was believable. She grabbed a can of pop from the cooler and after popping the top she took a sip, trying to come up with something that would satisfy Grizz's curiosity.

"I was thinking about opening up my own computer store. Fixing computers, making the club a little extra green."

He raised a bushy brow. "Instead of workin' with Ace and Dex?"

God, she hated lying to Grizz. It was like lying to her grandfather. But truth was, she really had thought about opening her own shop. Too many times to count. So it wasn't a complete lie. "Yeah. It'd be something small. I could control my own income, not have a set salary."

"You ain't hurtin' for money, are you?"

Shit. "No. I was just thinking about moving out of the apartment and getting a bigger place. Maybe getting a dog."

His gnarled, arthritis-filled hand swatted in her direction again. "Your ass lives for free in that place. Why you wanna saddle yourself with a mortgage an' all that extra bullshit?"

"You and Mama Bear have a nice house."

"So? We're hardly there." That was true. They both practically lived at church. Grizz's ass welded to his bar stool, Mama Bear in the commercial kitchen that was sandwiched between The Iron Horse Roadhouse, the public side, and the private club side of the bar.

"When I leave work, I'd like to *leave work*, not just walk up the steps."

"Gettin' customers buggin' you after hours?"

"Sometimes. Not much."

"Rude assholes."

She agreed. There was no reason to show up at someone's residence hoping to pawn something for some cash. Usually it was

CHAPTER 8

people who were hard up for cash, but still... She didn't work twenty-four seven and customers needed to respect that.

"Get Ace to give you a raise an' get your own place. Still work at the shop."

Ivy shook her head. "I'm not taking advantage of my college education."

"That's why school's a waste of fuckin' money. None of us are hurtin' an' look at all the businesses the club owns an' runs. No college needed. Just a fuckin' scam. We take care of our own."

Ivy sighed and took a sip of her cola. Something was off. Ah. A shot or two of spiced rum would fix what was missing. She leaned down to grab the Captain Morgan and a large, white paper caught her eye. It was tucked in between two bottles of liquor under the bar.

She pulled it out and stared at the drawing. "What's this?"

"What's it look like, girly?"

"A professional drawing." It was a pencil drawing of a Harley, but one that was all tricked out, completely customized and it was badass with a capital B. Every small detail was carefully drawn, though it wasn't finished. Some shading was missing, some lines incomplete. But it was well on its way to being one of the nicest bikes she'd ever seen. Nicer than the custom sled that Jag had built for himself and he had worked on that one for a couple years.

Too bad the Warriors had to go destroy it last night. Nothing good ever happened when they came out of the woodwork.

"Yep," was all he said.

"Yep? Who drew it?"

The old man tilted his bearded chin toward the empty shot glass that remained on the bar. "Jag was here early this morning hittin' the bottle, depressed about his sled bein' trashed. Was sittin' here doodlin'."

Doodling? This was no doodle. The sketch reminded her of something a professional designer for a concept car company would draw, but on a computer and not by hand. The details Jag had put into it were exquisite.

"He plans on building this bike?"

"How the fuck do I know? He wasn't sayin' much. Wanted to be left alone. Wasn't gonna bug the man like you bitches like to do. Jeez, woman."

She looked toward the back of the clubhouse at the stairway that led to the rooms upstairs. "He up there?"

"I look like his keeper?"

Ivy bit her bottom lip to keep from freaking out on Grizz. She loved the old man, so she didn't want to give him a taste of her temper. But it was spiking.

"Why was it down here?"

"Left it on the bar an' Mama tucked it away so it wouldn't get ruined."

"This is really good," she murmured, staring at the drawing once more. "Like *really* good."

Like completely amazing. She knew he was an expert at custom body work but she never considered that actual art. But what she held in her hands was art for sure.

Jag was a freaking *artist*.

"Have you seen him draw like this before?"

Grizz's answer was a scowl in her direction.

She carefully rolled up the thick drawing paper, grabbed a discarded hair band, probably left behind by one of the sweet butts that hung out at the club, and secured it. She headed toward the back door of the club where her car was parked.

"Where ya goin' with that?"

"I'll bring it back."

"He ain't gonna like it," he shouted at her back as she pushed open the metal door and stepped out into the daylight.

"Probably not," she whispered as the door latched closed behind her.

Not even fifteen minutes later she was standing in Sophie's Sweet Treats with the sketch rolled out on top of the bakery's counter. She stood shoulder to shoulder with her sister Bella, Zak's ol' lady

Sophie, and Jewel, who rushed over after Ivy texted her and told her to get her ass over there pronto.

She obliged without even a question. Because that's what the club sisterhood was about... having each other's back.

"Damn," Bella whispered, her eyes wide. "That's fucking great."

"I know," Sophie also whispered.

There was no reason for them to whisper, but clearly they were in awe of Jag's talent just the same as she was. And, apparently, being in awe made you whisper.

Ivy slid her gaze to Jewel. "You ever see Jag draw like this before?"

She lifted one shoulder. "Sure. He doodled when we were kids. Never saw nothing like this though. His doodles weren't bad."

"This is no doodle," Bella said, her eyes landing on Ivy. "Where'd you find it?"

"Under the bar at church. Grizz said he was working on it this morning while he was downing shots of Jack."

"Downing shots of Jack already this morning?" Bella frowned, then she nodded, a sad look coming over her. "Oh, the shit with his bike."

"And other things," Ivy added, not wanting to bring up the crap that went on between them at her apartment and she'd promised Pierce not to talk to anyone about the Knights thing. Though, Jewel knew. She lifted her eyes to Jag's sister, trying to give her an unspoken message not to open her mouth.

Jewel just gave her a look, then scrunched up her face in answer. "Saw the remainders of his bike this morning. Didn't think you could trash a sled so badly by just dragging it."

"I saw it last night. It looked like they drove over it, too."

Ivy realized her mistake when both Sophie and Bella's eyes shot to her.

"Last night?" Bella asked. "You were with Jag last night?"

"Not what you think. Can we get back to his sketch?" She leaned her hip against the counter and crossed her arms over her chest, looking directly at Jewel. "Seriously now... Jewelee, you ever see him draw anything like this before?"

She shook her head. "No."

"He never brings in any sketches of the bikes he's building into the shop?"

"Not like this. I've seen some rough sketches taped up in the bay he works in, but that's about it. This one is pretty detailed."

"I bet it's for the bike he'll build to replace his trashed one," Sophie said, moving over to the display case and pulling out a tray of cupcakes. She slid it onto the glass top and handed one to each of the women, none of them refusing her amazing baked goods. "Key Lime," she murmured before taking a big bite of her own.

Ivy tentatively licked the merengue topping, and when the tangy but sweet lime touched her taste buds, she shoved half of it in her mouth, her eyes rolling in ecstasy as she chewed. "Damn, that's good," she said as soon as she swallowed.

"Your sister made them," Sophie answered, waving a hand toward Bella.

Bella just shrugged, her mouth full of cupcake.

Just then, Jewel and Jag's sister Diamond walked in, the little bell clinking over the front door as it opened then closed.

"So what's all the brouhaha that I have to haul my ass over here?" She stepped up to the counter and eyeballed the cupcakes. "New flavor or something?"

Sophie handed her a cupcake and immediately Diamond peeled the paper off the bottom and shoved half of it into her pie hole. Or cupcake hole more like it. "Holy fuck, that's damn good!" Di said, with a mouth full of cake.

"I know, right?" Jewel said. She took the last bite of her own then wiped her hands on her jeans. "Come back here and look at what our brother has done."

Di rolled her eyes. "What's that shithead done now?" She walked through the counter opening and came up next to Ivy, her eyes immediately dropping to the drawing. "Jesus," she whispered. "Jag do that?"

"Yeah," Ivy breathed.

"That bonehead drew *that*?"

"Yeah," Ivy repeated, a little louder.

"No fucking way."

"Yeah, he did," Ivy insisted. "It should be framed and on someone's wall, right?"

"Hell yes, once it's finished." Diamond stepped back and faced Ivy. "Where'd you find that?"

"Under the bar."

"Under the bar? At church?" Diamond asked, surprised.

"Yeah, Mama Bear found it and put it there for safe keeping."

Diamond shook her head, then pursed her lips. "So, what's the issue?"

"Think any of the brothers know?" Ivy asked her.

She hesitated, studied the drawing closer, then shrugged. "Doubt it. You think Jag would want to get ribbed about a talent like that? Being an artist?"

"Crow's an artist," Sophie pointed out.

Di snorted. "That handsome hunk of man-meat shoves needles and ink into skin and causes pain. Calls himself an ink slinger not a tattoo *artist*."

That was true. No one called Crow an artist to his face. And she would assume that to the brothers a tattooist would be considered more manly than someone who sketched with pencils. Even if the sketches were motorcycles.

Sketches.

Most likely there were more than just this one. He certainly didn't get this good overnight. Maybe he had a whole stash of them tucked away somewhere.

Hidden from all of them. Hidden from the world.

The man should be sharing his talent. Be proud of his skills.

Whatever. Typical biker, wanting to hide anything not "biker" worthy. They always have to act the ultimate badass. Keep their "rep."

Pretty much all the brothers in the club did only the basics: grunted, burped, ate, drank, shit, fucked, and raised hell. They *rode* motorcycles, didn't draw them.

Ivy frowned.

She needed to show the world Jag's talents. She needed to find more of his drawings and show them to an art dealer, or post them online for sale, or... or... something.

Something needed to be done. She'd have to give this some serious thought.

Jewel whispered close to her ear. "I see trouble."

Yeah. So did Ivy.

"Don't do anything stupid."

She faced her close friend and DAMC sister. "I'm not going to do anything stupid."

What she really wanted to do was drag Jewel into the back of the bakery and grill her on how Jag found out that she was at Dirty Dick's the night before, but she thought about what Pierce said, and would deal with Jewel the next time they were alone. Not with their sisters standing around and their ears perked.

The bell above the front door jingled again, and all eyes pointed that direction as Axel walked in. He froze and his blue eyes widened when he saw the group of them.

"Fuck," he muttered, then unfroze himself and moved closer. "A gaggle of biker babes. What's going on here? You ladies up to no good?"

"At least you didn't call us bitches like the rest of them do," Jewel mumbled and elbowed Bella, giving her the *what's up with him?* round eyes and brow raise.

Bella ignored her and broke away from the group. "You here for your daily sugar rush?"

"Yes," he leaned into the display case, eyeing up the Key Lime cupcakes. "You bake those?"

Ivy eyed Axel in his police uniform like he was a cupcake. Maybe she should chase cops, be a badge bunny and stop bringing home geeks. They may be more up her alley. They might like a little rough sex, but not treat their women like property.

"Yes," Bella answered him, handing him one. Then all eyes were

CHAPTER 8

glued to the cop as his tongue came out and he slowly licked off half of the merengue.

"Jesus," Diamond whispered next to her. "If he wasn't my cousin..."

Ivy elbowed her, but inconspicuously squeezed her own thighs together. Jag had left her hanging last night. He made her come once with his mouth, but she needed more than that. So watching Axel—who looked so much like his brother Zak, who Ivy had a crush on for most of her youth—use his tongue like that while pinning his gaze on Bella, just about made her come in her pants.

Bella was one lucky woman if she'd let Axel in.

But she wouldn't and she won't.

Bella wasn't letting anyone in.

Plus, the brothers would shit a brick if Bella hooked up with a cop, even if he was Zak's blood brother and related to a few of them.

Blood or not, Axel and his father Mitch were the law. And the law and the DAMC didn't mix very well.

Not one of the women moved as they watched Axel finish licking all the merengue off the top of his cupcake. Then when he bit into the cake it seemed that the spell was broken and all of them relaxed, sighing in unison.

Then when the radio on his duty belt squawked, the women all blinked at each other with color in their cheeks.

"Fucking Axel," Bella grumbled, turning away and shaking her head.

Jewel clutched her chest and leaned into Ivy, saying under her breath, "Holy fuck, that's my cousin. Something's wrong with me."

The corner of Ivy's lip twitched. "I think I hear banjos."

Jewel's eyes widened, then she laughed, smacking Ivy on the arm. "Gross."

Ivy shrugged. "You need to go bleach your brain."

"That's for sure."

Axel finished up a quick conversation full of cop-speak into the mic on his shoulder, then stepped closer to the counter. "What's that?"

Shit.

His eyes were on Jag's drawing. She rushed over to it and began to roll it up.

Axel held out his hand. "Give it to me."

Double shit.

"No."

"Ivy," he said in a cop's tone, full of warning.

Ivy sighed and handed the sketch over. Since he hardly ever talked to any of the club brothers, even his own blood brother Zak, she wasn't worried about him spilling the beans.

He snagged the drawing from her and laid it out on the counter, studying it. "What are you doing with one of Jag's sketches?"

Ivy blinked. Diamond blinked. Hell, all the women just looked at Axel and blinked in surprise.

Ivy shook herself mentally. "You know Jag draws?"

He nodded, his short military style haircut not even moving a little bit. "Yeah. He did a sketch like this when he built my bike. Not quite this detailed but just as good. This looks like it's going to be a nicer bike than mine. Or even his. Who is he building this one for?"

Ivy's gaze swept over the women then landed on Axel, who was staring at Jewel. Which made sense. Not only was Jewel Jag's sister, but they worked together at the body shop. If anyone should know, she should.

Which she didn't.

But that was not here nor there.

"Probably himself," Jewel finally answered.

"Why? He's got a bike he spent like forty grand on."

Forty grand?

Holy shit. And the Warriors just reduced it to a pile of rubble in minutes.

"Needs a new bike," Jewel said.

His dark eyebrows pinned together. "Why? What happened to his old bike? Not that it was old..."

Ivy knew the cops weren't called last night. No one reported what happened. Axel's interest may be innocent, but if he found out the Warriors were involved and stirring up the beef between them and DAMC, he'd go into cop mode. And that wouldn't be good for anyone.

Ivy shot Jewel a look, then stepped forward, laying a hand on Axel's arm to draw his attention. "I think he's just playing around with some ideas, that's all."

Axel nodded and took Ivy's words as truth.

That was the second time she lied today. Well, she might have *sort of* lied to Jag early this morning in her apartment, too. "Sort of" didn't count.

"Yeah, well, I'd love a bike like that. Can't afford it on a cop's salary, that's for damn sure. Already paid Jag out the nose for the one I have." He turned to Diamond. "Tell your brother, if he builds a new one, I'll consider buying the one he has now. Upgrade my ride."

Yeah, that wasn't going to happen. But Ivy bit her bottom lip to keep her thoughts to herself. Jag would be lucky to get a few cents a pound for the scrap metal that used to be his sled.

Then Ivy noticed her hand was still on Axel's arm and Bella was staring at it with intensity. She raised her gaze to her sister. When Bella finally glanced up her whole body jerked causing Ivy to quickly pull her hand away and curl it into her chest.

She stepped away from Axel, taking the drawing with her. Once again she carefully rolled it up and slid the hairband around it to secure it.

She needed to get it back to church before Jag discovered it missing.

Suddenly, the door from the bakery's kitchen swung open and Zak swaggered out. The man could certainly swagger. It was one of the reasons Ivy had a crush on him for so long. That loosey goosey hip movement and just his all-around badass coolness. But as soon as he noticed his estranged brother, he stopped and went solid.

Axel sighed loudly, his hands loosely resting on his duty belt. "*Brother*," he greeted.

"Had that conversation before," Zak muttered, stepping behind the counter, wrapping a hand around the back of Sophie's neck and pressing his lips to her temple. "Babe," he murmured softly.

Sophie smiled up at her ol' man and laid a palm flat against his chest. "Axel's here," she said, her voice husky.

Zak's gaze bounced to Axel then back to her. "No shit."

"He did this *thing* with his tongue on a Key Lime cupcake and now we need to go upstairs for a few minutes." She'd lowered her voice a notch but everyone could still hear her.

Both Axel and Zak made a strangled sound and their eyes met then slid away uncomfortably.

He stared down at Sophie, one brow cocked. "Right now?"

"Yeah," she whispered.

He lifted a shoulder. "You got it, babe." Then he steered Sophie by the neck to the swinging door and flipped two fingers up over his head in sort of a badass wave as they pushed through it.

Ivy looked at Jewel, whose mouth was hanging open, and she doubled over in laughter.

"No shame in that game," Diamond said, her words also choked with laughter.

Axel eyed up Bella. "You need to go somewhere, too?"

"Not with you. I can take care of myself."

"Damn," Jewel whispered.

"On that note, I have to go patrol my zone," Axel announced, his eyes still on Bella.

"You do that," she said.

Axel frowned at her, turned on his heel, and stalked out.

As soon as the door shut behind him, Diamond turned to Bella, "Girl, you're crazy. There is no reason to take care of your own business when you have someone like him breathing down your neck. You ask him to drop to his knees, that man would do it in a second for you. I know those two are my blood cousins, but I *swear* their hips are double-jointed. You're going to turn that action down? You're a fool."

"Let it go, Di," Bella muttered, grabbing the tray of Key Lime cupcakes and sliding them back on the shelf in the display case.

"I'm just saying—"

Bella slammed her hands on her hips, her brows low, her eyes heated. "And I heard you. Enough."

Diamond threw up her hands and huffed. "Fine. The day someone that looks *like that* throws himself at me *like that*, doing shit *like that* with his tongue... I'm not saying no." Her gaze caught her sister Jewel's. "You hear me? I turn someone like Axel down, just get my head examined. Or shoot me."

Jewel snorted. "Will do. Long as I get to pull the trigger."

"I'll hand you the damn gun," Di said, making her way out of the bakery.

Ivy waited until the bell above the door quieted, then looked down at the rolled-up sketch in her hand.

She needed to get the hell out of there and get back to church before the day went even more sideways.

CHAPTER NINE

Ivy glanced at her cell and read the text. The coast was clear; Jewel confirmed Jag was busy working at the shop. Now Ivy just needed to sneak into church without anyone seeing her and break into his room without getting caught.

Simple enough. Though, going undetected might or might not happen at this time of the day. Normally by eleven, most of the brothers were up and out doing their thing... which was usually working. For Dawg, it meant getting things prepared for a busy evening and night at Heaven's Angel's Gentlemen's Club. For Hawk, it meant stocking the bar and checking on supplies and other stuff for The Iron Horse Roadhouse. For Crow, it meant beginning his day at In the Shadows Ink since customers started rolling in right before lunchtime.

Ivy opened the back door and stepped into the dim interior of the clubhouse.

As for the prospects...

The clack of pool balls hitting each other came from her left. Her head spun in that direction and she saw three prospects standing around the pool table with a sweet butt.

What the fuck?

If anyone should be working, it would be them. Her eyes fell on one of the newer sweet butts who went by the name of Tequila. Her nickname was rightly earned from her clothes "falling" off every time she drank the liquor. Not that she ever wore much to begin with, so it never took very long for her to lose her clothes.

Today she was a fashion plate wearing a red stretchy tube top, her dangling belly ring showing, short cut-off shorts that were low enough to hint at a hip tattoo, and… cowboy boots. It made more sense she was wearing her Daisy Dukes today since the weather had turned hot, but Ivy had seen her wearing something similar when it was certainly inappropriate. Like when there was frost on the ground.

She was hanging off Rooster, a prospect who had been around for a while now and was close to getting patched in if the rumor was true. If Rooster was sticking his dick in her, then he better sanitize it with some Tequila, the actual alcohol, so he didn't catch the clap. Or crabs.

All eyes swung to Ivy, and she sighed at this little snag. She needed to take control of the situation and make it so they believed she had the right to be there in the middle of the day and not them.

Slamming her hands on her hips, she scowled at them and projected her voice laced with annoyance. "What are you fuckers doing here in the middle of the day? Weren't you given something to do?"

Their faces went from carefree and happy to slightly worried.

"Hawk know you all are in here playing?" She tipped her head to the pool table and then to Tequila. Her meaning was clear.

Dead silence greeted her.

"Just takin' a break," Weasel finally said, picking up a nearby beer bottle and tipping it to his lips.

"Yeah? Someone tell you that you could take a break? You want a break go get a union job. You want to be patched in, your ass better be breaking a sweat."

Squirrel's eyes narrowed, and he straightened. "Since when do club bitches tell us what to do?"

Oh. No. He. Didn't.

Ivy stepped closer to the table, but still kept enough distance where she could keep an eye on all of them. "I may be a club 'bitch' but I have more power in this club than you, prospect. Remember that. My granddaddy—"

He cut her off. "Same ol' shit we always hear. My granddaddy this. My granddaddy that," Squirrel sneered. "Women hold no power here."

As Ivy took a step closer, her hands balled into fists, but instead of her knocking some sense into Squirrel, she was knocked to the side by a large moving object. She only got a glimpse of the prospects' eyes widening and their faces becoming pale before she caught her balance.

For a bulky man, Diesel moved surprisingly fast. One second Squirrel was on his feet, the next he was on the ground in a ball, blood gushing from between his fingers which he held to his face.

"Get up, *club bitch*," Diesel barked.

Rooster and Weasel backed away quickly, leaving Tequila where she stood, raking her gaze down Diesel's massive body with excitement.

"Damn, Diesel," Tequila said, giving him "fuck me" eyes.

Without even turning his head, he shoved his finger in her face and grumbled, "Shut the fuck up."

She did.

Diesel's narrowed gaze landed on Rooster. "What're you assholes supposed to be doin'?"

"P-Preparin' for tonight's p-party."

"What *were* you doin'?"

"P-playin' p-pool."

"Hawk give you a list?"

"Yeah," Rooster grumbled, avoiding direct eye contact with the larger, very pissed off man.

He pointed a finger at Weasel. "You've been pushin' my limits for a while. You wanna be a member of this club?"

"Yeah."

"Sure don't look like it. Get gone."

Weasel only hesitated a moment before Diesel took a threatening step towards him. The recruit caught some sense and jogged toward the side door of the clubhouse that led to the courtyard and disappeared.

He swung his attention and his finger toward Rooster. "How 'bout you?"

"Yeah."

D tilted his head toward Tequila. "You stickin' your dick in that twat?"

Rooster opened his mouth but nothing came out.

Diesel took another menacing step closer.

Finally, Rooster answered, "No."

"Dawg's girls, not sweet butts. Got me?"

Rooster nodded. "Got you."

"Now get gone."

Rooster hightailed in the direction Weasel went, almost tripping over his own feet in his rush.

D shook his head and pinned his gaze on the sweet butt who now wore an outraged look. "You lettin' prospect dick in you?"

"He just said no."

Diesel's chin jerked at her back-talking him. "Maybe not Rooster dick, but there's other prospect dick 'round here. Don't be doin' them or you're out. Got me?"

Tequila frowned while yanking her tube top up over her very generous, but very fake breasts. "Not enough dick to go around when it comes to the members."

"Don't like it then there're plenty other clubs you can land. Heard the Knights are looking for some fresh pussy."

At the last of his words, his eyes landed on Ivy.

Oh shit.

Diesel knew.

That meant everyone probably knew.

"Prospects got work to do. Get gone, Tequila."

The woman, who couldn't be more than twenty-one or twenty-two, made a face like an angry pout, and pushed past Diesel, heading toward the front of the club and the door to The Iron Horse.

"No." The one word came out so harshly, Ivy even started and Tequila stopped dead in her tracks. She looked over her shoulder at him. "Stay out of The Iron Horse. Hawk don't need you hangin' all over him. He got work to do."

Her pout turned even darker as she spun on her heel and marched the opposite direction toward the back parking lot.

"Want dick, come back tonight for the party. Don't want to see you here until then. Got me?"

Tequila waved a dismissing hand over her shoulder and stomped her pointy-toed cowboy boots out the back door, slamming it behind her.

Ivy's gaze landed back on her angry cousin, but his attention was now focused on the bleeding recruit still on the ground.

"Gimme your cut."

Squirrel pushed himself up to a seated position with a groan, still holding his smashed nose with one hand. "Can't just kick me out. Gotta go to the table for a vote." Blood dripped down his chin and his words came out muffled.

"Fuck it does."

Ivy finally unfroze her feet and quickly moved to the bar, snagged a handful of napkins and went back over to stand over Squirrel. She held the wad of paper napkins out.

"Don't be nice to him," Diesel grumbled. "Insulted you, Doc, an' the rest of us."

"Yeah, well, I think he learned his lesson."

"Not yet," he said with a grunt.

"D..." Ivy started.

But Diesel gave her a warning look and then his eyes dropped back to Squirrel. "Gimme your cut. Not gonna repeat myself again."

Squirrel yanked the napkins from Ivy's fingers and pressed them to his face as he pulled himself up from the floor using the pool table.

He stood, swaying slightly, but he eyeballed Diesel, probably trying to figure out how serious the man was about kicking him out of the club.

Ivy could attest that Diesel didn't joke around about stuff like that. She stepped up and tugged on Squirrel's vest. In one way, she wanted to help him so he'd hurry up and leave, in another, she didn't want Diesel losing his patience, which was thin as it was, and kicking the former recruit's ass even more.

She did that more for her cousin's sake than Squirrel's. The club needed their Sergeant at Arms too much to be able to do without him if he ended up sitting in jail for assault.

Squirrel reluctantly shrugged one shoulder and then the other as Ivy pulled the cut off his arms. She handed the bloodied vest over to Diesel.

D fisted it, then said, "Done here. Get gone."

Squirrel made his way slowly to the door and walked out without another word.

Once it was just her and Diesel left, he swung his attention to her. "Whadya doin' here?"

Shit.

What seemed like lie number fifty in the last couple days slipped easily off her tongue. "Dex needs something from his room."

"Since when you do his biddin'?"

"I needed a break from the shop, so I offered."

Diesel stared at her for a hard moment, then nodded.

"Pierce won't be happy with you kicking out a prospect."

"Don't give a shit what Pierce thinks. He's fucked."

Ivy swallowed hard. "What do you mean?" This was not good. Dissension among the ranks in the club was not good at all.

"Know exactly what I mean. Go get Dex's shit an' get gone. Don't want you alone with the prospects. Or Pierce."

Ivy glanced over her shoulder toward the closed meeting room door. "He here?"

Diesel's bulky shoulders rose and fell in a heavy shrug. "Probably at the gun shop. Don't matter. Don't want you alone with Pierce any more. Not ever. Got me?"

Ivy's gaze flicked to his. He was dead serious.

"Yeah, I got you," she said softly.

"I hear you've been holed up in that meetin' room with him... or anywhere..." He shook his head, the tight mohawk not shifting even the slightest. "Ivy, it ain't gonna be pretty."

She nodded and went to move past him, but he grabbed her arm and stopped her. "Serious, Ivy."

She tugged at her arm, but his grip tightened. "I hear you, Diesel."

He did a chin lift and released her. She headed toward the stairs, then ran up them when she got there.

She paused at the top until she heard the back door slam. With a sigh of relief, she headed down the hallway to Jag's room, sliding the small lock pick kit out of her back pocket. She slipped a tension wrench and a pick into the lock, applied slight torque to the wrench, wiggled the pick, felt the pins set and *Voila!* the door was unlocked.

She never thought she'd need the skill she learned so long ago. Ace had thought it was funny when he taught the then ten-year-old Ivy to pick locks. It was entertaining for him. Little did he know she'd use what he taught her for the reasons she did.

She grinned and turned the knob, letting herself into Jag's room. She flipped the switch and closed the door behind her, locking herself in. She wouldn't put it past Diesel to come up and check on her.

She put her tools back in her back pocket and looked around. She'd been in his room only twice before. And both times she had been a bit... intoxicated, so she had never taken the time to inspect it closely.

Though the room was one of the larger ones in the clubhouse, it still was nothing to write home about. There weren't a lot of secret hiding spots in a ten by twelve room with a tiny bathroom attached.

She stepped over the piles of dirty clothes that had been simply thrown on the floor and stared at his unmade bed. There was an impression still in the pillow where his head normally laid. The top sheet was in a wrinkled ball. The fitted sheet pulled up on one corner, exposing a mattress she did not want to inspect any closer. And none of the linens matched.

Martha Stewart had definitely never been here.

The sweet butts usually stayed behind and cleaned a brother's room and bathroom for them after getting a good fucking. But it looked like no one had touched Jag's room in a long while.

Huh.

He said he hadn't been with anybody since the last time she broke into his room drunk. Maybe he'd been telling the truth.

A warmth stole through her. She sat on his bed, ran a hand over his pillow, then sank her elbows to her knees, dropping her head in her hands.

He hadn't been with anyone but her since that night.

No Goldie, no Tequila, no Lola. None of them. Not one.

Damn.

She hadn't been with anyone else either.

But that's not what she came for. She had a mission, and she needed to stick to it, then clear out before she got caught.

She slipped to the floor onto her knees to peek under the bed, then regretted doing so. The sweet butts may clean the rooms, but they clearly didn't do a very thorough job. She wrinkled her nose and pushed to her feet. She lifted the mattress slightly. Her eyes widened at the pistol, the blade, and the brass knuckles that were tucked between the mattress and box spring, but she shouldn't be surprised. She dropped the mattress back down.

Her head twisted as she looked around the room again for any indication of a good hiding spot. A place where he could hide pencils and a large drawing pad. She went to his beat-up dresser and pulled out drawers, feeling around under his boxers, his balled-up socks, his T-shirts, thermals, long-sleeve tees, and Henley's. She lifted out the blue-grey Henley he wore that emphasized the color of his eyes and held it to her nose.

Her pussy clenched as she inhaled his scent.

Fuck. Her body was such a traitor.

With a sigh, she shoved it back into the drawer and moved on to the next one and then the next. Finally, in the bottom drawer, under a folded pair of jeans, she found the box she was searching for. She pulled it out and lifted the lid.

Graphite and colored pencils, erasers, blenders, anything used to make a drawing like the one she found was stuffed into the box. She brushed a finger over them, imagining him bent over a drawing pad, concentrating on his work, his dark hair falling over his forehead.

Her core clenched again. Harder this time.

Fucking Jag.

After tucking the box back where she found it, she slid the bottom drawer shut, then peeked behind the dresser. Nothing.

Kneeling down once more, she checked underneath it. Nothing.

She groaned in frustration as her gaze swept the room again. Hands on her hips, she blew a chunk of hair out of her face. When it landed over her eye again, she swiped at it and looked up at the annoying red strand.

Then it hit her. The drop ceiling.

She detested them, but they made excellent hiding spots.

Her heart began to thump hard in her chest. They were up there. She just knew it. No other place they could be unless he hid them at another location completely.

But they couldn't be far from his pencils.

She grabbed the rickety wooden chair in the corner of his room and dragged it next to the bed. The chair shook and shimmied when she climbed up and reached her arms up. She could barely touch the ceiling tile above her with the tips of her fingers.

Shit.

She did a little jump, knocking it to the side and... nothing.

Damn it.

She wanted to scream. Instead, she bit her bottom lip, knocked the tile back in place into its metal frame and climbed off the chair. She shifted it farther from his bed. Climbing back on the wiggling chair, she knocked the next tile to the side, hoping the piece of shit chair wouldn't collapse underneath her.

Suddenly, she was pelted with loose papers, rolled up drawings, and last but not least, a drawing pad bounced off her noggin.

"Ouch!" She rubbed the top of her head and glanced down around her.

Holy shit.

There were more than she expected. They had spilled onto his bed and the floor.

The ones that landed right side up were in black and white, some in color. They seemed endless.

Endless.

She scooted to the floor, watching where she stepped, gathering as many into her arms as she could without crushing or wrinkling them. She piled them on his bed and when she finally collected them all, sat next to the large pile, looking at each one, her jaw hanging, her eyes wide.

Her mind spinning.

Custom bikes, Harleys and more, old muscle cars, new sports cars. All customized. Some of them looked like concept cars.

But all of them, *all of them*, were as detailed as the one found under the bar.

When did he have time to do these? It must be years of work.

Years.

Once she finished looking through the pile, her gaze landed on the rolled drawings. The ones secured by wide rubber bands. She grabbed the nearest one, slipped off the rubber band and unrolled it.

Holy shit.

Holy shit.

Holy shit.

Her own portrait stared back at her. She quickly grabbed the next one, opened it. The next one. The next. There had to be at least twenty.

Twenty fucking pictures of her. Not one other woman. Not one other portrait. Only her.

Again, some black and grey, some in color with her hair a fiery red, her eyes a bright green.

She pressed her fingers to her mouth as she laid them out over the bed, her eyes bouncing from one to the next.

She was naked in almost all of them. But they were tastefully done. The realism and details incredible. She looked flirty, sexy, smoldering in almost every one of them. The way he had her posed, none seemed obscene at all. They were *artistic,* tasteful.

Then one caught her attention, and she pulled it closer, her fingers trembling. She was sitting, maybe on a bed or something similar, and she peered over her shoulder, like a model would gaze at the artist, smiling softly, her hair like a soft cloud falling around her shoulders.

She wasn't completely naked in this one. Oh no. She was wearing only his cut. *His* cut. A vest with the patches clearly stating, "Property of Jag."

One like the ol' ladies wore.

Her heart stopped for a second then slammed against the front of her chest.

Most of the drawings were signed and dated. The signature just a squiggle, but the dates clearly marked.

She inspected the date of this one. Over a year ago. A couple months before she dragged him upstairs that first time.

Holy shit.

She swept her hand through the sketches, peering at the dates. A few were recent, in the last few months.

Most were from years ago.

Years.

Like the cars and bikes, he'd been sketching her for years.

She shivered as both a warmth and a coldness ran through her. Warmth because she could sense the intensity of his feelings for her in each one of his sketches. Cold because she had pushed him away, fought him at every turn. Denied both of them, denied what they could be for one another.

Before she could stop it, a tear ran down her cheek and dropped to the rumpled sheet, barely missing one of the drawings.

She swiped at her face so she wouldn't get them wet. She needed to protect them, put them back in their hiding spot. But she didn't want to. She wanted to take them with her. Show the world his talent. It shouldn't be hidden. Not like this. Talent like this shouldn't be tucked away in a ceiling.

She needed to confront him, but she didn't know how. How did she explain her breaking into his room and finding years' and years' worth of his drawings, something he clearly poured his heart and soul into?

She needed to grab that original sketch she found, the one she had tucked back under the bar yesterday morning after showing it to the girls.

That's the one she had to confront him with. Tonight. Maybe after the party.

Grabbing her cell phone, she snapped pictures of some of the drawings as she neatly put them back into a pile. Then she photographed every one of her before rolling them back up and securing them again.

She hated putting them back in that black hole in the ceiling. That's not where they belonged.

He also didn't belong in this clubhouse, in this club. He could be something way bigger than he was.

By being DAMC, he was holding himself back.

And that hurt her heart.

CHAPTER TEN

Jag flipped his pillow over and punched it, trying to get it adjusted just right. He sighed. He wasn't going to be able to sleep. The music was still way too loud, and he wasn't drunk enough to pass out.

Hell, he wasn't drunk at all.

Nope, he was stone cold sober. He'd made sure to remain that way as he watched Ivy flit around the party in the courtyard, laughing and joking with some of the brothers, talking to her girls, but giving Dawg's strippers and the sweet butts a wide berth.

He'd finally went upstairs when he couldn't take anymore. He couldn't watch her and not touch her. He couldn't hear her laughter and not want to kiss her, then drag her upstairs to his bed. He couldn't bear her laughing and joking with one of the brothers and not want to slide his dick deep inside her.

Jag flipped over, shoved his face into his pillow and bellowed. Not that anyone would hear him, the music was way too loud. Strains of a Bob Seger song seeped through the floor and walls into his room indicating the party was still in full swing.

Typical Friday night.

He needed to move out of church and get his own place where he had privacy. A place he could escape to when Ivy showed up for club gatherings.

He needed to avoid her as much as possible. At least until the pain dulled to a point where he could bear it.

He shot straight up when his door rattled. The lock clicked, and the door opened, a dim strip of light sliding across his bed. His hand automatically reached between his mattress and box spring, but he froze and curled his fingers into fists.

No mistaking the curves silhouetted in the doorway. He cursed under his breath as the door closed and the room became dark again.

Jag listened to the rustling as she moved about his room. Then he heard a gasp and a searing curse as she knocked what he could only imagine was a knee into the bed frame. He pinned his lips together. He didn't want to get stabbed in the dark for laughing.

"Should I get you a key?" he asked, pulling himself up to lean back against the wall, arms crossed over his chest.

The shadowed figure halted in place and after a heartbeat or two, she said, "What fun would that be?"

"I'd say it'd be faster, but you're pretty damn skilled with pickin' a lock."

There was another curse as she stumbled over his boots.

With a sigh, he rolled out of bed, pressed past her and hit the light switch. The room lit up and so did all that fucking red hair of hers.

His heart stopped and his breath left him in a rush. She stood in the middle of his room naked, holding a bottle of whiskey. He pushed past the urge to throw her onto the bed and pump into her until his nuts were dried up raisins.

Instead he grumbled, "Told you I was done with you."

Her gaze dropped from his face—after pausing on his lips—then slowly ran down his chest and stomach. By the time she hit his dick, there was no hiding the fact he wanted her.

"I'm not done with you," she whispered, then bit her lip.

Watching her teeth dig into her plump bottom lip made his balls tighten. He was proud of himself for not immediately grabbing his dick and stroking it.

She lifted the whiskey in her hand. "Brought Jack for a threesome."

His gaze flicked to the half-empty bottle. "You drunk?"

She tilted her head, her green eyes spearing his soul. "No. You?"

"Hell no." He stepped closer, so she was now within arm's reach but refrained from touching her.

His willpower was being sorely tested, though. His fingertips itched, his cock flexed, his balls were crying for relief. "You only end up in my bed willingly when you're drunk, Ivy. Gotta be drunk to be with me?"

She glanced at the bottle in her hand, then stepped behind him to place it on his old, scarred dresser.

He didn't have to turn to know she was directly behind him. His nostrils flared as he inhaled her scent, and her heat warmed the skin of his back. He steeled himself against the shiver that wanted to race down his spine.

When her hands cupped his shoulders from behind, and her lips pressed to the top of his spine, he bit back a groan.

He wasn't going to let her do this to him. He wasn't going to let her pull him back in.

He had given her a choice: in or out. And she couldn't do it. She couldn't be all in. She couldn't be with him.

So why was she here now torturing him like this?

Because her touching him, kissing him, wearing nothing but that hair that drove him fucking nuts, was nothing but torture.

"Sorry about your bike," she murmured against his skin. She leaned slightly away as her fingertips outlined the rockers and large DAMC logo tattooed onto his back.

His fingers clenched into fists and he dropped his head, closing his eyes. He needed to keep his shit together.

He struggled to suck in air as she finished tracing every line of that tattoo. The tattoo that mirrored the patches on his cut, that tattoo that covered his whole back and signified his club, his family, his brotherhood, his loyalty, and represented every aspect of his life.

He *was* DAMC.

Never once in his life had he wanted anything different.

And never once in his life had he wanted anyone but Ivy.

Any other woman had been a temporary fix, only a balm to soothe his needs.

"You showin' up here mean you're all in?"

His stomach felt empty and hollow when she wrapped her arms around his waist, pressing her cheek to his back, but not answering him.

He opened his eyes and circled her wrists with his hands. "You all in, Ivy?" Her answer would determine if he pulled those arms tighter around him or pulled them away.

"I—" she started.

Disappointment bubbled up, making him squeeze his eyes shut once again. He shook his head.

"I have a favor to ask," she finished.

He glanced over his shoulder, though he couldn't see her since she was still pressed to his back and she was much smaller than him. "What's that, baby?"

"Can I— Can we take it one day at a time? Can you give me that?"

He'd already waited too long. His patience had hit its limit a long time ago. If she didn't understand that... "Ivy—"

"Mick..."

He stiffened and tightening his grip on her wrists, he removed her arms from around him, stepping away. He turned to face her, shaking his head. He tamped down his temper. "No."

"Just listen—"

"No."

She moved forward, her eyes pleading, her hand outstretched like she was going to cup his cheek. Against his better judgment, he met her halfway and stepped into her touch. Her fingers gripped his jaw as he stared down into her breathtakingly beautiful face causing the ache in his chest to turn into a sharp pain.

Her little pink tongue slipped out as she licked her lips. She began again, "Listen, give me that. Give me time. Give me Mick. Let Mick be mine and mine alone. Let everyone else have Jag. The club, the brothers, your customers, everyone... But, please... let Mick be mine."

It was hard not to give her anything and everything she asked for when she looked at him like that.

"Just a name," he grumbled.

Her hand trailed down his chest. "Not to me."

And that's why it bothered him so much when she used it. "Can't deny who I am. Not only that, who you are."

"I've lived it my whole life," she answered softly. "So, you're right, I can't deny it. But sometimes I need a change."

"Not going to change." He captured her hand under his when it reached his lower stomach and pressed it to his erection. "Right now, don't care what you call me. Call me Mick, call me Jag, call me asshole. Just call me yours."

Her fingers encircled him, squeezing him tight at the root. Fuck, he wanted to do nothing but thrust into her fist.

"Promise me you won't take it to the table, you won't claim me. Not yet. I'm asking for you to give me the time I need."

"How much time?" And what if at the end of that time, she decided that being his ol' lady wasn't for her and she walked away? Then what? He'd be worse off than he was now. Seeing his Harley as a metal scrap pile would be nothing compared to losing Ivy forever. To finally have her and then watch her slip through his fingers...

That couldn't happen.

But was it better to have her for a little while than not at all?

Hell yeah, it was.

"Don't answer that. Give you all the time you need." It went against every fiber of his being to say that, but he knew it was for the best. For him. For her. For both of them.

She melted against him, his arm automatically circling her shoulders as he tipped her face up to his and dropped his head, taking her lips.

She tasted like Ivy, *his* Ivy, as his tongue swept through her mouth. He deepened the kiss, and a groan bubbled up from the back of her throat. He swallowed it but quickly gave it back to her as one of his own.

He dug fingers into her hair when her tongue tangled with his, encouraging him to kiss her harder, deeper. He complied but managed to shift her around without breaking their kiss. Or her grip on his throbbing cock.

And if she didn't stop stroking it, he was going to shoot a load all over the both of them.

Finally, he pulled away enough to say, "Gotta stop, baby. Wanna come in you, not on you."

She gave him a wicked smile that he felt all the way to his dick. "On me isn't bad, either."

"Not this time." With that, he picked her up and tossed her onto the bed. He climbed on after her, crawling up the bed, like a jaguar stalking his prey.

Her laugh was low and throaty as she swept her hair out of her face and met his eyes. "Whatcha gonna do to me, *Mick?*"

"Probably not much this first time, baby. Make up for it during the second."

"Promise?" she asked breathlessly, her eyes hooded, her nipples peaked and begging for his mouth.

"Fuck yeah. Also promise to make sure I lick an' kiss every one of those fuckin' freckles on your body before that time I'm givin' you runs out."

"Mmm." Her smile widened. "That's a lot of freckles."

"Damn right."

"Might take you awhile. You better get started."

He grunted and sucked one of her nipples deep into his mouth.

"I see you're starting with one of the bigger ones."

He couldn't help but smile against the fullness of her luscious tit. He rolled the other nipple between his fingers and tweaked it hard, making her back arch and her head roll back, giving him access to that long, delicate neck of hers. He took advantage by nipping her from the hollow of her throat up, then kissing along her smooth ivory skin on the way back down.

He pulled himself forward on his elbows until he was face to face with her. "Hope you're wet. Gonna test it in a sec. Just want you to know, if you're not, might not have the strength to hold off until you are."

And, fuck if that wasn't the truth. If he didn't sink into her pink, tight cunt soon he would explode. And it wouldn't be pretty.

He reached between them, not breaking eye contact, and watched her face change and mouth part when he brushed her clit on his way down to dipping a finger inside her.

She was soaked.

Thank. Fuck.

He guided the head of his dick between her wet folds and pressed slowly inside, feeling her take him all, her inner muscles squeezing him tight. He stilled and pinned his forehead to hers, once again trying to keep his shit together.

He needed to take a moment.

Just a moment.

"Fuck me, Mick," she whispered, her green eyes hazy, unfocused.

He grunted as he ground his hips against her. The hot silk that surrounded him made him just about lose his mind. And when she grabbed his ass and dug her nails in while pulling her knees back, he began to move.

He wanted to let loose, slam her hard, spill into her as quickly as possible, but he forced himself to keep a steady rhythm that would make it last more than seconds. Not that it was going to last much longer than that.

He needed a distraction, something to keep him from falling completely into her wet heat and never being able to escape.

But the slower he went, the deeper her nails dug. She arched up, crying out his name, and sank her teeth into his shoulder.

He grunted again, jammed his face into her neck and just let it happen. His body meshed perfectly with hers and they did the age-old dance in their search of satisfying their hunger, both of them racing to their release but trying not to leave the other behind.

She clawed his back, the little noises escaping her lips making him squeeze his eyes shut, fighting the uncontrolled rush that went through him.

Too soon.

Too soon.

His breath caught when she let out a wail as she slammed her hips against his.

"Fuck, baby," he groaned.

She rippled, pulsed, and if he wasn't already on his knees, he would've been brought there.

"Ivy," squeezed past his gritted teeth and he pumped hard one more time before spilling inside her, making her his.

As he came down, his senses returning, he mumbled, "Sorry," into the crook of her neck.

When her body shook against him, he realized she was laughing.

At him.

He lifted his head and stared at her profile. "Nothin' like laughin' at a man who just shot a load way too quickly."

"You come?"

"Yeah."

"Did I come?"

"Yeah."

"Nothing to be sorry about then."

Jag grinned, sliding out and settling against her side. "Yeah," he said on a satisfied sigh.

———

Ivy rolled, and an arm snaked out to grab her and yank her back. Her heartbeat went from zero to sixty in a split second.

His chest rumbled when he said gruffly, "Almost fell off the bed."

She glanced over her shoulder at a heavy-eyed Jag. "Were you watching me sleep?"

He didn't answer, instead just tucked her closer into his side.

His bed was a twin and definitely not big enough for the two of them to sleep comfortably. Nor was there a lot of surface space to get down and dirty. "Next time we're in my bed instead of this tiny thing," she announced, twisting in his arms to go face to face with him. One of his long, heavy legs wrapped around hers and his erection pressed hard between them. "You've been hard all night?"

He grunted, which she interpreted as a yes, then said, "Waitin' for you to wake up."

The corner of her lip curled. "Sure you didn't try to kick me out of the bed just so I'd wake up? Think I feel a footprint on my back."

"Wanted to force you awake, would've found a more agreeable way to do it."

"Mmm. Should've then."

"Though, wouldn't mind sleepin' with my dick inside you all night."

"Not sure if that's possible, honey."

His whole body jerked against her at the nickname "honey." His voice sounded a bit thick when he finally said, "Can't hurt to try."

She brushed a finger over his forehead, then traced it along his jawline, down to the hollow of this throat to the silver DAMC pendant he wore on a black cord around his neck. She fingered it, finding it warm to the touch.

Without looking, she knew he stared at her as she studied the tattoos over his shoulders, down his chest, over his arms.

"Crow do them all?"

"No."

She nodded, even though she was surprised. Crow did almost all of the brothers' ink. His body art reminded her of the other "bodies" he worked with. "Ever think about doing something other than custom bodywork?"

"Like what?"

She lifted a shoulder slightly. "Anything."

"Good at what I do. Make good bank."

"I know you are and I know you do. Not sure what you spend it on though."

"Don't spend it. Savin'."

She lifted her head and asked, "For what?" She could imagine the club members all had a wad of cash hidden somewhere if they lived at church. They didn't have to pay rent, just their club dues. Most didn't have many expenses except their bikes, fuel, all that silver and brass jewelry they wore. Tats, too, though Crow didn't charge his brothers much. They could pretty much eat and drink for free for the most part. Yeah, she could imagine them being able to bank some cash.

"Now a new sled."

No surprise there. "And before?"

"Think I wanna live here forever?"

"Your own place? Like a house?"

He grunted.

She pursed her lips as she took that as a yes. He was saving for a house. An actual house. Damn. "White picket fence?"

He snorted. "Big-ass garage."

"A house is a better investment than a bike," she mentioned.

"Baby," he said, a brow cocked.

"I know. Bike, brotherhood, then bitches, and *then* everything else after that."

"Can't be Road Captain without a sled. Can't be DAMC without one, either."

No, he couldn't.

"Can't have my *bitch* behind me, squeezin' me tight while ridin' free, if I don't have a badass sled."

"I know you're looking to fill that spot on the back of your bike."

"Not lookin'." He flicked the ends of her hair with his finger. His eyes raised to hers. "Found her."

Ivy drew in a shaky breath. "One of the things about giving me time is not pressuring me, honey."

"Say that again."

"One of the things—"

"No," he cut her off. "Last part."

She hesitated, thinking back to what she said. "Honey?"

He pressed his mouth to her ear. "Call me that... not Mick. Call me that... not Jag. Call me that whenever you wanna make my dick hard."

She closed her eyes, his warm breath tickling the hair by her ear. "I'll tuck that away for future reference."

"Do that." He rolled to his back, taking her with him. She straddled his waist, her hands propped on his chest. "Nice to see this," he brushed his fingers along the long strands of hair that fell over her nipple, "matches this." His fingers continued a course down her belly to the small patch of hair she kept neatly trimmed over her pussy. "Fire everywhere."

"Going to use your hose to put the fire out?"

He grinned. "Don't ever want to see that fire burn out, baby. Like to see it burnin' red hot."

He wrapped a hand around the back of her neck and pulled her down into a deep kiss, his tongue teasing hers. "Guess you're ready for round two?" she murmured when he finally released her. Though, she seemed to be a little more breathless than him when he did.

"Get rid of those boots yet?"

His question caught her off guard. Should she admit she didn't? Should she lie? She lied way too much this week.

Fuck it. "No."

A smile crept over his face. "Good."

She raised her eyebrows, surprised once again. He made it pretty clear he wanted her to get rid of them. Maybe that had been his temper talking at the time. "Good?"

"Yeah, want you to wear them with a sexy bra and panties. For me. And me only. Got me?"

"Any particular color?"

He didn't even hesitate. "Black. Match the boots. Make the panties easy to rip to the side so I can just bend you over an' fuck you from behind."

Ivy buried her face in his neck to smother her laugh.

"Supposed to be makin' you wet an' horny, not makin' you laugh."

"What's making me laugh is you being so bossy about it."

"Baby, that ain't ever gonna change."

Yes, she knew that. That's why she needed time to make sure she could deal with that shit on a daily basis. It was one thing to have one of her blood relatives or one of the other club brothers, or even a prick of a prospect, try to boss her around. She could just flip them off and walk away.

It was very different when you had to deal with it on another level. Like the ol' lady level.

Her sister Bella got sick of being treated like property and being told what to do. That's why she ended up on the receiving end of a horrific shit storm. One she was still recovering from.

One she might not ever completely get over.

Ivy watched her sister deal with that mess and it was only one reason why she shied away from being tied to a biker.

Their mother, Allie, had also avoided getting sucked too deeply into the DAMC lifestyle, always skirting the edge. Though, she didn't look down on it since she, too, was raised second generation DAMC, she never wanted to make the complete plunge. Neither did Ivy's aunt, Annie. After Allie, Annie and Ace watched their father Doc get sent away for murdering a Shadow Warrior in retribution for killing club co-founder Bear, only Ace lived the club lifestyle completely. But then, Ace was a man and a club brother and would never be treated like property.

Jag grabbed her hair and used it to pull her face out of his neck. "You rethinkin' the me givin' you time thing?"

Ivy sighed. If she was in her right mind she would. But no one in their right mind would waste that hard-on that currently pressed against her ass. Or no woman, anyway.

She planted her palms on his chest and pushed to a seated position, grinding her pussy into his belly. He grunted and grabbed her around the waist.

"Should I be?"

"Not gonna hide who I am, baby. Never have, never will."

Yes, but he had no problem hiding his artistic talent in the ceiling above them. "Never, huh?"

"Nope. Get what you see."

Would she get what she didn't see? What he kept buried from everyone, including her?

He reached around her, grabbed his cock, and thumped it against her ass. "Right now, though, you gonna get some dick. Gotta problem with that?"

Ivy bit her bottom lip. She definitely had no problem with that. "Are you going to last longer this time?"

Jag slapped his other hand on his chest in a dramatic show of being wounded. "*Damn.* My woman cuts me deep."

My woman.

There was something so satisfying about hearing that claim coming from him. But it also scared the shit out of her.

She opened her mouth to respond, but her breath hissed out of her instead. No point in arguing, since, like he said, he was never going to change. She had to accept him the way he was or not.

Right now, she was going to accept his hard cock deep inside her. Deal with the rest later.

Leaning over, she nipped his pec, then moved down until she caught the flesh around his nipple in her teeth. She sank them in gently and he plunged his fingers into her hair. Not to pull her away, no. He groaned as his hips raised beneath her, thrusting his cock between her ass cheeks.

He liked her biting him.

A lot.

She moved to the other one and wasn't so gentle this time, making sure to bite him hard enough to leave her mark in his flesh.

He barked out a curse and thrust against her again, the precum from the tip of his cock lubing the cleft of her ass, making it easier for him to slide up and down. Heat and wetness slipped from her as he pushed his hand between them, teasing her sensitive clit, slipping a finger inside her.

"Fuck, baby," he groaned. "Get so fuckin' wet."

She flicked each of his nipples with the tip of her tongue, then traced his silver pendant before moving her way down. But he stopped her by pulling on her hair and yanking her up.

"C'mere," he demanded. "Want your tits."

She smiled, cupped them, and brushed her thumbs over the hard nubs. "These?"

"None other."

She shifted forward until one hung just above his face, teasing. He arched up and snagged it in his mouth, sucking hard. She gasped, the pull from his mouth went directly from her nipple to her core, which clenched violently. She needed him inside her. Soon.

Fuck that. Now.

She reared up, lifted herself, grabbed the root of his cock and sank down on him. He grunted and her mouth fell open, her breath ragged as she basked in the fullness and stretch of his cock deep inside her.

Yes, *this*.

This was worth him calling her his woman.

At the surface, the man beneath her was a misogynist biker set in his ways who worked with his hands, shaped metal, painted it, and made a good living at it.

Under the surface, he was so much more.

That's what she wanted, what she craved. The man underneath the tough, gruff exterior. The artist who saw the beauty in that metal and created something unique with it. The artist who could draw something breathtaking without a day of professional training.

The man she'd known her whole life who wanted to claim her as his.

Who hinted at buying a house, moving her in. Waking up together, drinking coffee, eating breakfast before they both went their separate ways for the day, only to join up again at night. Fall into each other's arms, satisfy each other's needs. Make each other groan, moan and grunt until they were spent, and then later do it all over again.

Would she get tired of him, of his ways?

She couldn't answer that honestly, even to herself.

But no matter what, there was more to Mick Jagger Jamison than met the eye. More than what he showed the world, his brothers, his family.

And if he only ever showed it to her, she would consider it a special gift to hold on tightly to.

But it would be a damn shame if it ended up being only her that knew him completely.

Her eyes flicked to his and held as she ground her hips hard against him, taking everything he had.

"Beautiful, baby."

No, he was the one who was beautiful. His lean muscles, his tattoos, his dark hair falling across his forehead, his steel-blue eyes that searched her face.

"Somethin' wrong?"

She sucked in a breath, then shook her head. "No. Everything's right."

His face changed then, became intense, his gaze heated. He lifted his hips to meet her every time she lowered herself.

"Waited for you a long time, Ivy," he murmured, his fingers teasing, circling her clit. His other hand cupped one of her breasts, squeezing, kneading. *Worshipping* her. "Long time," he repeated softly.

Her head fell back, her breath rushed in and out between her lips, her eyes rolled back as his length entered and left her. Driving her to that spot right before the climax would overcome her.

"'Bout time you got some sense."

Her pace hiccupped and she landed heavily, stopping and dropping her chin to stare at him.

He continued, "I saw it, others saw it. You belong with me."

At least he didn't say "to me."

"Just because we're compatible in bed, doesn't mean it's going to work... out there," she swung her arm toward his bedroom door. "Out in the real world. If you expect me to change, Mick... If you expect me to suddenly bow to you, become meek and mild, then I won't need any time at all. This can end right here, right now. Because that's not me. Never will be me. What you see is what you get," she parroted him from earlier, feeling the ice run through her veins.

"Know who I got sittin' on my cock right now. Know who I want on the back of my bike. Know who I want warmin' my bed every night. Know who I want havin' my kids an' raisin' 'em."

A mix of amazement, fear and warmth rushed through her. Kids…

Kids.

This man wanted her to bear his babies. She closed her eyes and whispered, "Mick." She pictured her belly protruding with his child inside her.

Then it hit her and it hit her hard. She wanted that. She fucking *wanted* that. She felt that all the way deep into her soul with how much she wanted it.

Maybe not now, not tomorrow, maybe not even next year. But eventually. She wanted a little Jag clinging tightly to her hand as he learned to walk. A teenaged replica of Jag by his father's side learning how to turn metal into something special.

Jesus.

She needed to think this through and not when he was buried deep inside her.

"Though, havin' babies might stretch out that tight pussy of yours."

Ivy blinked a couple times, stunned, then fell forward, collapsing onto his chest, her body shaking uncontrollably.

He swept her hair off her cheek, trying to see her face. "You laughin' or cryin'?"

"I should be coming right about now."

His chest rumbled under her cheek and she gasped in surprise when he grabbed her hips and rolled them both over, him ending up on top.

"You got it, baby."

CHAPTER 10

He grabbed her bottom lip between his teeth, tugged it, then kissed her hard, stealing her breath. She hitched her knees back, tilting her hips, encouraging him to hit *all* the right spots as he took her hard and pounded her deep.

All his words, all her thoughts melted away, leaving just the two of them. Two people who fit together so perfectly, who constantly butted heads and probably would continue to do so for the rest of their lives.

Their lives would never be boring.

"Honey, I'm coming."

"Say it again," he grunted into her neck.

"Honey... I'm... *coming*." The last word turning into a wail as she jammed her hips up and he met her thrust for thrust. Her head fell back as her toes curled when the orgasm radiated through her, rippling around him, squeezing him tight. Her thighs, her arms, her core held him tight, not wanting to let go.

Never letting go.

In the moments after she came down, reality hit her.

She was screwed.

She let him in. He only needed to lodge one little piece of himself into her life, into her heart, and she'd never be able to get him back out.

She trailed her fingers up his back, which rose and fell quickly as he tried to catch his breath, his face still pressed into her neck. Most of his weight crushed her, his cock still pulsed deep inside. Her inner thighs had become slick from their fluids intermingling, reminding her that it wouldn't take much for her to get pregnant, to carry his baby. Only a little pill taken daily would keep that at bay.

But she could have that if she wanted.

She had a feeling if she asked for a house, he would bend over backwards to provide it for her. If she asked to become his ol' lady, he would call an executive meeting tomorrow to bring it to the table. If she asked him to give himself to her completely... he would.

"Baby," he mumbled against the damp skin of her neck.

"Yeah?" she asked softly, raking her fingers through his hair.

"Gonna try to stay like this as long as possible. You good?"

"Yeah, Jag, I'm good."

"Mick."

"What?"

"Mick."

She smiled up at the ceiling, her gaze landing on where his drawings were hidden. "Yeah, I'm good, Mick."

Ivy laid on her side, her head propped in her hand, just waiting... and waiting. It would be any second now, the shower had turned off, the toilet had flushed, the squeal of the pipes from the sink running had quieted.

Any second now...

The door flew open and Jag, wearing nothing but a towel around his waist, stepped out.

Oh hell yeah, it was worth the wait.

Damp skin, a few beads of water clinging here and there over his sinewy muscles and tattoos, his hair wet and combed back out of his face, which was freshly shaven. Baby smooth. Kissable. Lickable. In between her thighs doable...

He stopped, his steel-blue eyes landing on her, his gaze running over every curve and line of her body.

She fought the shiver, but her nipples peaked anyway.

"That's a sight," he said, his voice low and husky.

He should see what she was looking at. *That* was a sight.

"If I hadn't knocked the bottom outta you little bit ago, I'd be ready to do it again."

Always the romantic.

"Not sure I have time for that, anyway," Ivy said, regretting that she didn't. She had to get to the pawn shop at a reasonable hour. But she needed to hit her apartment first to clean up and get fresh clothes.

"Could make it quick," he suggested.

"Going to take longer than that to get your motor started."

"Yeah, ten years ago could've come an' stayed hard 'til I came again."

Ivy didn't want to let her mind wander to every woman he's ever stuck his dick in. It was bad enough she knew he stuck it in Goldie.

She needed to wipe those thoughts clean. "What are you going to do today?"

"Gotta bead on an old Harley frame gonna go look at."

"Already?"

"Baby," was his answer.

Right.

A biker was nothing without a bike.

"Bad enough it'll take me a couple years to do it right."

"Are you going to find something temporary in the meantime?"

He shrugged and Ivy watched to see if the towel would hold. It did. Damn it.

"Keep lookin' at me like that, ripping this towel off an' you can blow me 'til I'm hard again."

Though that sounded like a plan... "It's my Saturday to work."

He lifted his chin, then jerked his head toward the bathroom behind him. "Gonna shower?"

"Here?"

"Yeah."

"Hell no. I'll head back to my place. Who knows when the last time your shower's been cleaned."

He shrugged again, the light reflecting off his damp shoulders. The ones she wanted to lick dry.

"When I get a house, I'll get a house mouse."

Ivy's eyes bugged out, and she pushed herself to a seat. "You want to repeat that?"

"Said—"

She raised a hand, palm out. "I heard what you said."

His brows dropped low as if he was confused on why she suddenly had attitude. "House mouse ain't a sweet butt."

She frowned. "Jag."

"Baby."

"Don't 'baby' me."

"You movin' in an' cleanin' my house? Since I gotta keep my dick outta sweet butts, who's gonna clean? Not me."

Ah fuck, these men. "*Jesus*."

"Jesus ain't gonna clean, either."

Ivy blew out a breath. A long, long, shaky one. "Jag."

"Baby." His eyes slid away from her and landed on the nightstand. She knew exactly what he looked at without even turning. She had placed it there on purpose. "Baby," he repeated but this time it didn't sound the same.

Not at all.

"Where'd that come from?" he growled.

She pushed herself up to a seated position, dragging the sheet with her. Not that a mismatched sheet would be much protection if he got angry enough.

She leaned over, grabbed the rolled up drawing and removed the hair band. She held it up and opened it toward him. "You draw this?"

He took a step closer to the bed, his shoulders stiff, his face a blank mask. "Where'd you get that?"

"Answer me."

His gaze rose to hers and it burned through her. "Why does it matter?"

"Because it's crazy good."

Jag scrubbed his palms over his face and Ivy watched as his body softened and he visibly relaxed. Something switched inside of him. He was going to blow it off like it was no big deal. She just knew it.

And she was right.

"Just a sketch of my next bike."

She raised a brow at him. "That's not *just* a sketch, Jag."

"Then what is it?" He reached for it and she moved it out of his range.

"Art."

He snorted in disbelief.

"Honey… Art you could sell for big money."

"Right."

"I'm serious."

"People would pay big for this kind of quality pencil drawings. Framed? You could make a name for yourself."

"Got enough work doin' customs."

"Need to show this to some art dealers or something."

"Or somethin'? Fuck that shit. I'm no artist. Don't be callin' me that in front of the brothers, Ivy."

"You have talent, Jag." She shook her head. "Real talent."

"Yeah, with my tongue." He grabbed his junk through the damp towel. "And my dick."

She sighed, though she really wanted to roll her eyes at him instead. "Fair enough. But with a pencil, too. You got more of these?"

He hesitated, dropped his head and shook it. "Nope."

Lie. And he couldn't even look her in the eye when he did it. She took a deep breath. "You do this for all the bikes you customize?"

"Yep, just somethin' to follow when buildin' it."

"What do you do with the sketches after? Give them to the bike owners?"

He hesitated again. "Sure."

Again lying.

"You draw anything other than bikes?"

Something flashed behind his eyes. "Let it go, Ivy."

That wasn't going to happen. But at this moment, she could either call him out on it or let it go. However, she'd give him a reprieve for now since she really needed to get to work before Dex and Ace started blowing up her phone.

She rolled the drawing back up and held it out to him. He snagged it, grabbed the hair band from her fingers and secured the sketch.

Slipping out of bed, she snagged her panties and tank top off the pile of clothes on the floor. "Can you do me one thing, honey?"

His gaze followed her every move as she yanked up her panties and slipped the tank over her head. He bent down and hooked her bra, then tossed it in her direction. She caught it. "Gotta put that on if you're gonna walk outta here. Bra when you're out. None when you're home with me. Got me?"

Ivy opened her mouth to argue, but he cut her off. "Ain't gonna have words 'bout it. Don't' wanna hear no shit 'bout it, either. Got me, Ivy?"

Instead of answering, she ripped her tank back over her head and put on her bra, then finished getting dressed. As she tugged her ankle-high boots over her jeans, she said, "I do that for you, you show me that sketch when it's done. *Got me?*"

A smile tugged at his lips. "Gotcha, baby. Can do."

With a nod, she leaned in, gave him a quick kiss and turned to leave. Before she could open the door, she was pinned against it, his chest tight to her back. His mouth brushed her ear. "Lettin' you go now, baby. But tonight, your apartment, gonna fuck you good. Dinner first, though."

"Are you cooking?"

"Nope. You are."

"Right. If you expect me to cook for you, you better do more than just fuck me."

His low, warm chuckle made goosebumps break out all over her. "Deal."

Suddenly, he smacked her ass hard, reached past her to yank the door open and shoved her out into the hall.

Before the door slammed shut, he said, "Gonna jerk off thinkin' about smackin' that ass some more."

Ivy stared at the now shut door with her mouth open. She snapped it shut, smiled and rolled her eyes as she walked down the hallway, hoping she didn't run into anyone this early on a Saturday morning.

Most of her day ended up being a blur since all she could do was picture Jag laying on his bed naked, stroking himself.

She might have short-changed a few customers.

CHAPTER ELEVEN

Jag wanted to growl and punch his fist through a wall. Instead, he snapped his response every time one of his brothers dared to say anything to him.

He was supposed to be over at Ivy's, filling his belly with her surprisingly good cooking and draining his balls like he'd done last night. But he wasn't.

Fuck no.

Diesel called in everyone for a late Sunday church meeting. And when he wanted everyone, he meant *everyone*. Even the fresh, wet-behind-the-ears prospects. Their Sergeant at Arms wasn't fucking around.

Pierce pounded the gavel on the bar top and all heads turned toward their current president.

Though, Jag wanted to rip the man's throat out for letting Ivy go into the Knights' territory alone.

Rip it out and then shit down it.

He turned his head to where Zak stood, leaning against one of the walls, arms crossed over his chest, watching Pierce carefully. Jag caught his attention and Z did a chin lift his direction. In answer, Jag tilted his head toward the front of the clubhouse and his cousin just did a little shake of his head.

Now was not the time to take Pierce out as head brother.

But that day was coming.

It certainly was.

Zak needed to take his rightful place back at the head of the table. And Pierce wasn't gaining any loyalty by making club decisions without bringing it to a vote.

Doing shit like that was anarchy.

Anarchy could implode a club. Destroy a brotherhood.

"Lookin' a little edgy there, brother," Ace murmured low as he sidled up to Jag.

Jag just grunted. Last thing he wanted to do was tell him the reason why.

"Just so you know, I sometimes leave the shop late. Know there's some stray cats around, but damn, last night I heard some shit that certainly wasn't anythin' of the feline variety."

Oh shit.

"Actually was a little disturbin' since she's my niece an' I gotta look her in the eyes almost every day."

Jag stared at his boots, his jaw tight. "Gonna get my own place."

"Yeah? When?"

"Soon as I get enough scratch."

"Got a bike to build first."

That was true. "Yeah."

"In the meantime, I'll text you when Dex an' I are clear of the shop. Don't wanna hear that shit again. Got me?"

Jag finally looked Ivy's uncle in the eye since he had a lot of respect for the older man and Ace deserved all his attention. "Got you."

"Rather it be you than any of those others, but don't wanna hear it, brother. An' Dex don't wanna hear his sister squealin' like a stuck pig, either."

"Got you," Jag said more firmly, hoping Diesel would soon start talking so they could get off this subject.

With relief, Jag heard Diesel bark out, "Listen up. Been takin' it in stride, but can't do that anymore. Gonna look weak, vulnerable if we do. Gotta hit fast an' hit hard. Leave a mark. Teach a lesson they won't soon forget."

Hoots and hollers rose up from the brothers and prospects standing in the common area and hanging up by the club bar.

Diesel continued, his words projecting through the large room, "Gotta keep vigilant. Two things your enforcer can't stand... The Warriors touchin' our bitches or our sleds. We let shit go for too long now."

The sound of boots stomping on the concrete floor became deafening.

Diesel's powerful deep voice rose above. "All right, fuckers, listen up. No matter what, gotta remember where we came from, where we're goin'. Don't want anyone else catchin' a murder wrap an' endin' up in Greene. But gotta make a statement. One that's gonna last."

"Down an' dirty 'til dead!" Nash screamed their motto at the top of his lungs nearby. Hoots, piercing whistles, and "fuck yeahs" followed it.

Adrenaline flowed through the room and anger electrified the air around them. The excitement of getting vengeance on the Warriors was spreading.

"Gotta bead on a place in South Side where a few of 'em's been hangin'. A couple of us gonna go in colors flyin', let 'em know what an' who hit 'em. Some of you need to sit tight, sit watch on the businesses, on the families. Hawk will let you know your place. No lip, no shit. Do whatcha told."

"Consequences for those who don't," Pierce added, standing on a chair next to Diesel, surveying the crowd. "Keep your shit tight."

"Who's goin' to South Side?" Abe, one of the prospects, asked loudly. He looked ready for a challenge. But the guy was still young and green. He'd end up babysitting one of the businesses or have to head out to Ace's farm to protect Ace's family.

"None of you pencil dicks. You turds are a step above pussy. Short one prospect, so you all will get watch somewhere."

"I'm goin'," Jag muttered. It was his bike that was trashed, so there was no way Diesel was going without him. He was sure Zak would go since it was his ol' lady that was almost snatched recently.

And he expected both of Ace's sons, Diesel and Hawk, to head the ass kicking operation. They never backed away from a fight. Hell, Diesel started fist fights as early as kindergarten. He got tossed from school after giving some kid a black eye for breaking a little girl's crayon. Luckily, the teacher stopped him before he shoved the broken crayon up the kid's asshole.

The only person D was ever afraid of was Ace. And that changed when Diesel outgrew and outweighed him at sixteen. Ace had to start using his wits instead of a cuff upside the head to get his son in line.

Diesel had a good head on his shoulders, but he was also a hot head. And he enjoyed someone challenging him. Facing off with some Warriors would be pure pleasure for him.

"'Nuff talkin'. See Hawk for your task. Z, Jag, Dex, meet me an' Pierce at the table."

Zak cupped his mouth and yelled, "Down an' dirty..."

A chorus rose up. "'Til dead!"

"Fuck yeah," Jag murmured as he made his way to the club's meeting room. If he wasn't going to get to eat Ivy's food or pussy tonight, at least he'd get the chance to bash some Warriors' brains.

They did end up taking a prospect with them. They decided on Abe since he was good with his fists and smart to boot. They left him standing guard at the bikes around the corner from the Gypsy Rose, an Irish pub in the city where Diesel had gotten word that some of the Warriors had been hanging out.

Warming stools and wreaking havoc in a pub that wasn't theirs. But that was typical Warrior mentality... wanting or even taking something that didn't belong to them.

They had noticed a line of eight bikes with no prospect guarding them. Stupid fools.

As nomads they had no home territory, which was the reason they wanted Shadow Valley so badly. They thought since they were the Shadow Warriors, they belonged in the town whose name started with Shadow and where DAMC had planted roots back in the early seventies. The fledgling outlaw club didn't ride through town until two years later. But founders Doc and Bear weren't giving up their home base without a fight.

And here they were over forty years later—not to mention, numerous deaths—and the Warriors were still being a thorn in the Angels' side. Tonight it was DAMC's turn to stick them where it hurts. Draw first blood. Though, it probably wouldn't be last blood.

Before going to prison, Zak fought hard to take the club all legit, and they were still headed in that direction, but shit like this kept dragging them backward.

Z had good reason to want vengeance, even though he was still on parole. Not only did a Warrior try to snatch Sophie right in front of him during daylight on a public street, but they had set him up years ago. He had been charged with felony possession when they planted a chemical used to make meth in his apartment at the time. He did ten years for a crime he didn't commit.

Ten fucking years. Parole or not, Jag would want to bash their heads in for that alone. He patted one of the back pockets in his jeans to check for his brass knuckles and the other to make sure his knife was still there after the ride over on a borrowed bike.

He had hated every second of being on a bike that wasn't his. Didn't feel natural. But every mile reminded him of who forced him onto that sled. Every time he pictured his baby in pieces he got a little hotter under the collar, his grip got tighter on the throttle, and his jaw turned to stone.

Now he was raring to go.

Diesel was taking point with Pierce following up at the rear as they entered the dive bar. Dex spit on the rusty metal sign out front that stated, "No colors allowed."

He doubted the Warriors removed their cuts before going inside, either.

The pub was narrow but deep. Not a lot of room to move if shit got ugly.

And it was going to get ugly. Guaranteed. Because of how narrow the bar was, Jag couldn't see shit with Hawk and Diesel's massive bodies taking lead.

But Jag didn't miss when the two men tending bar ducked for cover.

Smart.

Jag, Dex, and Zak kept their heads on swivels, eyeing customers sitting at both the bar and at a few of the high tables along the dark, dank walls.

"Warriors?" Jag heard Diesel grumble.

"Upstairs," someone said and then rushed past them to escape the upcoming mayhem.

"Probably know we're here by now, not good to head single file up those narrow steps. Could pick us off one at a time," Zak said, his hand planted on Hawk's shoulder.

Without looking behind him, Diesel grunted. Jag figured D was ready to run upstairs and take on all eight of their rivals single-handedly. Though, they might end up with a dead enforcer.

"D, think hard on that," Hawk said to his brother.

Diesel grunted again.

"Smarter to wait an' let them come down those steps. Be at an advantage. Can't wait up there forever."

Jag waited for D's answering grunt, but surprisingly none came. He had to be considering Hawk's suggestion.

"How 'bout I go up there an' throw them down the stairs one at a time."

That would be effective, too. As long as the Warriors didn't plug him full of holes first. Diesel was tough, but he wasn't tougher than a bullet.

None of them were, so they had to play it safe.

Diesel swung a meaty hand out toward the swinging door behind the long bar. "Dex, make sure there's no other way down."

Dex nodded and made his way through the door, disappearing. He was back in less than a minute. "Nothin' back there but roaches an' shit I wouldn't feed a dog."

More patrons pushed past them in their effort to escape the pending conflict. The next few minutes pretty much cleared the bar. One guy was passed out in the corner, his hand still wrapped around what looked like warm, flat ale.

Diesel went over and unplugged the old jukebox that was along the back wall by the stairs. When he straightened up, he raised his face and bellowed, "Ain't waitin' all day, motherfuckers! Bring it!"

As one, his brothers' spines stiffened, their shoulders straightened, their stances widened. There was no mistaking the stomp of biker boots rushing down the old, creaky wood steps.

They were coming in hot.

Amazing how a man as large as D could flatten himself against a wall and make it look easy. As soon as the first Warrior hit the landing, Diesel's hand snaked out to grab the older, beer-bellied biker by the neck and he flung him in a half circle until the man's head cracked into the corner of the jukebox. Blood ran over the glass and onto the floor as the guy's forehead split wide open. With an elbow to the kidney, Diesel took him down as easy as swatting a damn fly.

Jag smiled and so did the others, Hawk met the next one before the bottom of the landing. Both of them began to grapple and they tumbled onto the pub's filthy floor, rolling and getting in a punch whenever and wherever they could.

Pierce rushed up the two steps to the landing, then ducked as he shouted a warning. The shot made them all flinch and duck for cover as one bullet, then another struck the wood panel too close to Pierce's head.

Pierce leapt off the landing and hugged the wall, his chest heaving as he sucked in oxygen. He pulled a revolver from under his cut at the back of his jeans and glanced down at the heavyset biker that Diesel was finishing off with a few kicks to the ribs.

Stools crashed to the ground as Hawk and the Warrior continued to roll across the floor, bumping into the high tables, knocking over abandoned beers, mugs shattering as they hit the floor.

Diesel paused, looked up, held up a hand, signaling them all to wait and not rush in.

Jag pulled the switchblade from his back pocket, engaging the blade. He got close to Pierce.

He tried to push past the urge to slice their president's throat right then and there. But it wasn't worth it. They had a bigger fish to fry in this fight. They could deal with Pierce at a later date that didn't involve bloodshed.

With a last glance at Hawk and the now bloodied Warrior grappling on the floor, Jag took a flying leap on top of the jukebox and waited for the gun to appear near the stair banister. And predictably, it did.

Jag kicked the banister, crashing it into the gun and the hand holding it. The gun bounced down the steps, Dex ran to snag it and cleared the stairway in a flash. He checked the clip, then pointed to the ceiling, his eyes on Zak. Z nodded and everyone, except Hawk, who was still wresting on the floor with a Warrior, covered their ears as Dex shot up into the ceiling.

Even with plugging his ears with his fingers, Jag's head rang from the close shots. But shooting up through the floor had the remaining Warriors running down the steps. Dex clocked one of them in the back of the head with the Warrior's own handgun, knocking him down and out on the stairway which tripped the next one, bringing him to his hands and knees. Jag snagged a nearby heavy beer mug and clobbered the Warrior over the head, knocking him out cold. He gave him a good kick to the gut as he waited for the next one to come down the steps.

He tackled the next one, slugging the guy in the face, but before he could do it again, he received a kick in the ribs from one of the downed, but apparently, not out, Warriors. He grunted in pain, elbowed the first guy in the ribs, then punched him in the face again. The guy went down like a bowling pin.

Jag shook out his hand and glanced toward Hawk, who was now

wiping at his bloodied nose with the sleeve of his shirt and straddling a knocked out Warrior beneath him.

Five down, three to go.

"Get the fuck down here," Diesel shouted up the steps.

"Go fuck yourself," came the answering shout.

"You gonna pussy out?"

Diesel got no answer.

"Yep, you gonna pussy out. Jump outta window if you ain't gonna face us head on."

"Fuck you!"

Diesel grinned and slapped a palm to his chest. "Wounded by that."

Zak and Hawk chuckled.

"Think 5-0's en route yet?"

"Probably," Diesel grunted. "Gotta finish what we started before they get here." His eyes swung to Zak. "You're on parole, need to get the fuck outta here." He moved his gaze to Jag. "Go. Take Z. Leave Abe with the sleds. We'll clean up here."

Cleaning up didn't mean with a mop and bucket. It meant leaving a mark on any Warriors who still stood vertical. And maybe even some that didn't.

D or Hawk wasn't going to leave without making sure the job they came for wasn't completed.

"Sure?" Jag asked. He hated to miss the rest of the fun. He still owed them a lot more for his bike being totaled.

"Yeah. Fuck up their sleds on the way out."

Jag smiled and nodded. He'd enjoy doing that for sure. "One more for good measure, though." He said as he heard another warrior coming down the steps slowly and trying to be quiet, though the old steps were nothing but.

Diesel's arm snaked out again around the broken banister, snagged the unseen as of yet Warrior and pulled him down the remaining steps, flinging him in Jag's direction. "There you go."

The Warrior couldn't stop his momentum before Jag clocked him in the eye, then the chin. He kicked him in the shin, taking the biker down to knees where Jag kneed him in the face. Blood spurted from the guy's nose and split lip and before he collapsed like dead weight to the floor. Jag booted him in the chest, making the now unconscious biker smash into a table.

"That's what you get for fuckin' up my sled, motherfucker."

Jag wiped his bloody hand off on the Warrior's cut and then straightened, meeting his cousin's gaze. "That's for Sophie, too," Jag muttered under his breath. "Let's get the fuck outta here before you get busted for violatin' parole."

"Wish we had one of Rig's rollbacks with us so we could plow their bikes over."

"Yeah, but we don't," Jag said, a last look at the brothers they were leaving behind as they made their way to the front door.

"Stay safe," Zak yelled, flipping them a two-finger wave over his shoulder.

Jag pushed through the pub door and sucked in the fresh night air. He could hear sirens screaming from a distance. "Don't gotta lot of time, let's do this."

They both kicked at the end bike and watched it topple into the one next to it. And one by one they fell like dominoes. Their actions wouldn't do enough damage to the Harleys, not nearly like the damage done to Jag's bike, but it made them feel better. A few scratches and dents were better than nothing.

It was more of a message than anything else.

When the last one fell, Zak and Jag looked at each other and nodded, then hightailed it back to their bikes and Abe.

"Stay here. Call me if shit goes sideways. Got me?" Zak told him.

Abe nodded. "Got it covered."

That boy would make a good fully patched member one day.

If it was up to Jag, he'd patch him in before Rooster or Weasel, even though he had been a recruit for just a fraction of the time.

"Saddle up, brother. Let's ride," Jag said to Zak. The roar of their straight exhaust pipes rose into the night and they rode back to Shadow Valley.

CHAPTER 11

Ivy flung open her door and stepped out, meeting Jag on the landing outside. "You know what time it is?"

Jag gently chest bumped her backwards into her apartment. "Shut up, woman. Get in the house."

Luckily, the man's tone didn't match his words. And he wore a shit-eating grin. So he was lucky.

Very lucky.

She noticed the blood splattered all over him once he stepped inside and into the light.

"Don't need you harpin' like a nag if I'm out takin' care of shit." He laid a sloppy kiss on her lips as he pushed past her deeper into the living room.

She spun, hands on her hips. "What kind of *shit* involves blood? I'm assuming that isn't yours?"

"Fuck no."

"What happened?"

Jag cocked an eyebrow in her direction.

"If you tell me 'club business,' I'm going to throw you right back out of here, you hear me?"

"You're yellin' in my ear, so I hear you, woman."

She helped pull his cut off his shoulders and tossed it onto the couch. She circled, inspecting him. "Are you hurt?"

"Don't think so."

She grabbed his hand and lifted it, looking at his busted and bruised knuckles. "In a fight?"

"Yeah."

Ice rushed through her veins. "Were you by yourself when this happened? Were you jumped?"

He headed back toward her bedroom. "No, baby. Shit went down with the Warriors, that's all."

The Warriors?

She jerked into motion and followed him. "That's all?" she echoed as he sat on the edge of her bed and started to unlace his boots.

"Yeah. Need a shower."

He needed more than a shower.

"You've got blood on your jeans, you've got blood on your shirt. And what are you going to wear after you shower?"

He lifted his head to stare at her. "Shoulda went back to church first."

But he didn't. His first instinct was to come here which made her belly warm, but her next thought turned her cold. "Are the cops going to be knocking at my door?"

"Hope not."

"Not sure though?"

"Nope."

She sighed and planted her hands on her hips. "This is not a way to convince me to become your ol' lady."

He ignored that. "Ace downstairs watching the store?"

Ivy tilted her head. "He called me and said he'd be down there doing paperwork. That's not normal on a Sunday night. Figured he just needed to get away from his mother for a bit." Then it hit her. "This all had to do with whatever went down with the Warriors, didn't it?"

"Baby."

"Fucking Jag." She shook her head. "It's this shit… This… And everyone wondered why I would date anyone but bikers. Seen this shit all my life, Jag. Seen your father and my grandfather go to prison. Seen Zak go to prison. D's been shot at several times. Don't know if I can handle this kind of stuff happening to a man I allow in my bed. Allow in my heart. Actually considering having *children* with. I don't want to be a mother raising my kids on my own because their father is in jail or dead. I can't do it, Jag. I can't."

"You're DAMC, would never raise our kids on your own."

"Oh, well, that makes it all right then," she said bitterly, swiping at a lone tear that ran down her cheek. It was stupid to cry over children they hadn't even had yet. "Long as I have DAMC raising my kids, everything will be all right then," she said, the sarcasm thick in her voice.

"They're fuckin' family, Ivy. You know it. Family takes care of each other."

"Yeah, like Mitch and Axel. They have Zak's back, now don't they?"

"Different, baby."

Maybe so. But she saw how Zak's exile from the rest of his immediate family wounded him deep. He might not admit it out loud, but she's known him all her life, and they had always been close. Watching him hurt made her hurt for him.

"Speaking of family..." She grabbed her cell phone off her nightstand.

"Whatcha doin'?"

"Texting Dex to bring you a change of clothes."

"Dex is busy, don't bug 'im."

"Doing what?"

"Baby," was all he said, shaking his head and yanking one boot off then the other, tossing them to the side.

"Jag."

"Dex ain't bringin' me clothes," he muttered.

"Why?"

Ivy moved directly in front of him and after he yanked off his socks, he straightened up, meeting her gaze.

He grabbed her hips and pulled her in between his spread thighs.

"Was he involved in this, too?"

When he didn't answer, she realized more than a couple of the brothers had been involved in whatever went down tonight.

She pulled away from him. She needed distance. "You have to be honest with me, or this isn't going to work," she warned him.

He sighed, leaned his elbows on his knees and wrapped his hand around the back of his neck.

"Baby..."

Ivy raised a palm toward him. "Fine. I'll let what I just said sink in. I'm going to go run you a bath. If you were in a fight, you're going to be sore. You'll need to soak."

With that, she turned on her heel and walked out of the room. She hit the hall bathroom, turned on the spigot and tested the water until it was the perfect temp. She closed the drain plug before heading back into her bedroom where Jag was now sitting on her bed only wearing his tattoos.

Every time she saw him like that, she lost her breath. But this time, it was due to the bruise that was starting to bloom over his ribs, darkening the tattoos in that area.

"Shit," she muttered. Then her eyes dropped to the switchblade and brass knuckles he had thrown on her dresser. "Jesus, Jag."

Those were the same ones she had discovered under his mattress back at church.

"Takin' care of business."

"Right." She swung an arm toward the door. "In the bathroom. Now."

He blinked at her bossiness. But she didn't care.

"Now," she repeated when he hadn't moved.

With a groan, he stood and pushed past her, heading for the one and only bathroom in her apartment.

The tub was half full when she followed him in.

"Before you get in there, let me see your hand. I don't want you soaking in blood."

She turned on the warm water in the sink and grabbed both his wrists, guiding his hands under the running water.

He hissed at the sting she was sure he was feeling.

"Don't be a pussy."

He tugged his hands, but she tightened her grip on them as she washed away the crusty blood, seeing how bad the actual damage was.

"I guess you didn't use those brass knuckles," she stated.

"Didn't get a chance."

"Maybe that was a good thing. Anyone dead?"

"Not when I left."

Ivy's head jerked up, she caught his gaze and held it. "When *you* left? Who did you leave behind?"

"Baby..."

She shut off the sink faucet. "Oh, fuck that. Get in the damn tub and start talking."

Jag frowned, but looked toward the tub. "You gettin' in with me?"

"You're way too big for me to fit in there with you."

"Can sit on my lap."

"Right," she said sarcastically.

"Haven't taken a bath since a little kid."

"Get in." She squeezed past him and shut off the water.

He reluctantly climbed in the tub, acting as if soaking in bathwater wasn't manly and he didn't want to do it.

But as soon as he sank into the warm water, he sighed and closed his eyes. "Fuck yeah," he groaned.

Ivy squeezed some of her shampoo into her palm. "Slide down and get your hair wet."

His eyes popped open, he glanced at her hand, then slid down the tub far enough to dunk his head. When he resurfaced, he leaned back against the tub. His eyes just followed her as she dropped to her knees, leaned in and began to scrub his hair.

"Jesus," he whispered, his eyes closing as her fingers worked his scalp. She smiled.

"You're going to owe me one of these," she murmured knowing how good it felt when someone else washed your hair.

"You got it. Gonna both be naked, though."

That was fine with her.

"Dunk your head again."

He didn't hesitate to listen this time. When he came back up he wiped the water off his face and out of his eyes.

Goddamn, he took her breath away again. And again. Just watching him slick and sitting in her tub, made her wet and her nipples hard. She suddenly wished she had a bigger tub.

But she didn't, so she grabbed the loofah and squeezed out a good portion of her scented body wash onto it. She dampened it and squished it until it got sudsy.

"For fuck's sake, 'spect me to sit still while you wash me?"

"Yep," she said then bit her bottom lip. Leaning in farther, she started wiping the loofah over his broad shoulders and down the expanse of his back that sat out of the water, then she brushed the rough loofah over his nipples.

His heated gaze followed her, but she tried to ignore it and concentrate on her task instead. But drawing the soapy loofah over his broad chest made more than her hand wet.

Leaning forward, he murmured into her ear, "Gonna smell like you, baby."

That he was.

She dipped the loofah under the water as she worked down his tight stomach and encountered what she suspected she'd find under the soapy, opaque water.

He was as ready for her as she was for him.

He was naked and wet. She was clothed and wet. She let the loofah go, and it floated to the surface of the water as she wrapped her fingers around his slick, hard length.

She began to stroke him slowly, creating ripples at the water's surface and when she heard a strangled noise, she looked up. His eyes were hooded, his mouth parted.

"Wearin' too many clothes, baby."

True. And wet, too. Her tight camisole had water spots all over it and the crotch of her boxer shorts was soaked. Though, not by bath water.

"Want me to stop, honey?"

He blew out a breath. "I tell you to stop?"

She chuckled and moved her hand faster, the water beginning to splash. "Think it's clean yet?"

"Nope."

"'Kay."

His head tilted back against the shower wall and he closed his eyes, his hips rising and falling with each stroke of her hand.

"Fuckin' baby, gonna blow my load in this water if you don't stop."

She ignored him and continued, watching as his jaw tightened, his brows lowered and his body tensed.

"Baby," he moaned. Then his eyes popped open, he pushed to his feet, the water sloshing over the side of the tub and onto her. And suddenly, he was out and pinning her to the slippery, drenched bathroom floor.

He tugged her damp boxer shorts off her legs, flinging them to the side. Then he pushed up her cami, and she gasped as his mouth latched onto one of her aching nipples. He shoved a knee between her thighs, spreading her legs wide enough to take the breadth of his body.

She realized in that moment she never got him to reveal what happened earlier with the Warriors. Her mistake. His hard, wet body had been her downfall.

She dug her fingers into his dripping hair and pulled him down into a deep, thorough kiss, taking the lead, pushing her tongue into his mouth, showing him how much she wanted him right there on the bathroom floor.

His erection pressed against her inner thigh and she tilted her hips and groaned into his mouth, encouraging him to shift forward, to take her, to make her his.

He grabbed her wrists, yanking her hands from his hair and pinned them above her head with one hand. The other gripped her cheek as he pushed back against her tongue, taking the control, taking her mouth, until finally, they both had to pull away to catch their breath.

His hand slipped down over her breast, squeezing and kneading for a moment, before continuing down and finding her swollen, needy clit, so ready for his fingers, for his tongue.

But she didn't need much prep, she was ready for him now. His slick body was all she needed for foreplay. She ached for him.

"Fuck me, Mick."

He nipped the tender skin at the base of her throat, then stroked it with his tongue, before moving back down, flicking at one of her nipples with the tip, circling her areola.

With a gasp, her body rocked as he shifted to a seated position, he grabbed her hips and brought her down hard on his lap, impaling her. Then they both stilled, the only sound in the bathroom was dripping water and their ragged breathing.

He was so deep inside her that when he murmured, "Where I belong," she agreed one hundred percent.

He buried his face into her neck, grabbed her ass and began to guide her up and down his shaft.

"Where I belong," he mumbled again against her damp skin.

She wrapped her arms around him, holding him as close as she could get him, as she used her knees for leverage to take over, to control the rhythm, the age-old movement of bringing two people together and making them one.

"Mick..." she whispered into the hair at the top of his head. "Could've lost you tonight."

He pulled his face away from her neck enough to say, "Quiet, baby."

"No, it's true."

"Quiet," he said more firmly.

"Mick..."

"No, Ivy, *enough*." He shifted them both quickly until she was again on her back and he was above her as he took over the control, slamming his cock into her as hard and fast as he could.

Showing her just how alive he was. How alive they both were at that moment.

The faster he moved, the slicker she became, meeting him thrust for thrust. Then without warning, she exploded around him, clenching down hard, arching her back, crying out his name.

His motion stuttered, and he barked out a curse, but he slowed his pace as the ripples subsided and she floated back to Earth, returned to the bathroom, to the man who knew just how to bring her back up to that peak once again.

"Gonna come soon, baby. Gonna come again?"

She struggled to answer, but he heard her and smiled down into her face.

"Nothin' like feelin' that hot, wet cunt squeezing my dick. An' that little patch of red hair, that fire above your pussy makes my balls want to explode."

She was never going to hear one romantic thought come out of that man's mouth. But it wasn't the words he uttered that squeezed her heart, it was the emotion in his eyes, the way he looked at her. Like she was everything to him. Like he believed with all his heart and soul that she was meant for him. That they truly belonged to each other.

Always and forever.

Everything she fought so hard to avoid, all that effort she spent resisting for years. It was all for nothing.

It should bother her.

But it didn't.

She should feel defeated.

But she didn't.

Jag felt right and she no longer wanted to resist or fight him. She truly opened herself up to the possibility of spending the rest of her life with this man. Taking the shit that came along with the good. Dealing with club business in another capacity. As his ol' lady.

As the mother of his children.

Even as his wife.

"Baby..."

Not realizing her eyes were closed, she opened them and met his dark, worried gaze. "Yeah?" came out on a sigh.

"You okay?"

"Yeah."

He smiled and her heart clenched in response. "Good. Gonna bust a nut soon. Gonna come?"

"Yeah." She wrapped her legs around his hips, angling them just right so he hit that perfect spot.

Within seconds, the waves of another orgasm rolled over her, dragging him under with her. He captured her lips as he came, his cock pulsating as he held himself still and deep inside her.

He broke the kiss, pressed his forehead to hers. "Love ya, baby."

Fuck. He just slayed her.

CHAPTER TWELVE

Fuck. She got what she wanted and didn't even have to say a word. She used her pussy as a weapon of mass destruction.

After their second round of fucking in her dry, much softer bed, he spilled almost everything that happened earlier in South Side.

If word got out that he told his woman that shit, he would never hear the end of it. But he blamed it on a moment of weakness, due to drained balls and a happy dick that made him do it.

That was his excuse, and he was sticking to it if need be.

Right now though, they should be sleeping, but neither of them could. He was waiting to hear what went down after he left and to make sure that everyone got out in one piece.

Of course Ivy was worried not only for her brother, but for her cousins and Zak, though not so much for Pierce.

Finally, his phone chirped, and he grabbed it off the nightstand, the screen illuminating the dark room and Ivy's worried face.

He read the texts from Zak and cursed.

Ivy slapped his arm. "What does it say?"

He studied her for a moment in the glow of his cell phone, then took a deep breath before saying, "Everyone's good." He shook his head. She needed to know the truth, and she'd find out in the morning, anyway. "No, everyone isn't good."

He heard her suck in a breath.

"Mean that everyone's in one piece, baby."

"So what's wrong?"

"D and Hawk got busted. 5-0 snagged them. Sittin' in jail."

"Aaah shit."

"Yeah. Zak gotta call in to Pannebaker." According to Z's texts, he had to leave a message since the attorney the club had on retainer didn't normally answer his phone at three o'clock in the morning.

"Do we need to go bail them out?"

He eyeballed her. "You got that kind of scratch?"

She frowned. "No."

"Didn't think so. Gotta go in front of the judge in the morning, then Pierce and Zak will handle it."

"Pierce," Ivy muttered.

He felt the same way. "Still the prez, baby."

"Yeah."

"Might be for a while yet, until shit gets sorted." Eventually, everything would get straightened out. Hopefully, sooner than later.

"Well, thankfully, no one's dead or in the hospital, right?"

"Yeah, baby, could've died tonight. Any one of us."

"Wasn't smart."

"Had to make a statement. No one's safe with their hit an' runs on us."

"Do you think this so-called 'statement' is going to do any good?"

"Dunno." He tossed his phone back onto the nightstand and gathered her into his arms. He shoved his nose into her hair and inhaled her scent. Though, now he knew where she got that scent, her shampoo and her body wash. And he smelled the same after that bath. "All I know is that my woman's in my arms tonight an' got to bust a nut in her."

"Jesus, so romantic," she whispered, but she snuggled in tighter and a feeling of deep contentment rushed through him. "Have to ask you something, Jag."

He grunted because knowing her, it'd be one that he wouldn't want to answer.

"One of the things I have to insist on is you not hiding anything from me. You want me to be your ol' lady and from what you said, the mother of your children, so you can't hide shit from me. You can't do that and have this work. I know it, you know it. Club business or not."

He rolled to his back, and she wrapped around him, pressing her cheek to his chest. He drew his fingers through her loose hair, then traced the delicate outer shell of her ear. "Didn't hear a question, baby."

"Maybe not."

He sighed, her head rising and falling with his chest. Her fingers traced along his pecs and collar bone, making it hard for him to think. "Can't share everything. Know that."

"Yeah, but you can share a lot more that you do… If you know what I mean."

He tipped his eyes down toward her. "Whadya mean?"

Her warm breath blew across his chest before she admitted, "I found your drawings."

She *what*?

He tensed as what she said sank in. He pulled himself up on his elbows and stared down at her shadowy figure in the dark. "My drawings," he finally repeated.

"Yeah."

"Not just the one." The one he had stupidly left on the bar the morning his bike got trashed. The one he left behind in his drunken stupor as he made his way to his bed to pass out and forget about both his bike and Ivy.

"No."

"The ones in my room?" He knew it, he just needed to hear it.

"Yeah."

"You fuckin' broke into my room an' went through my shit?"

"Yeah."

Damn. "Fuckin' Ivy."

She reached up and cupped his cheek. He wrapped his fingers around her hand but didn't pull it away. "Jag... *Mick*. I needed to know. I saw the talent in that partial drawing of your new custom. I knew that couldn't be the first time you drew like that. Not sure why you're hiding it."

"So I don't take shit from anyone. That's why. Easy to understand, Ivy." And it should be since she was raised DAMC and knew what a man should and shouldn't be. "Do me a solid an' just forget whatcha saw."

She lifted her head finally and rose up on her elbow, too. She pulled her hand from under his and laid it on his chest. "I'm not going to forget what I saw."

"What *did* you see?"

"All of it." She reached over him and grabbed her cell phone, hitting the power button to activate it and then pressing the photo gallery app.

Shit.

Shit.

Shit.

Her finger swiped across the screen until she found what she was looking for. She turned the screen toward him. "All of it," she repeated.

His stomach dropped as his eyes fell on the phone. One of the many drawings he did of Ivy smacked him right in the face. The one she showed him was one of the firsts ones he ever did. The one of her wearing his cut. "Fuck me," he muttered.

"Honey, you shouldn't hide these. You shouldn't hide *any* of them."

He closed his eyes for a moment. There was no way she was going to keep this under wraps. "No one's business."

She swiped at her phone once more, then shoved it in his face again. His stomach churned. "Need to tell you something..." She swiped and turned it toward him. "Seeing these..." Swipe. Turn. "Mick... seeing these..." Swipe. Turn. "All the drawings of me..." Swipe. "Years' worth..." Swipe. "Made me realize something..."

Problem was, he didn't need to see anything she was showing him. He knew what they all looked like. He remembered in detail doing each drawing. And why he did them.

"What?"

"You mentioned in the bathroom that you love me. But you didn't say for just how long."

His nostrils flared and his lips flattened as he dropped his head back and stared up at the ceiling.

"You going to hide that, too?" she asked softly.

He rolled over and onto her, covering her body with this weight. Digging his hands into her hair, he pressed his forehead to hers, he grumbled, "Not gonna hide it, baby. Was just waitin' for you to figure it out."

"Figure out that you love me?"

"No. Figure out how much you love me."

"Mick…" she whispered. Her voice trembled, making his chest tighten.

"Baby, loved you a long time. Wanted you even longer. Dreamed about you when we were teens. Jerked off all the time to you, too. Hell, still do."

Her mouth dropped open. "Nice."

He shrugged. "Hell, can't remember a time I didn't want you. You just needed to figure out what you wanted."

"Yeah, I did."

"You want me?"

"Yeah."

"You love me?"

"Yeah, Mick, I do. It hit me hard tonight when I realized you could've been killed. Realized that would've left a hole in my heart. Honestly, I've kept my head buried. When I found the sketches, it started to become a little clearer how much I mean to you, how much you mean to me. You've always been around and I took you for granted. I realize that now."

"Fought me at every turn. If I'd have shown you the pictures a long time ago, you would've been in my bed sooner?"

She bit back a smile. "I can't say that. Needed to do my thing first. You know, like college and—"

"Nerds."

"Nerds," she echoed in agreement.

He sighed. "Should've been your first, baby." Should've been, could've been, if she had just let him in a long time ago. He couldn't do anything about that now. Maybe make up for lost time. Which he would gladly do. Even if it killed him.

"My first time sucked," she said.

He should feel bad for her, he should. But he didn't. He was kind of happy it sucked for her. Once again he couldn't help thinking that it should've been him. "Coulda made it better."

"Doubt it."

He grunted. She was probably right. Took him awhile to learn how to pleasure a woman. It would've killed him to disappoint her. Instead, someone else did it for him. "Gonna be your last, though."

"You think?"

Ivy's giggle made him smile. "I know."

She grabbed his ear and tugged. "No more Goldies?"

He snagged her hand away and laced his fingers with hers. "No more man-boys? Wanted to stomp that fucker into the ground with my boot."

"Adam was nice... until you Neanderthals scared him away."

That they did. "He's lucky I allowed him to continue to breathe."

"*Jag*," she scolded him.

"*Baby*," he teased back, taking her mouth.

He decided they were done talking and needed to do something about it.

EPILOGUE

Ivy paced the clubhouse, the Long Island Iced Tea that Bella made sat ignored on the bar.

She had heard they were holding an executive meeting today, which made sense because they were still dealing with the aftermath of Hawk and Diesel being arrested the other night.

But it was what happened afterward in her apartment that made her nervous.

With all the shit that went down due to the fight with the Warriors, they hadn't had a chance to talk about what steps they were taking next after admitting to each other that they loved one another.

She figured Jag would go full bore ahead on claiming her as his ol' lady. And to do that he needed to bring it to a vote. But he hadn't discussed it happening so soon. So she didn't get the opportunity to discourage him from doing so before she heard about this meeting.

She headed over as soon as she could once she saw Dex and Ace leaving for the meeting. She couldn't leave the pawn shop until she got someone there to replace her. Luckily, her mother and Ace's wife, Janice, rushed over to help once she explained to them what her panic was about.

However, by the time she got to church it was too late. The meeting room door was shut and the remaining executive members were inside.

Now, as she paced and her eyes kept landing on the closed door, she debated whether to bust inside and tell Jag that now was not the time to bring it to a vote.

She wasn't ready.

She wasn't ready at all. And she didn't give her permission.

Not that he needed it. He certainly didn't. If he claimed her and everyone voted yes on it, she was screwed, no matter what she thought.

Her head swung toward the door again and she stopped, hands on hips.

Grizz slammed his pint glass full of beer on the bar, making the draft spill over the rim onto his hand. He cursed, shook off his hand, then pointed one crooked, gnarled finger toward the closed meeting room door. "Remember, girly, a woman don't belong in that room *ever*."

"But—"

"Nothin' in that room's your business," he grumbled.

If Jag was in there claiming her, it *was* her business. She had to stop him.

She took one step toward the door, then suddenly she was there, hand on the knob, turning it, flinging the door open...

"Goddamn women!" Grizz shouted at her back.

All eyes landed on her and she froze. Ace, Jag, Pierce, Dex... And Zak? He wasn't a board member anymore. Why was he in there?

Her brother frowned at her. "What the fuck, Ivy?"

Her gaze landed on Jag and he cocked an eyebrow at her, a small smile pulling at his lips.

"You do it?" she asked him from the doorway.

"Do what?" he returned.

"Ivy get outta here," Ace yelled. "We're talkin' business."

"I know! Don't let him bring it to a vote!"

Her uncle looked at her funny. "What are you talkin' about?"

EPILOGUE

Her gaze bounced to Jag and back to Ace. "The vote."

"On what?" Ace asked, clearly confused.

Jag pushed to his feet and approached her. "Just what do you think we're votin' on?"

"Me being your ol' lady," she whispered.

He shook his head and laughed.

Ace swept a hand around the table, looking a bit peeved. "We got two members missin', we ain't votin' on shit."

"Oh." Heat crept into her cheeks.

"Bitches," Pierce griped, shaking his head. "Heard the crazy ones are the best in bed. That true, Jag?"

Jag's head spun toward Pierce and his shoulders visibly tightened. Ivy placed a hand on his arm, pulling his attention back to her.

"I thought you were in here claiming me."

"Should I be?"

"No!" she shouted a little too loudly. She cleared her throat. She looked at Zak. "Can you not vote with two missing members?"

Zak shrugged, but it was Pierce who said, "We can do whatever the fuck we want."

"Good." Her answer had them all twisting their heads back to her.

"Good?" Ace asked, clearly confused. Again.

"For fuck's sake," Dex grumbled under his breath.

"Yeah," she stepped closer to the table. She looked Pierce in the eye. "I need to bring something to a vote."

"You can't bring shit to a vote."

"You just said," she lowered her voice to sound gruff like Pierce, "'We can do whatever the fuck we want.'"

"Know what I said, woman! *You* can't bring shit to a vote."

"Baby, you gotta go," Jag started, grabbing her arm. She yanked it free and looked at each one of them sitting around the table. "Jag ain't claiming me."

"Ever?" Ace asked, his brows raised in surprise.

"Ever."

"Sucks to be you, Jag," Dex muttered.

Ivy shot daggers at her brother. "Are you going to ask me why?"

"Baby..."

"Nope," Pierce barked.

"I'll tell you why..."

"Baby," Jag said more firmly, grabbing her arm again. She shook her arm, but he didn't release her this time, he just held on tighter.

"I'll tell you why..."

"Ivy," he said, the warning thick in his voice.

Pierce let out a long, loud dramatic sigh. "Tell us why an' then get the fuck outta here."

"Because I'm claiming him."

She could have heard a pin drop as everyone stared at her wide-eyed. Even Jag.

Then Ace barked out a laugh and slammed the table with his palm, making her jump.

Dex groaned and shoved his face in his hands.

Zak smirked at Jag, shoved away from the table and came over to pound Jag on the back. "Congrats, brother. Got yourself a ball an' chain. Welcome to the club."

Ivy turned slowly toward Jag, afraid of what she was going to see.

It wasn't as bad as she thought. He seemed kind of shell-shocked, but his gaze was heated as he stared at her. And he sort of looked... proud.

Huh.

"All in favor?" Ivy asked loudly, her gaze holding his.

"It wasn't even brought to a motion yet," Ace laughed through his words. She was glad he was finding this amusing.

"So make the damn motion," she said impatiently.

"How about I just second the motion?" Ace suggested.

"Whatever," she muttered. "All in favor?" she asked again.

"Ayes," rose up, the loudest coming from beside her.

She bit her bottom lip as Pierce slammed the gavel on the table and yelled, "Motion carries. Jag's officially now pussy-whipped. Good luck there, brother."

Jag yanked her to him and dropped his lips to hers. But instead of

EPILOGUE

kissing her, he murmured, "Now, get the fuck outta here so we can finish talkin' 'bout your cousins' legal troubles."

Oh.

He gave her a quick kiss, then pushed her out the door and slapped her ass. "Deal with you later," he said gruffly.

Before she could turn around to address him, the door slammed in her face. She wandered back to the bar where Grizz just shook his head and Bella gave her a knowing smile.

Her cell phone dinged, and she glanced at it.

Love ya, baby.

She texted back. *Love you, too... ol' man.*

———

Jag, wearing nothing but his boxers, wandered past Ivy sitting at her kitchen table. He threw open the refrigerator door, contemplated the interior, scratched his balls, then snagged a beer, twisting off the cap and tossing it into the sink.

He tipped the bottle to his lips and let the cold brew slither down his throat as he waited for her to bitch at him for the hundredth time about where the garbage can was located. But she remained quiet. He cocked a brow and approached the table, the bottle hanging between two fingers.

Apparently, she hadn't noticed because she was too engrossed in whatever she was looking at on her laptop.

"Watchin' midget porn?"

"No," she said distractedly, not even bothering to look up. "Working."

"Watcha workin' on? It's late."

"Something for you."

"Me?"

"Yeah. Something that will make you enough to build the custom bike of your dreams as well as put a down payment on a house." She finally looked up over her shoulder at him, and with a smile added,

"So we don't have to wait for the 'all's clear' text from Ace before we can have sex."

"We can have sex. Your uncle just don't wanna hear you squealin' like a pig."

"He say that?"

"Yeah."

"Damn," she whispered, color flooding her cheeks.

"So, if you can stay quiet…" his voice trailed off. "Never mind. Okay, how you gonna make me a lot of scratch so we can get our own place?"

She turned her laptop so he could see it clearly. He leaned over her shoulder to get a better look. He blinked.

"What's that?"

"A website."

"For what?"

"For you."

He read the fancy header at the top of the page: *M. Jagger Jamison*.

"M. Jagger?"

"I knew you'd be pissed if I used your first name."

He set the beer down on the table and swiped his finger over the touch pad on her laptop, scrolling up the page. The page was full of photos of his sketches. And there were outrageous prices under each one.

"This live?"

"No, I wanted to show you first and get your approval."

"Think you can get that for my drawings?"

"Yes. I emailed an art dealer, and he was impressed. He actually was the one who suggested some of the prices. He said you'd make more if they were framed professionally."

"When you doin' that?"

Jag watched her jaw drop and her eyes widen. She wasn't expecting that response from him. But she was right. No use hiding them away in a ceiling. He might as well sell them and build the dream bike he wanted as well as buy her a house.

EPILOGUE

Get her a ring.

Start a college fund for their kids. Since they'd most likely be super smart like her.

"You're okay with this?"

He lifted a shoulder and picked up his beer. "Yeah."

"You won't care what any of the brothers think?"

"Didn't say that."

"You can handle it."

He thought about what she said for a moment as he took a pull from the beer bottle. Finally, he said, "Yeah, I can handle it."

He stepped behind her chair, wrapped a hand around her neck and pulled her head back. He dropped a kiss onto her forehead.

"Gonna buy that house an' fill it with green-eyed, redheaded lil' girls like their momma."

She reached up to cup his cheek. "Nope. Badass little boys with grey-blue eyes like their daddy."

He stared down in her eyes, and the warmth that ran through him reached all the way to his toes. "Do me a favor, baby."

She smiled up at him, a dreamy look on her face. "What's that?"

"Don't sell any of the ones I did of you."

"You can draw more."

He shook his head. "Don't. Don't want no one but me to have you. In two-D or three-D."

"Okay," she said softly, her eyes suddenly shiny.

"Ready to go start makin' those kids, baby?"

"I'm on the pill, honey."

"I know, but could practice in the meantime."

She slapped the top down on her laptop and pushed away from the table. "That we can."

"Can I fuck you while you're naked wearin' my cut?"

"Like the drawing? No."

"*Baby.*"

"*Jag.*"

He smiled to himself as he dragged her down the hall. It might not be tonight, but one of these nights he'd get her to agree.

He'd dreamed about her wearing his cut for what seemed like forever. And if she only wore it while they were in the bedroom, that would be fine with him. But he was going to make sure she was screaming his name when she did.

Turn the page to read the first chapter of book three in the Dirty Angels MC series:
Down & Dirty: Hawk

DOWN & DIRTY: HAWK SNEAK PEEK

Turn the page for a sneak peek of the next book in the Down & Dirty: Dirty Angels MC series.

DOWN & DIRTY: HAWK SNEAK PEEK

Chapter One

Hawk grunted.

About fucking time.

As the annoying high-pitched buzz sounded, the magnetic door lock released and the reinforced steel door clanged open, he glanced up and saw a guard pushing through the door.

He'd been sitting here long enough, waiting in this sparse room that only housed a bolted-down, dented and scratched metal table and two chairs that sat unevenly on the concrete floor.

Not that he had anywhere else to go. He was stuck here until the club's attorney showed up and did his legal hocus-pocus to get him the fuck out of county jail.

All he knew was that he did not look good in an orange polycotton blend. He preferred denim and leather. He'd rather not be wearing a *one-size-does-not-fit-all* jumpsuit at all. It wouldn't take much flexing for him to split the seams with the one he currently wore.

Like the Hulk.

He grinned.

But that grin was quickly lost as the person following the guard into the room did not look anything like his lawyer.

Not unless the Dirty Angels MC's attorney had a sex change operation, lost at least fifty pounds—which included a gut—and slapped in colored contacts. Not to mention, found some sense of style.

Hawk closed his dropped jaw before he started to drool like a fool. Because, for fuck's sake, slobbering all over himself wouldn't be very badass biker. Not. At. All.

He drew himself up straighter in the uncomfortable metal chair and puffed out his chest until the top snap of the jumpsuit popped open.

Then he let his gaze slowly run down that fine piece of ass from top to toe.

Oh, fuck me, he thought as he took in the woman's long, wavy dark brown hair, her plump *suck-my-cock* lips, her bouncing tits that wanted to bust out of the blood-red blouse that fit her like an *if-you-can't-acquit* glove, her narrow waist, her *not-so-narrow* hips, which were encased in a black skirt that only came down mid-thigh—thighs that would fit perfectly around his ears—those long-ass, lickable calves, slim ankles, and... *fuck... higher-than-hell* heels.

She could walk all over him as long as she wore those fucking shoes.

He heard the clearing of a throat and reluctantly lifted his gaze to flashing, but amused, deep blue eyes.

He hadn't even realized the guard was gone and the door had been closed. They were alone.

With a hard-on that wouldn't quit, he now couldn't wait to get back to his cramped cell to rub one out. He didn't even care if his cellmate watched. Fuck that strung-out weasel dick.

"Where's Pudwhacker?"

And when that vision opened her mouth to speak... Yeah, he just about creamed in his county-issued tighty whities. "I was assigned to your club by Mr. Pannebaker."

"Why?" came out sounding more like a grunt than a question.

"Because I'm good—"

In bed? I'll be the judge of that.

"And he's busy," she finished.

The woman yanked the chair away from the table and the metal legs screeched along the filthy, pitted concrete floor. She smiled when he winced at the sound.

"You gonna be able to sit down in that skirt?"

She proved it when she slid that ass, which he had yet to get an eyeful of, onto the seat.

He was jealous of that scrap of metal. No doubt. She should be sitting on his face instead.

"Sure thing, Mr..." She flipped open his file, ran a long blood-red fingernail—one that matched her blouse—along a document inside and then tapped it. "Mr. Dougherty."

"You wear that for all your clients? Or am I special?"

She plastered on an *I'm-only-here-because-I-have-to-be* smile. "All my clients are special, Mr. Dougherty."

"I'm sure," he muttered. "Bet everyone who pays those fuckin' high hourly fees feels special." He reached around and rubbed his ass. "Feelin' *real* special right 'bout now."

She tilted her head and considered him. "You wouldn't have to pay anything if you hadn't been arrested."

Well, that was true. But sometimes statements had to be made and he, as well as his club brothers, had to be the ones to make them.

"Shit happens."

"That it does. So here we are. Can we get started, Mr. Dougherty?"

"Hawk."

She pursed her lips for a moment. And in that moment his balls tightened painfully. Damn, didn't he want to shoot his load all over her face.

Suddenly, she dropped her torso beneath the table and then popped back up. Hawk watched as her tits also bounced back, testing the top button of her deep V-neck blouse.

He blinked. Since when were threads so damn strong?

Then his breath rushed out of him loudly when she slipped on a pair of glasses.

Holy fuck. She just became every man's sexy librarian wet dream.

I've been a naughty boy, Ms. Librarian.

She placed some sort of flat computer that didn't have a keyboard on the table. What Ivy would call a tablet or some such shit. Not that he cared. He didn't fuck with those types of things. He barely knew the basics when he used the computer at his bar and even then, he let his computer whiz of a cousin do the rest.

He didn't have time for that shit.

She dropped her gaze to the folder. "So, I went over your charges—"

"Read my last name without your glasses."

Her head rose and those deep blue eyes blinked at him. "What?"

"Read my name without your glasses, now you need 'em?"

She stared at him. "I forget to put them on sometimes since they're just for reading. Your name was a bit blurry, but I could make it out. Does it matter if I'm wearing my glasses or not?"

Fuck yeah it does. Especially if you're naked.

And in my bed.

"Gotta name?"

Her mouth opened and closed once before she said, "Sorry, I should've introduced myself. I'm Kiki Clark."

His brows shot up his forehead. "Kiki?"

"Yes, sir," she said on a dramatic sigh.

Hawk muttered, "What the fuck."

She shrugged. "Ask my parents."

"So, you ain't lyin'."

"I never lie."

His brows shot up once again. He had a hard time believing that coming from an attorney.

"Okay, maybe sometimes. But only when it's important. Like when someone's freedom hangs in the balance."

Well, damn. "You lie to judges," he stated.

Without even the slightest hesitation and a fleeting smile, she answered, "I plead the fifth."

Hawk leaned back in his chair and barked out a laugh. "Yeah, you're just like a real super hero rightin' wrongs." He shook his head. "Damn, wanna get in your skirt."

"I'll dry clean it for you first if you would like to wear it. Might be a bit tight on you, though." She lifted a shoulder slightly. "No loss for me, since I've never been fond of it anyway."

"Fuckin' goddamn," he whispered.

She arched a brow. "Does that mean good?"

"Fuck yes. For me, anyhow. But I'll make sure it's good for you, too."

"I'm relieved," she said, sarcasm dripping from her voice. "I've already had too many selfish pricks in my bed."

"I'm not a selfish prick."

"So you say."

He studied her, wondering how many notches she had on her bed post. "How many is 'too many?'"

"You first, Mr. Dougherty. How many women have *you* had in your bed? I've heard rumors about those biker parties."

"If you're talkin' about at the same time... then a few. Wanna be one?"

She adjusted herself in her chair, then pushed her glasses higher on her nose. "How about we just agree to keep our relationship on a professional level. Me as the lawyer and you as the defendant."

Hawk gave her a half-assed grin. "Doubt that's gonna happen."

She made a noise. "It'll happen."

"You say so, babe."

Now she gave him a *Do-I-really-have-to-tolerate-this-asshole?* smile. "I certainly do, *pumpkin*."

Hawk snorted and his grin widened. He liked a challenge. And she was pushing all his buttons. In the right way.

She again arched a perfectly shaped eyebrow at him. "Now, can we get down to business?"

He wasn't ready to get down to business. Or at least the business she was here for. He liked playing with her. And she didn't seem to mind it, either. He liked that. No, he fucking *loved* that. "Right here on the table?"

She shook her head and sighed, then ran her gaze over his head before switching gears without a warning. "Did it hurt to get your head tattooed?"

It hurt like a bitch. "Tickled."

Now both of her brows rose. "You're ticklish?"

"Wanna find out?"

"Another time, but thanks. The guards might frown upon it if we get into a tickle fight."

Hawk's grin widened. They'd probably be jealous, if anything. "Not scared of bikers, are you?"

"Should I be?"

"Depends how bad they wanna fuck you."

"You want to fuck me..." She glanced down at her file. "Hawk? Is that your real name?"

"Yeah. On both accounts."

"*Ah*. Okay. I'll take your uncontrollable desire into consideration before I step into a dark room alone with you."

Once again, Hawk sat back in his chair, crossed his arms over his chest, and smiled. She was a feisty one. Classy. Curvy. A lot of hair to pull. Smart and a smart ass mouth, as well.

Right up his alley.

Yeah, he liked a good challenge.

He might have to taste her between her legs to see if she was sweet as well as spicy.

"Gotta get outta here. Got a bar to run."

"Right." She peeked back at her paperwork before meeting his gaze directly. Head on. Nope. No fear at all in those eyes. "The Iron Horse Roadhouse. Maybe you should have thought about that before you kicked that biker's ass."

"Just defendin' myself."

She leaned forward, giving Hawk a better view of her tits. "So, let me get this straight, the man that you knocked out and badly injured put his hands on you first?"

Shit.

"He put his paws on DAMC property."

When she noticed where his eyes had focused, she sat back. "Him specifically? Or someone in his club?"

Hawk shrugged, then stretched his neck out toward the left and then toward the right, cracking his spine, before answering, "Don't matter. All the same."

"Not in the eyes of the law."

"Justice is blind," Hawk grumbled, thinking about the ten years the former club president, Zak, spent in prison for a crime the Shadow Warriors set him up for.

Fuckers. They deserved everything they got and then some.

"I can't disagree with you on that. That's why I got into criminal defense."

Speaking of defense... "Where's my brother?"

"The other Mr. Dougherty has been released."

What the fuck? "How'd he get sprung an' my ass is still sittin' in here?"

Kiki lifted a shoulder, one he wanted to sink his teeth into as he was making her come. "He didn't waste my time trying to get down my pants. Or up my skirt."

Right. He was sure Diesel would take a shot at that if given half the chance. "Doubt that's the reason."

"And you would be correct. Though this can't be proven, I have a feeling your brother's size alone intimidated the witnesses. No one saw him do anything but hold the front door open to the pub to let the rest of your crew in."

Lucky fucking bastard.

"What did these so-called witnesses see me do?"

"They saw enough that you would be held responsible for the damage."

"So, has nothin' to do with crackin' some Shadow Warriors' heads. Just the damage to that bar?"

"Sort of, but not exactly."

"That's clear as fuckin' piss."

"I agree."

Hawk grunted. "Club'll pay for the damage."

"Already done."

He cocked an eyebrow. "So what's the hold up?"

"I have to go before the District Justice and plea for leniency. He seems determined to make an example of at least one of you. You came into his jurisdiction and wreaked havoc, Mr... Hawk. Judges tend to frown upon that. They tend not to like motorcycle gangs—"

"Club," he corrected her.

"What?"

"Club," he barked. "DAMC's a fuckin' club, a brotherhood, not a gang."

"Okay, well," she pushed her glasses up her nose once more. "Club, then. Judges tend not to like *clubs* going to war in their area. Can you see where he's coming from?"

"You know this DJ?"

"Yes."

He narrowed his eyes as he watched her face carefully. "Good?"

"Very well, yes."

Hawk leaned forward over the table until they were almost face to face. "You fuck 'im?"

He couldn't miss the uncomfortable swallow and the flash of shock that crossed her expression. Finally, he got a reaction from her. But it quickly disappeared as a blank mask slipped over her face.

"I'm not going to answer that. That's simply ridiculous."

"You gonna wear a skirt like that when you plead my innocence?"

When she sighed with impatience, Hawk's gaze became glued to the rise and fall of her chest.

"I'm not pleading your innocence. I'm shooting for a reduced sentence."

"Then you plan on fucking me an' not in a good way."

"I'm going to do my best to get you out of here and back to your *club* and your *brotherhood* as an 'upstanding business owner who made an unwise decision that won't be repeated.'"

"An unwise decision." Hawk snorted. "In self-defense."

"No. I'm not going to insult the judge that way. You've learned from your time here and you've learned from your mistake. You're taking this as a life lesson and will be a better citizen because of it."

Damn, she was good. She almost convinced him with that bullshit. "Sure, babe. Sounds like a plan. Long as it works."

"It'll work if you keep your mouth shut in the courtroom and you don't stare down the judge in defiance. You let me do all the talking, while you're as quiet as a church mouse and looking as harmless as one, too."

"Mice can do a lotta fuckin' damage."

Hawk bit back a laugh when she slapped a hand to her forehead and her eyes bugged out behind those sexy little glasses. "Fuck my life," she said under her breath.

Damn, that was hot. "Love a classy lady with a dirty fuckin' mouth. Wanna wrap my fist in all that hair when you're suckin' my cock with it."

She opened her mouth, blinked, sucked in a deep breath and then sighed loudly before saying, "You really know how to sweet talk a lady."

"Don't want you to be a lady. Want you to be a hellcat. Not prissy. Sweatin', screamin', bitin', scratchin', fuckin'. Comin' so hard you see spots."

"Well, all righty then. Let me pull up my calendar so we can schedule that." She held up a finger as she tapped an app on her computer/tablet/electronic thingy. "Date?"

"First night I'm outta this joint."

"Location?"

"On the floor, against the wall, on a table, in my bed."

"Well, that's a lot of typing." *Tap, tap, tap.* "Okay, let me make sure I got this down correctly... *Suckin', scratchin', bitin', sweatin', fuckin'*, and..." She glanced up from her tablet.

"Screamin'. Forgot screamin'."

"Ah." She nodded, tapping the screen. "*Screamin'.*" She lifted a brow his direction. "Anything in particular?"

"My name."

"Got it. Screaming *H-A-W-K*. All that against the wall, on the bed, the floor and hanging from a ceiling fan. Right?"

He smirked. "That'll do for starters."

"Right. I can't wait."

"Me neither." She might be taking all of this like a big joke, but she was going to find out just how serious he was.

She focused her pretty blues on him. "Can you promise me one thing?"

"What's that, babe?"

"It's going to be the best fuck I've ever had?"

Fucking goddamn. "Have a feelin' it's gonna be the best fuck I ever had."

She tapped her finger against her bottom lip—which he had the urge to bite—then tilted her head. "Okay, I lied. I need another promise."

His lips twitched. "Shoot."

"If I get you out of here, you're not going to punch anyone else."

He studied her a couple beats. "Can't promise that, babe."

"Why?"

"Got enemies."

Her eyes narrowed. "Who?"

He zipped his lips shut.

"Who?" she prodded. "Those bikers you beat up in that bar?"

Hawk leaned forward, no longer amused at the direction the conversation was going. "Know you're new to this. Know you're here to help me, help all the brothers when we're in a jam. Know it. Appreciate it. But you'll learn… Club business, babe, ain't a woman's business. When you're needed, you'll get the info we can give you an' no more. Got me?"

Kiki abruptly shoved her chair back with a squeal and stood. "Sorry, but no, I don't *got* you. You want me to stick my neck out for you and your boys—"

"Brothers," he cut in.

She ignored him and continued, "Then you need to be open and honest with me or you can hang out to dry for all I care. *Got me?*"

Hawk smiled, leaned back in his chair and ran his gaze over her once more. Yep, he was going to get a piece of that hellcat. "Damn, woman, can't wait for that appointment."

"We have to get you out of here first."

"You do that."

She stepped closer to the table to look down at him. "Are you going to be checking out my ass when I leave?"

"Fuck yeah."

With a nod, she spun around, strutted her way to the door and pressed the buzzer.

Hawk didn't miss the guard checking out her ass, either.

Son of a bitch.

Get *Down & Dirty: Hawk* here: www.books2read.com/Hawk

BEAR'S FAMILY TREE

BEAR Jamison
DAMC Founder
Murdered 1986

- **MITCH Jamison**
  Blue Avengers MC
  b. 1967
  - **ZAK Jamison**
    DAMC (Former President)
    b. 1985
  - **AXEL Jamison**
    Blue Avengers MC
    b. 1987
  - **JAYDE Jamison**
    b. 1993

- **ROCKY Jamison**
  DAMC
  b. 1964
  - **JEWEL Jamison**
    b. 1989
  - **DIAMOND Jamison**
    b. 1988
  - **JAG Jamison**
    DAMC (Road Captain)
    b. 1987

DOC'S FAMILY TREE

- **DOC Dougherty**
  DAMC Founder
  b. 1943
  - **ACE Dougherty**
    DAMC (Treasurer)
    b. 1963
    - **DIESEL Dougherty**
      DAMC (Enforcer)
      b. 1985
    - **HAWK Dougherty**
      DAMC (Vice President)
      b. 1987
  - **ALLIE McBride**
    b. 1968
    - **DEX McBride**
      DAMC (Secretary)
      b 1986
    - **IVY McBride**
      b. 1988
    - **ISABELLA McBride**
      b. 1987
  - **ANNIE Dougherty**
    b. 1971
    - **Kelsea Dougherty**
      b. 1991

IF YOU ENJOYED THIS BOOK

Thank you for reading Down & Dirty: Jag. If you enjoyed Jag and Ivy's story, please consider leaving a review at your favorite retailer and/or Goodreads to let other readers know. Reviews are always appreciated and just a few words can help an independent author like me tremendously!

ABOUT THE AUTHOR

JEANNE ST. JAMES is a USA Today bestselling erotic romance author who loves an alpha male (or two). She was only thirteen when she started writing and her first paid published piece was an erotic story in Playgirl magazine. Her first erotic romance novel, Banged Up, was published in 2009. She is happily owned by farting French bulldogs. She writes M/F, M/M, and M/M/F ménages.

Want to read a sample of her work? Download a sampler book here: BookHip.com/MTQQKK

To keep up with her busy release schedule check her website at www.jeannestjames.com or sign up for her newsletter: http://www.jeannestjames.com/newslettersignup

www.jeannestjames.com
jeanne@jeannestjames.com

Blog: http://jeannestjames.blogspot.com
Newsletter: http://www.jeannestjames.com/newslettersignup
Jeanne's Down & Dirty Book Crew:
https://www.facebook.com/groups/JeannesReviewCrew/

facebook.com/JeanneStJamesAuthor

twitter.com/JeanneStJames

amazon.com/author/jeannestjames

instagram.com/JeanneStJames

bookbub.com/authors/jeanne-st-james

goodreads.com/JeanneStJames

pinterest.com/JeanneStJames

ALSO BY JEANNE ST. JAMES

Made Maleen: A Modern Twist on a Fairy Tale

Damaged

Brothers in Blue Series:

(Can be read as standalones)

Brothers in Blue: Max

Brothers in Blue: Marc

Brothers in Blue: Matt

Teddy: A Brothers in Blue Novelette

The Dare Ménage Series:

(Can be read as standalones)

Double Dare

Daring Proposal

Dare to Be Three

A Daring Desire

Dare to Surrender

The Obsessed Novellas:

(All the novellas in this series are standalones)

Forever Him

Only Him

Needing Him

Loving Her

Temping Him

The Rip Cord Trilogy:

Rip Cord: The Reunion

Rip Cord: The Weekend

Rip Cord: The Ever After

Down & Dirty: Dirty Angels MC Series:

(Can be read as standalones)

Down & Dirty: Zak

Down & Dirty: Jag

Down & Dirty: Hawk

Down & Dirty: Diesel

Down & Dirty: Axel

Down & Dirty: Slade (Coming Soon)

You can find information on all of Jeanne's books here:

http://www.jeannestjames.com/

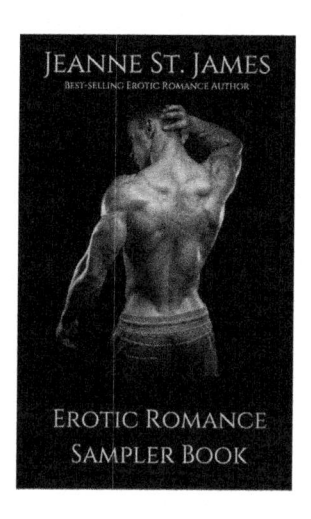

Get a FREE Erotic Romance Sampler Book

This book contains the first chapter of a variety of my books. This will give you a taste of the type of books I write and if you enjoy the first chapter, I hope you'll be interested in reading the rest of the book.

Each book I list in the sampler will include the description of the book, the genre, and the first chapter, along with links to find out more. I hope you find a book you will enjoy curling up with!

Download the sampler book here: BookHip.com/MTQQKK

Printed in Great Britain
by Amazon